Books

Single Titles

A Creative Guide to Getting a Life
Thirty Lessons Learned

A Creative Guide to Getting a Life

ISBN # 978-1-78651-927-6

©Copyright MJ Eason 2016

Cover Art by Posh Gosh ©Copyright 2016

Interior text design by Claire Siemaszkiewicz

Totally Bound Publishing

Published in 2016 by Totally Bound Publishing, Newland House, The Point, Weaver Road, Lincoln, LN6 3QN, United Kingdom.

Printed in Great Britain by Clays Ltd, St Ives plc
1

A CREATIVE GUIDE TO GETTING A LIFE

MJ EASON

Dedication

To my Aunt Mable, who has gone on to be with God. At five-foot-one, Aunt Mable could be both a free spirit and a force to be reckoned with. She taught me many lessons in life. The most important being that no matter how old you are, you don't have to act your age. I miss her dearly and I hope this book does her proud. This one's for you, Aunt Mable.

Chapter One

There are the Things you Think You Want...Success

When it comes to men, Aunt Mable always said there are good ones, bad ones and the worst possible kind—the kind that steal your heart and leave you wondering what happened. The kind you can't change.

Through the years I'd certainly seen my fair share of the worst possible kind. In fact, I often wondered if there wasn't some sort of hidden sign written across my forehead announcing, 'Come on in! Open for business! Give it your best shot!'

I guess I'd never fully appreciated the wisdom of my aunt's advice until I met David Martinez, the man who broke my heart and destroyed most of my self-esteem. It had taken a year of intense therapy just for me to regain some of my confidence. Forget men. I wasn't anywhere close to being ready for men again.

Or so I thought until I looked into the prettiest blue eyes in Texas.

It happened the night I was catering my first major event for a woman who'd fired some of the biggest names in the business. This was my chance to prove myself.

I believed I could handle anything that came my way as I stood hopeful before the world dressed in my perfect little caterer's outfit—starched white shirt, black skirt and sensible shoes. I was ready for any challenge.

After all, I'd certainly spent enough years preparing for this moment. I'd attended all the best culinary schools in Paris, New York and Texas, put in endless hours, worked multiple jobs in preparation for the time when my small pride and joy, my baby, Carrie's Creative Catering, would finally become a success.

For someone on the brink of thirty-five, single and living in Austin — one of the most exciting cities in Texas — success was all around me. So far, it had remained just out of my reach — until tonight.

"Carrie?" The sound of my name coming from the most gorgeous lips around made me weak in the knees. His voice sounded like pure romance. The Cary Grant kind of romance.

Unfortunately, the voice addressing me now came attached to one of those worst possible kinds.

Turn around. Walk away. Before it's too late, my mind virtually screamed, while my heart seemed to have a will of its own. It kept me standing there, foolishly smiling back at what was undeniably the sexiest man alive.

"Are you okay?"

"How did you know my name?" Too late, I remembered the nametag pinned to my crisp white shirt. It announced to the world that my name was Carrie Sinclair in bold, black lettering. Everyone at this party knew my name by now, especially since Martina Hilbert, the woman hosting this little get-together for a few hundred of her closest friends, had informed me that I lacked any real talent whatsoever as far as crab puffs were concerned. My skills in every other area were still questionable.

Once Martina had finished my thorough dressing-down in front of most of her guests, not to mention all three of my staff members, she'd proceeded to politely smile and simply walk away, as if she were merely commenting on the weather, not condemning *my* best hors d'oeuvres as garbage. I'd wanted to disappear right there into her spotless Italian marble floor.

This party was supposed to be my big moment. A client like Martina held parties like this all the time, according my best friend, Stephanie Monroe-Jennings. I'm embarrassed to say Steph got me this gig in the first place.

In her opinion, if I got in good with Martina and all of her well-to-do friends, it could really put Carrie's Creative Catering on the map.

I was now utterly humiliated. If I didn't escape to some quiet place soon, then everyone here would witness my childish reaction to Martina's insult. That's when I all but ran into Tyler Bennedict's arms.

The second he'd smiled at me with a little lopsided grin, the first warning whistle along the path to my destruction blew. It would be the first of many to come from that fast moving train headed my way, warning me of the disaster waiting ahead if I was foolish enough to listen to my heart.

I was.

"Don't listen to her. Martina doesn't know what she's talking about most of the time. These just happen to be the best crab puffs I ever tasted. And, if I'd known *the* Carrie of Carrie's Creative Catering was *this* talented, not to mention beautiful, I would have booked your services long ago."

Damn, he was good! Charming, sweet and unbelievably handsome. All the things that made me push aside my first uneasy feelings about him and ignore those whistles going off inside my head.

What did it hurt to simply talk to the man? He was a guest. I couldn't go around pissing off the guests, now could I? And besides, he was gorgeous.

I took a moment to assess his...attributes, from the dark brown hair streaked with highlights no salon could perfect — those babies came from spending lots of time outdoors — past laughing blue eyes, down to the perfect male nose. The only hint of imperfection I could find in him was a tiny little bump at the bridge of his nose. After a second glance, I decided it gave him character. The icing on the cake came when he smiled at me again, revealing two charmingly boyish dimples.

I returned his smile, Martina's nasty little comments all but forgotten. This was one great looking guy. Where exactly had he come from anyway, and why hadn't I spotted him earlier?

Suddenly it seemed as if it were just the two of us in this crowded room, like some old romance movie. He looked at me as if I were the only woman in the world. Later I would come to understand the reason behind this look.

"Carrie, do you want me to serve the desserts now?" Allison Richmond, my right hand woman, had apparently been asking this same question for quite some time, if the annoyance in her voice was any indication. The world around me came back into sharp focus the second I got a good look at Allie's smirk. Belinda and Janet, the two high school girls who worked part time for me, were practically drooling over Tyler.

I forced myself to remember why I was at this party in the first place. I wasn't one of the rich guests. I was the hired help. Somehow, I untangled my eyes from Handsome Guy and faced the woman who had been with me almost as long as Carrie's Creative Catering had been in existence.

"Huh? Oh, y-yes, Allie, that's a good idea and I-I'll help you." I turned back for one more look — what did it hurt? — just to make sure the gorgeous man I'd just encountered was actually real and not part of some twisted fantasy cooked up by my deprived body simply because I was currently in the middle of what must be a world-class sexual dry spell. I blushed as I imagined breaking that dry spell with him and stammered to cover up my overactive imagination. "I-I should go. I, uh, d-do have work to do."

Then he smiled again and I forgot everything I'd been about to say — forgot Allie, the dessert and Martina entirely. This was one dangerous man. He could make me forget just about everything, including the fact that my relationship with David had begun just this innocently.

"I understand, but maybe you'd consider having dinner with me sometime?"

I looked around the room. *Am I the only one hearing those whistles?*

8

"Did you hear that?" I asked. His only answer was another little grin.

At least he's finding me amusing.

I stalled again, trying to recover some of my composure. "I don't know. I don't even know your name. You might be anybody."

"Tyler Bennedict, and I'm not anybody. I'm just a guy asking you out to dinner. Will you have dinner with me on Saturday night?"

"Carrie, are you coming?" Allie's less than patient voice reminded me this was a job, not a place to pick up men.

"Right, Allie. Yes, I'm coming." I turned back to Tyler as levelheaded Carrie tried to convince in-lust Carrie to refuse flat out. Save herself the heartache. But the word "no" just would not come out of my mouth.

"I'll meet you at Sedona's at eight on Saturday night." Tyler promptly dismissed both Carries' arguments.

"But you don't know who I am either."

Tyler Bennedict turned back to me one more time and grinned. I didn't care who he was at that point. I was in lust and I wanted to kick myself. This was the last place I needed to be right now. Since David, I'd promised myself to focus more on the business and put aside my personal life—aka sex—for the time being.

"Don't worry. I'll find out all about you on Saturday."

The rest of the evening went by in a mindless blur of activity. Nothing penetrated my euphoric state, not even seeing Tyler, my date for Saturday night, chatting with a stunning redhead who was actually a guest and not the hired help. What did it matter? He'd asked *me* out. I mean, she could even be his sister, right? The fact that I was already making up excuses for him should have been my first clue of the trouble I was walking into—if I had actually been looking for clues.

By the time the party had ended, the cleanup finished and all the equipment safely stored away in my little rented shop on Thirty-Eighth Street, it was after three-thirty in the morning. Exhausted, I finally trudged up the steps to my fourth-floor corner apartment. You can probably imagine my surprise as I stood before my bathroom mirror to face my best tangy raspberry sauce plastered across my cheek. I'd added the sauce to the white chocolate cheesecake minutes before my run-in with Tyler.

My heart sank. Now I understood why someone as breathtaking as Tyler Bennedict would ask me out in the first place. It wasn't as if he were interested in me. He just wanted to know what choice of food I would be wearing next.

* * * *

When the phone rang at exactly six fifty-nine the following morning, I wasn't anywhere close to being awake.

"Carrie, where have you been? I left you three messages on your machine last night! You were supposed to call me! This is important. I've had a feeling."

I certainly wasn't in the right frame of mind to deal with my friend Stephanie's frantic voice yelling in my ear.

Stephanie had…feelings. I'm not talking about the tender, emotional kind. No, Steph's always meant that something bad was about to happen. I avoided hearing about them like the *plague*.

You see, Stephanie is convinced she possesses some kind of psychic ability and these feelings of hers are not to be ignored. Me, on the other hand? Well, don't get me wrong. I love her and she's my best friend, but I just think she's looking for attention.

Steph's the only child of two very wealthy parents who gave her everything her little heart desired, but they were always just a little too busy to be there for her much emotionally. Steph's poor husband, Ed, tries to fill the void, but it's a full-time job, and he has a full-time job already, working as an attorney for Steph's father.

I'd met Steph by accident, literally, years earlier, when I

was still new to town. She'd almost run me over with her Mercedes while on her way to a private sale at one of the more exclusive shops in the Arboretum Shopping Center.

"Steph, I didn't get home until after three this morning. I was exhausted. I didn't even look at the answering machine. I'm going back to sleep now. I'll call you later, when I'm actually *awake* and you can tell me all about this feeling of yours, okay?"

"Don't hang up on me. It's about Tyler Bennedict."

This had me sitting up in bed, wide awake, my full attention focused on what she was saying. "What about him? Why would you even mention him to me?"

"Oh, don't play dumb. I saw the two of you talking last night at the party. I tried to get your attention to warn you, but you were too busy flirting with him."

Okay, this definitely wasn't good. If Stephanie was calling to warn me about someone like Tyler, then chances were my day was about to go south.

Mental note to self — try not to be so obvious next time. "I wasn't flirting," I brazenly lied to my best friend. "He was only trying to make me feel better after your nasty friend was so rude to me."

"Stop it, Carrie. Tyler Bennedict doesn't do *anything* for *anyone* without good reason. It's not in him. You *can't* go out with him!"

"What are you talking about? We just met."

"Meet me at Starbucks in half an hour." Steph cut across my feeble attempt at more lies. "I have so much to tell you, but I can't do it over the phone. I have to see your face. You can't lie to me if I see your face."

"Steph, I'm still in bed —"

"Half an hour or I'm coming over there and getting you out of bed."

Before I could think of a single snappy comeback, the sound of the dial tone hit my ear. Steph wasn't giving me the opportunity to refuse, as if I was actually considering it. The second she'd mentioned Tyler's name, I knew I would hear what she had to say, however bad it turned out to be. I needed to hear her tell me what deep down inside I already knew. Tyler was one of those worst possible kind.

Even though Starbucks is just around the corner from my apartment, I was still fifteen minutes late getting there. Not that I wasn't dressed in record time. I just didn't want to hear what Stephanie was going say.

I spotted my friend's *naturally* red hair, the shade she spent big bucks obtaining each month from one of the most expensive salons in town. She was sitting at our favorite corner booth, coffee in hand. She waved the second she saw me then smiled when I indicated I was getting a drink first before joining her. Something told me I needed a cup of really strong coffee before hearing about Stephanie's *feeling*. A slice of cranberry crumble cake couldn't hurt either.

"Okay, what's the dirt on Tyler?" I took my usual seat across from her, not bothering with pleasantries. We knew each other too well for such niceties.

"You can't go out with him."

"Steph, for crying out loud! You said as much on the phone already, but I still don't know what you mean. You have to give me more to go on than 'you can't go out with him', okay?" Silently I berated myself for not listening to levelheaded Carrie for just once in my life. All of this would have been avoided if I'd just listened to her and ignored my foolish side. Now, as I looked into Steph's worried green eyes, I feared the worst.

"Tyler's not interested in anything long term. Tyler Bennedict has been through more women than any other man I know. He's only looking to have a little fun."

I somehow pulled my thoughts away from my long, dry spell. Sex, ah yes, I remembered it fondly. Sex right now didn't sound so bad. "I'm not interested in anything permanent either—not after David. It's too soon. I'm focusing on work. Nothing takes priority over my business. I certainly don't have the time or the energy to deal with another serious relationship right now. And even if I did,

I'm not ready to."

"That's what I'm trying to tell you. You aren't ready, especially not for someone like Tyler. If you go out with him, you're going to fall for him. Every woman he's ever dated has fallen for him! They can't seem to resist him. And if you fall for him, you're going to get hurt. I don't want to see that happen to you again.

"I mean, you almost didn't survive David. You remember what a wreck you were for months after you broke up with him? Well, Tyler Bennedict will make David look like a choirboy! You know I love you. I only want what's best for you, but you don't exactly have the best track record when it comes to men. Trust me on this one. You're not strong enough to survive Tyler. Besides, he would never fit into the five-year plan, and the five-year plan is foolproof."

Stephanie invented the five-year plan years ago when she was still at university. She believed in it and followed it religiously.

Graduate from university in five years—check. Steph allowed herself five years because she didn't want to rush the experience, and after all, she wasn't actually planning on using her education to, like…get a job. What did she need a job for? Her parents were rich.

Marry the perfect man in five years—check. Although, technically, it took five and a half years to convince Ed he was worthy of her, but I wasn't about to point that out.

Spend five years helping your husband become successful—check. Ed was now a partner because he'd married into the position.

Have the first of two babies, which were to be—you guessed it—five years apart. Steph figured one boy and one girl, so big brother could look after little sister.

This is where Steph's five-year plan had gone a little off schedule. It was now seven years and no baby. Steph had reached the freaking out stage a few years back. She'd been to every fertility expert around and forced Ed along as well, only to learn nothing was wrong with either him or her.

Her doctor had suggested she needed to relax and give it more time. This, of course, did not fit into Steph's five-year plan.

Although my friend was adamant about the merits of the five-year plan, in spite of the baby thing, I subscribed to a slightly more creative and less structured plan for my own life. It was simple really — become very, very successful in my chosen career, someday meet the perfect man and live happily ever after. Sounds easy enough, right? Wrong! David's departure from my life after two years of serious, going-somewhere dating proved my plan still had a few holes in it.

"I'm not interested in working on the five-year plan, or any other plan right now. I know I'm not ready." Okay, so this was another lie, but, hey, I was still trying to believe I could control things at this point. Steph, of course, was not buying it.

"Oh please! You've been looking for Mr. Right since you started dating. Case in point — David! You ignored all those warning signs, put up with more than any other woman would in the same situation and he hurt you terribly because of it. You are the serious, committed, five-year plan type. You've just been waiting for the right one to come along. Tyler Bennedict isn't the one."

"How do you know this? And how do you know anything about him anyway?"

"For starters, I've met Tyler before and I've heard all about his exploits from my friends. Trust me, I know. Tyler isn't interested in marriage or any other type of relationship. You can't imagine the number of women who have tried to change his mind. I don't want to see you hurt again, Carrie. If you go out with him, you will be. He'll break your heart."

"It's only dinner. I'm a big girl. Surely, I can handle Mr. Bennedict. I mean, it's not as if I'm going to sleep with him or, God forbid, fall in love with him on the first date."

"Don't do it, Carrie. Please, I'm telling you this as your friend. Don't go out with him even once. I know what a hopeless romantic you are, but Tyler Bennedict is no Prince Charming."

I would have argued this point if weren't true. You see, back in my apartment in one corner of my bedroom, there is an old trunk that holds all the proof needed to confirm that everything Stephanie said about me is true.

Hundreds of happily-ever-after romance novels I'd first discovered at the tender age of thirteen lay tucked away in the trunk, hidden underneath a handmade quilt, a gift from my Aunt Mable, the woman who taught me to be strong and independent.

Aunt Mable certainly didn't believe in fairy tales. She was a no-nonsense kind of woman. This was why I'd never been able to tell her — or my concerned friend here — about my real passion.

Sure, I loved to cook and I was good at what I did, but my one true passion remained locked away like those novels. I was a secret romance writer.

I'd attempted my first venture into writing as a teen. It lay hidden away in my trunk as well. Another more recent attempt sat unfinished on my computer. I'd always promised myself someday — when I was older and more secure financially — I'd set my secret passion free.

Of course, everything Steph said about me was true, no matter how much I would have loved to deny it. I'd wanted commitment. I'd just been waiting for *the one*. David hadn't been the one. Clearly, Tyler Bennedict wasn't either.

"If you're seriously ready to start dating again, there are plenty of nice men out there. I can introduce you to some."

"Okay, I get it. So what do you suggest I do on Saturday — just not show up? He doesn't know where I live. It might just work. I mean, I could stand him up. What do you think?" I was only joking, trying to cover my disappointment. Steph was concerned about me and for good reason. She was right. I'd barely survived David.

"Joke all you want, Carrie, but I'm telling you these things for your own good."

"I know. I know you are. It's just… Well, I guess I was hoping…"

"I know what you were hoping, but it wouldn't have worked out like that. He isn't capable of anything more than a superficial relationship with a woman. You don't want that. Trust me. You can't expect someone to care about your feelings when they aren't capable of showing normal human emotions themselves. Tyler Bennedict doesn't have a heart."

I almost felt sorry for the man after hearing Steph's description of him. Was he really so cold and unemotional? Surely she was exaggerating.

"He's the worst possible kind and you're far too sensitive to survive him. Stick with the nice ones. Besides, even if you were capable of changing Tyler's mind, his father would never allow him to marry someone…" Steph suddenly stopped.

"Someone like what?" I was still trying to recover from hearing that another man of my dreams was turning out to be my worst nightmare. "You were going to say someone like me, weren't you? What were you going to say?"

"Carrie, don't make me say it!"

"No, I want to know. Someone like *what*?"

"Someone who doesn't have the right pedigree. Someone who doesn't come from money. Richard Bennedict is such a snob. He would never allow his son to become seriously involved with someone who doesn't travel in the right social circles."

"Well, gee, Steph, don't hold back. Tell me what you really think." Of course, Stephanie was only being honest and I had asked, but still. I'd gotten my hopes up with Tyler. Steph had managed to smash those hopes to smithereens in a matter of seconds.

David came from a similar background. I hadn't fit into his world either. Steph had known David for years. She'd tried to warn me against going out with him, too. I hadn't listened any better back then and look where it had gotten me. Had I really learned nothing from my past mistakes?

"I wasn't trying to hurt your feelings. You know that's not how I feel about you. You're my best friend, but Richard Bennedict comes from very old Texas money. He'd inherited the family's real estate empire from his father, and his father had inherited it from his, and Tyler will inherit it from Richard one day."

"It's okay, Steph. I get it."

"I'm only saying their business is one of the largest in the state second only to The Davenport Agency in Dallas and Richard just happens to be very good friends with the Davenport family. Tyler won't do anything to jeopardize his future. He'll do exactly as his father wants and no woman — not even you, my sweet friend — will change his mind. He stands to lose too much."

"All right, I get the picture. I'm the worst possible woman for him."

"I'm sorry, Carrie. I don't mean to be such a bitch. I'm only worried about you. You're my friend and I don't want to see you make the same mistakes with Tyler that you did with David."

In spite of my disappointment, I forced a smile. We might be worlds apart socially, but we had each other's back, which was why I couldn't disappoint her. I'd be crazy to go out with Tyler Bennedict, because for once, I trusted Steph's feelings. Not the psychic feeling she believed she possessed, but the best friend feeling.

I reached for her hand and squeezed it. "Don't worry. The last thing I need right now is his kind of trouble. If he's as bad as you say, then it can only do his ego good to be stood up, right?"

"Oh, thank you! I'm so glad. You have no idea how worried I was the moment I saw you two talking. I was so afraid…" She didn't finish. She didn't need to. She'd had that feeling.

"Okay, so let's just not talk about Tyler or David or any other man anymore. Tell me what you're doing today.

17

Because I was thinking…since you got me out of bed at the crack of dawn, the least you can do is spend the morning with me." I managed to say without cracking up.

Steph knew exactly what I was thinking. You see, she and I shared our own secret passion. We both loved watching those classic, corny romance movies.

"Oh, there's an old Cary Grant film showing downtown! You know…the one with him and the princess. What's it called?"

"To Catch a Thief," I supplied for her while mentally going over all the things I should be doing today, such as work. After all, I had another job coming up in less than a week and I'd been searching all over Austin for just the right ingredients for it — an engagement dinner party for one of Steph's old sorority sisters. Another job I owed to my rich friend here.

All of these things could wait. Cary Grant couldn't.

"Yes, that's the one. We still have time for one more coffee before it starts. I really should be working on the library fund raiser, but…"

"It's Cary Grant!" we both said at the exact same time, settling the matter once and for all. Cary Grant was the man of both our dreams. I'd been in love with him longer than I'd been reading those romance novels.

* * * *

"Carrie, thanks for coming with me," Steph told me once we had found our favorite seats in the empty movie theater. "And for agreeing not to see Tyler on Saturday. Do you want to come over to the house for dinner instead?"

I smiled at my friend's concern. She'd hate thinking about me sitting alone on Saturday night. After all, she knew all about my dry spell. ""No thanks. I have tons of work to do. Don't worry. I'll be fine."

Hours later, with one double feature behind us, I couldn't tell my best friend I still wasn't so sure I wouldn't walk into

Sedona's on Saturday night.

Of course, Steph had my best interests at heart and I trusted her judgment in business and in love. She'd never once let me down. Steph had been the one to hold my hand and keep me sane after David and I had broken up.

But no matter how much I argued those truths with myself, part of me would always wonder what *I* would be giving up by standing up Tyler Bennedict.

Chapter Two

Relief from a Long Dry Spell

"You were going to stand me up?"

For a minute, I couldn't believe my eyes. Tyler Bennedict was actually standing on my doorstep asking me this question. I blinked, then blinked again, but he didn't disappear. "You never intended to come to the restaurant tonight, did you, Carrie?"

Okay, I admit, just the sight of him dressed in that dark gray pullover that accentuated his very fit body was reminding me of how I'd felt the last time he'd looked at me this same way. It certainly had me rethinking all those promises I'd made to Steph.

"How did you know where to find me?" I tried corralling my wayward thoughts, which were clearly heading for places I had no business going. Not with Mr. Gorgeous standing in front of me, reminding me of my long dry spell.

"I told you I would find out everything about you. You didn't believe me?"

My conscience reminded me once more of all the dangers awaiting me if I let this man in my life. If I were smart, I'd push him out the door and lock it behind him.

"You were, weren't you? You were going to stand me up?" The look on Tyler's face said this was a first for him. I wished I could deny it or say something terribly coy like, "Oh gee, was that tonight? I completely forgot about our date!" As if! Instead, all I could do was nod.

"Why?"

If I hadn't heard the truth straight from Steph's mouth, I

might have been tempted to believe that the hurt expression on Tyler's face right now was real.

"What changed your mind?"

"I spoke to my friend. She told me you'd end up hurting me if I went out with you." I waited for him to deny what I'd said. Praying that he would, hating that he didn't.

"Your friend is probably right." As Tyler continued to watch me, that half smile of his disappeared completely. The look in his eyes took what was left of my breath away. Then I was in his arms. When he kissed me, his lips reassured me everything that Steph had told me about him was true. This man was going to break my heart.

It wasn't as if I hadn't known this truth from the moment my eyes had met his. I'd known his lips were going to taste good enough to leave me wanting more. I'd known, but I was powerless to stop it. It was fate, after all.

This is wrong, my conscience warned as the door closed behind Tyler.

I'd been so caught up in the touch of his lips against mine—strong, gentle, demanding—that even after he ended the kiss, it took me a minute to regain my bearings. Did he feel this same helpless, out-of-control passion?

When I opened my eyes, Tyler Bennedict stood perfectly still, looking down at me. I didn't even consider the consequences of our actions. I'd worry about those tomorrow. Tonight, I wanted him—wanted to feel him next to me—inside me. I took his face in my hands and claimed his lips. After a second's hesitation, he lifted me in his arms and I pointed the way to my bedroom.

He kicked the door closed hard enough to send pictures rattling against the wall with the force of a frustration he couldn't hide, before he laid me down on the bed.

Tyler wasn't giving me the chance to change my mind. I barely had time to do more than sit up when he was there beside me. His fingers threaded through my hair, forcing me to look at him.

"Carrie, I want you to be sure about this, because we

both know where this is heading. We've known from the moment we met. So tell me now if this isn't what you want."

He was right. I'd known the second our eyes met this was going to happen. I *wanted* it to happen every bit as much as he did, and no amount of false modesty on my part was going to change that truth, even if I wasn't able to admit it to myself.

I wanted Tyler Bennedict and I was willing to give him anything — everything, in fact.

So why was I crying now? I cried hot tears, making it impossible to see his reaction to them. He'd want to know why, but I couldn't even begin to explain my tears to him. I was disillusioned. I wanted to be loved. I wanted *his* love. I wanted this time to be special, but he only wanted sex.

Since I'd met Tyler, my actions had been motivated by my reaction to him, which was nothing akin to the way I would normally react to any guy's attention. Before Tyler, I would never have considered sleeping with someone on a first date, but then…this wasn't a first date. We hadn't even gone out once. This was as out of character as it got for me and that was what was really scaring me, even if I was powerless to stop it.

This was so wrong, my conscience continued, condemning me for a fool. But even as the words of retribution echoed through my mind, Tyler's gaze slid over me, taking away all rational thought. At that moment I didn't give a damn what was right or wrong. I wanted this — him.

"Are you okay? You're crying."

"No, please, I'm fine. It's just…" *That I'm scared to death because I've never felt this way before.* I shook my head. I couldn't share any of those fears with him.

That he didn't believe me was easy to read. For a breathless moment, I believed he'd simply get out of my bed and leave me desperate for him.

Tyler let go of the breath slowly and long before pulling me against him. His hands wandered over my body seductively and thoroughly, leaving little doubt how much wanted me.

I should have been thrilled—and part of me was. This was the man of my dreams, after all. But my head screamed just how sorry I would be once he was gone—and he would be. He would leave me and never look back. According to Steph, this was Tyler's style. He was not the type of man to pin my dreams on.

His kisses demanded responses from me that I didn't hesitate to give. No other man had ever made me feel this way before and I was unable to hide any of this from him.

Tyler moved away from me for a moment, his eyes searching my face once more. "Open your eyes, Carrie. Please, open your eyes for me."

I forced my eyes open to look at him. For the first time since he'd kissed me, my indecision returned.

Was I really going to go through with this? Was I going to sleep with a man I barely knew? Was I strong enough to survive this night? I couldn't answer any of those questions. I didn't know the answer to them, but the thought of all those things frightened me.

Tyler saw all my doubts and pulled me closer before I could act on them.

He slipped his fingers under my top and lifted it over my head. The second he touched my skin, I let go of all the doubts I'd still clung to, surrendering to this need inside me completely. I barely recognized his voice when he asked the question going through my mind.

"Tell me this is what you want."

I was shivering but I couldn't stop. He was doing dangerous things to my self-control with his hands. He felt my reaction, my excitement, and he smiled that crazy grin of his into my startled eyes.

"Yes, it's what I want. I only want you."

For a moment, Tyler went still. "I don't believe you."

There was a mocking quality to his voice that I had never heard before. Coming from him, it sounded sexy as hell.

He smiled once more before kissing me. He pulled me

closer, the movement of our bodies exciting.

He slid his hands across my breasts and down my stomach, dipping under the edge of my panties to slip them free of my body just as Steph's words of warning went through my mind again.

But as Tyler stroked his hands down the length of my thigh then slowly up again, I could no longer remember all the things Steph had told me about his guy.

The rhythm of his fingers moving over my skin threatened to shatter all of my self-control. I wanted this. I just didn't want to face myself after it was over.

Tyler slowed the movement of his touch, once more allowing the tension to ease within me before he released me. Slowly standing up, he slid his gaze over my frustrated expression.

He undressed quickly before taking me back into his arms. He took control of my body with a single movement.

"Don't stop! Please...don't stop," I whispered, and felt his shuddering reaction to my words. His lips never left mine and we moved our bodies in perfect rhythm.

There, in the arms of a man that I'd never even gone out with once, I gave in at last to my body's response—right before my Mr. Wrong lost himself at last in me.

Slowly Tyler eased his body away from mine, but he didn't let me go. He rolled over onto his back, taking me with him. I lay in his arms, too weak and exhausted to even think about moving away.

Tyler ran his fingers through my hair, forcing my head back, making me look at him as he searched my face. I couldn't meet his eyes. He released me and I lay against his chest, trying to breathe normally again.

Tyler switched off the lights and wrapped me in his arms.

Sometime later, I awakened as Tyler pulled me back against his body, his arms circling me once more. He moved his hands over me once again, igniting desires and longings deep inside us both. He brushed the hollow beneath my ear with gentle lips, thrilling me.

"Wake up, sleeping beauty. I need you again."

My body shivered in response to his words, his caresses... his lips. He made love to me once more and I tried to kill the voices of warning screaming in my head.

He'd come to me, after all. That had to mean something.

He lay next to me again and I put my arms around his body, clinging to him as if he were the only solid thing left in a world spinning out of control, both of us exhausted from the force of our lovemaking. I knew this man wasn't like any other man I'd ever met before or would meet again.

After tonight, my life would never be the same, no matter where Tyler went. Even if I never saw him again or held him close like this, I would never be the same. I couldn't. He'd touched a part of me that went beyond physical intimacy.

* * * *

Sometime just before dawn I awoke to an emptiness in my bed that I'd never felt before. The coldness beside me where he'd just lain told me just how long it had been since Tyler had left my side.

Fool, my conscience returned in full force to rebuke me, even as I tried to shut out the truth in those words. The tears that I swore I wouldn't cry again came easily as I turned away from the impression left in my bed from his body.

Even after I covered my head with his pillow, I couldn't shut out my own condemnation.

That damning word played round and round in my head, depriving me of sleep.

I'd never see him again, of that much I was almost certain. He hadn't felt any of the same helpless love I'd felt. He'd just needed me physically. That was all it had been for him, and I'd been only too willing to give him whatever he wanted, just to be close to him for a little while.

Steph had been right all along, but how could I bring myself to tell her about what had happened between us tonight? The answer to that came easily enough. I'd never be able to share this ugly little truth with Steph, not if I lived to be a hundred.

I dragged myself out of bed, showered and dressed in my favorite worn out shorts and T-shirt and sat watching the sun come up over the neighboring apartment complex with coffee in hand. Folgers coffee. Starbucks was my treat when I'd been good. I hadn't been very good lately, certainly not good enough to deserve Starbucks.

When the doorbell rang a few minutes later, I laid the unread paper aside and went to answer it. I opened the door without checking to see who might be calling at this hour of the morning. This was another one of my aunt's pet peeves. She was constantly reminding me anyone could be waiting for me to open the door, including a serial killer or worse. In this case, it was worse — far worse. It was Tyler.

"Hi. Sorry. I hope I didn't wake you, but I didn't have a key." He grinned at me as he held up two large cups of Starbucks coffee. All I could do was stare at them as if I'd never seen such a thing before.

"What are you doing here?" I hadn't been expecting to see him again, and yet here he was, smiling at me and handing me Starbucks.

"What do you mean? I went out for coffee. Did you think I'd just left without saying a word?" As much as I would have loved to deny it, Tyler had spotted the truth right away. "You did, didn't you? Carrie, I just went for coffee because I wasn't sure how to work your coffee maker. I wouldn't just leave you like that without saying goodbye."

He closed the door and stood, staring down at me. Suddenly I became conscious of just how pitiful I must look right now. I wasn't wearing a trace of makeup and my mutinous curls were going in all directions. This was *not* how I wanted Tyler to see me.

"But I thought—" I bit my tongue as hard as I could to stop those foolish words, but they were out before I could prevent them from escaping. I wanted to walk out my *own* door. He could keep the apartment.

"I know what you thought, but I wouldn't do that to you. Look, I know you've heard things about me from your friend, but please, I need you to trust me just a little. Give me a chance. Don't just write me off because of someone else's opinion of me."

"I'm sorry, but I have to go to church." At that ridiculous outburst, I started for the door. Yeah, he could definitely keep the apartment...and Max, if he could find my cat in whatever hiding place the furry brat had chosen to retreat to over the past few hours. Max would probably never forgive me for bringing a complete stranger into his sleeping quarters anyway.

I opened the door and was almost out free and clear when Tyler stopped me. There was no denying the laughter in his voice in spite of the uncertainty in his eyes. "Dressed like this? I know churches have become much more casual these days, but you are only wearing shorts and a T-shirt."

I turned back to look at him then, with my hand still resting on the door. As I listened, levelheaded Carrie warned me to snap out of it.

Tyler seemed to understand all about my indecision.

"It's okay. I could go with you if you'd like?"

This captured my full attention. Somehow, I couldn't picture Tyler in church. I started to laugh, but his expression told me he was serious.

"Have you even been to church before?" I tried not to smile while asking it.

"Don't laugh. Of course, I've been to church but I have to confess, it's been a while. Do I need to change?"

"No, you're fine. It's usually pretty casual."

"Just not casual enough for shorts?"

"No, not casual enough for shorts," I said with a smile.

Like Aunt Mable always said, there are good men and there are bad men—then there's Tyler Bennedict. He read my thoughts just as clearly as if I'd spoken them aloud. "We'll take it slowly, okay? Come drink your coffee."

As I looked into his eyes, I found I wanted to trust him. I

needed to believe he wasn't going to be like David. Surely I couldn't be that wrong twice in a lifetime.

"How did you know Starbucks was my favorite?"

"Because, Carrie Sinclair, you've got Starbucks written all over you."

* * * *

Stepping into uncharted territory and on little more than blind faith, I went to church with Tyler Bennedict — the man I'd just spent nothing close to a holy night with, doing everything my aunt warned me against doing.

It took me longer to figure out what to wear than I'd spent deciding to sleep with him the night before. I'd changed three times before settling on my favorite sleeveless black dress, which was about as out of character as it got for me, considering I rarely wore dresses. I was a jeans and T-shirt girl most of the time.

Today I needed all the help I could get to wipe the image of no makeup, bad hair and faded shorts from his memory. From the expression on Tyler's face when I finally emerged from my bedroom a few minutes before we were officially late for church, it was working. Or maybe he was simply remembering all the things we shouldn't have been doing the night before.

We found a vacant pew at the back where we sat close enough to touch, both looking very solemn in the small church I attended faithfully, thanks to my Christian upbringing.

"What are you so worried about?" my companion in sin asked as we left the church together. "Were you afraid maybe I'd be struck by lightning or something equally Biblical?"

"No," I somehow managed to get out with only a slight tremor in my voice. In truth, I was the one who was expecting the lightning bolt.

Tyler held the Range Rover's door open for me and stood

looking down at me in a way that made me very thankful we weren't back at my apartment right now.

"Will you have lunch with me?" He sounded so humble that I couldn't think of refusing. I found myself watching him curiously, as he maneuvered through the busy Sunday morning traffic, looking for a crack in his charm — some visible flaw — anything to keep me from falling any harder for the guy.

When Tyler stopped the Rover in front of Sangria's, I turned to him with my mouth hanging open. This just happened to be the hottest restaurant in town.

Sangria's was located in one of the more exclusive neighborhoods in the hills of Austin. Its clientele included a virtual Who's Who of Austin's elite. No one — absolutely no one, no matter who they were — simply walked in off the street to have lunch at this place, especially not on a weekend.

"You're kidding, right? There's no way you're getting *in there* today, buddy."

Tyler simply grinned at me before getting out of the vehicle to open my door. "Would you care to place a bet?" He handed the valet the keys to the Rover.

To my surprise, the kid actually called Tyler by his first name. I tried to keep my jaw from dropping any farther as Tyler escorted me inside. He probably had a table reserved here every single Sunday. I didn't much care for *that* thought.

The hostess seated us immediately at a table next to the windows, which provided a spectacular view of the city below. Within seconds, a waiter appeared to run through the specials of the day. It was difficult to make a decision, but once I'd chosen the Sangria Chicken, I sat back in my chair and took in the view.

I'd only heard about this place from people who knew people, who knew other people, who'd actually come here before. Even Steph was in awe of the people who could get a reservation at Sangria's. The food was perfectly placed on the plate when the waiter delivered it, and it looked delicious.

"Do you have any idea how sexy you look in your little black dress, Miss Sinclair?"

My reaction to those words was to choke on the piece of perfectly seasoned chicken I'd been trying very politely to chew like a lady.

For the first time in longer than I remembered, I was speechless. I couldn't think of one single clever remark to make in the face of the warmth in his eyes. Did he use this line with all the women he dated? Did it work as well on them as it had on me?

"Are you going to tell me who suggested you stand me up?"

It took a minute or two for what he'd just said to penetrate my befuddled brain. When he looked at me the way he was right now, I couldn't seem to concentrate on what he was saying, much less actually answer his question.

"Huh?"

"Who told you those things about me, Carrie?"

"No one. Just a friend."

"Somehow I don't think that's the case. It's clearly someone you trust. What did she tell you about me?"

"Nothing. Only that you'd be bad for me."

For a second, a hurt expression darkened his eyes before the teasing indifference returned, giving away nothing of Tyler's true feelings. "She's probably right, you know? If last night is any indication of how things are going to be between us, then..." He didn't finish. He didn't need to. The passion we'd shared last night had been unexpected for the both of us, but was it the kind of heat to last or would it fizzle out as quickly as it had ignited? If this were true, would there be anything left between us? I couldn't ask Tyler any of those things.

Tyler and I spent the rest of the day at my apartment, simply talking and reading the paper. Although it was late when he left me, it was still hard saying goodbye to him, even harder not asking him if I'd ever see him again. I'd promised myself I was not going to expect anything from Tyler. He was not the right man for me. He was just the one to relieve my dry spell.

I was actually starting to congratulate myself on showing so much self-control. Maybe he was just my relief guy after all?

Tyler had barely been gone a minute, when I heard a knock at my door. I opened it and he picked me up in his arms and carried me to my bed without as much as another word. Like it or not, I would accept our relationship on whatever terms he chose to give me, until I could no longer stand his terms.

* * * *

Sometime just before the dawn, Tyler got out of my bed, showered and came back to kiss me goodbye.

"Where are you going?" I hated the question, even if I couldn't stop myself from asking it.

"Shh, go back to sleep. It's still early. I need to go home and change before I go into the office."

"When will I see you again?" For a long time, he didn't say a word and I believed I had my answer in his silence.

"I don't know. Soon, maybe. I'll call you, okay? He left me then and I couldn't help but wonder if I would ever see Tyler Bennedict again.

* * * *

When my Monday morning alarm clock sounded its usual seven a.m. annoying time, I still didn't know how I was going to look Steph in the eye and not tell her everything. I was almost desperate enough to fake illness.

How could I explain to Steph that I'd moved beyond her 'You can't go out with Tyler Bennedict' mandate, to 'I had sex with him and he didn't even buy me dinner first'.

The problem was even if I didn't show up, Steph would

guess. I wouldn't even have to say a word and she'd know. I had to come clean.

Steph and I had first developed this routine of meeting for coffee on Monday mornings when I was still working two jobs, attending school and trying to get my business off the ground, and she was rushing off to all the parties and lunches of a single, well-to-do girl hoping to land the perfect husband.

Today, even before I walked in the door, I knew she'd seen the truth. Damn, she was good.

"You didn't! Oh, Carrie, please don't tell me you met Tyler Bennedict for dinner on Saturday? You promised!"

"Geez, Steph, give me a chance to at least get coffee before you start in?"

Stephanie shut up, but she didn't stop glaring at me until we were through the line and seated at our corner booth.

"You did, didn't you? You met him for dinner after you promised me you wouldn't!"

"No! No, I didn't go out with him. Well, not exactly."

"What's that supposed to mean? Which is it, Carrie? Either you did or you didn't. I don't understand."

It occurred to me then that Stephanie was mad — boiling mad, if the bright red patches of color in her cheeks matching the shade of her hair were any indication. I couldn't ever remember seeing Steph this particular shade of red or this angry before, except maybe at Ed, but never at me. This was definitely *not* a good sign.

"I didn't meet him for dinner, okay? He came to my apartment — "

"What do you mean he came to your apartment?" she interrupted before I could finish my excuse. "You called him?"

"Will you let me speak?" At this point, my anger was close to matching hers, but it didn't have anything to do with what she was saying, really. I was just scared to death I'd made a huge mistake and even more afraid that Stephanie was about to confirm all of this.

"No, I didn't give him my number, and no, I didn't meet him for dinner. He just showed up at my apartment. I have no idea how he found out where I live."

"You slept with him. Oh, Carrie…no. Not Tyler Bennedict."

"Steph! Geez, could you say it a little louder the next time? The old guy across the room didn't hear you." My cheeks turned bright red as I glanced around, hoping the people seated closest to us weren't as interested in our conversation as I would have been.

"Well, can you explain yourself?"

As I looked into my friend's disappointed expression, I did the one thing no self-respecting, almost thirty-five-year-old, hip woman of the world is ever supposed to do. I started to cry.

I caught Steph's expression before the tears took my vision away entirely. She was shocked. I never cried, at least not as far as she knew. I was the carefree one. Okay, so let's just disregard the whole David incident. Steph was the one given to emotional outbursts. Now, here I was crying my eyes out and all because of a man. I wanted to kick my own ass.

Steph's anger and disappointment vanished at the sight of my tears. I reached for my napkin.

"Oh, Carrie, I'm sorry. I didn't mean to sound so… judgmental. It's just… Well, you know I'm worried about you. I don't want to see you hurt again and I know you will be if you continue to see Tyler Bennedict. You already are hurt, aren't you?"

I could deny it—tell her she was so wrong, keep my heartache to myself—but something told me I was going to need Steph's strength more than ever in the days to come.

When I finally stopped crying long enough to look at her with some amount of self-respect again, I decided that the truth was the only way to go with this woman.

"I didn't intend for any of this to happen. I was really trying to do as you asked. And yes, before you even say it, I know he's the worst possible man for me. And no, I haven't forgotten about David. And yes, I know my record with men is terrible!

"I always seem to fall for the wrong ones, but what was I supposed to do? He just showed up on my doorstep then…I didn't know what to do. I think…" I was so close to telling her how crazy I was about Tyler, but Steph guessed as much. She was determined not to let me say those words aloud. They weren't real in her mind if I didn't actually say them.

"It's okay! Everything will be okay. You'll see," she rushed to assure me, before I could confirm her worst fears. "Let's just think about this calmly, okay? Are you going to see him again?"

"I don't know. We spent the whole day together yesterday. Tyler even went to church with me, but when he left this morning, he didn't say a word. So, I don't *know* if I'll ever see him again."

"Oh, Carrie! Well, maybe it's for the best. Trust me. You don't need another creep in your life right now." She caught my reaction to those words and reached for my hand before adding, "You'll find your prince someday. I know it hurts now, but maybe it's for the best." Steph meant well, but she didn't realize how painful those words were to hear.

"You know what you need right now? The one thing that always cheers me up when I'm down? Let's go shopping! I've been dying to go, but I hate going by myself. It's not the same, you know? Why don't you come shopping with me today? It will do you good. What you need right now is to spend a whole lot of money on yourself. Besides, it's too hot to do anything else."

Chapter Three

Someone like Cary Grant

By the time Steph and I left the Arboretum Shopping Center, she'd managed, at the cost of a whole lot of damage to my credit card, to put me in a slightly better mood.

Screw Tyler Bennedict! No pun intended. Did I really care if I ever heard from him again? No! I certainly didn't need him, or any other man, to make me happy. I had Steph and Aunt Mable — Max even. And I now owned half of Neiman-Marcus to boost my ego. What more could a girl want, really?

Besides, as my aunt was always fond of saying, men were just for fun. God, family and friends were for counting on in a crisis or when you just needed a little cheering up. She should certainly know. She'd divorced two husbands and buried one — all by the time I'd arrived on her doorstep at the tender age of ten.

At this point, men had become little more than a sidebar for Aunt Mable. Bringing me up right and spending time with her best friend, Trudy Wilcox, had been what made her happy.

She'd be so angry with me right now, if she could see me pining away over a man.

At the possibility of disappointing my steadfast aunt, I told myself I'd done enough worrying over Tyler Bennedict. According to Steph's calculations, there were some thirty thousand single men in the Austin area alone. I'd find someone right for me, someone who fit into my plan for life. I wouldn't compromise.

When I walked into my small shop hours later, Allie and the girls were actively working on the final preparations for tonight's event.

My little business was hosting its first corporate function for some poor soul forced into early retirement against his will after putting in more years than I could ever imagine spending at one job.

"Hey, boss. Geez, you look terrible," Allie announced once she'd gotten a good look at me. "Did you have a rough weekend?" This was just her way of reminding me that she hadn't forgotten my behavior from the other night at Martina's party. She'd probably been saving that little remark.

It wasn't as if Allie meant anything by it really. She had stood by me through thick and thin, when the business had almost failed at least half a dozen times and I'd almost run home to Aunt Mable just as many. Because of this, I chose to ignore Allie's somewhat rude comment, because, well, that was just her way.

"Everything all set for tonight?" This was to be Allie's first time catering an event without my help. She'd been training for months and was ready, even though she wasn't quite as convinced of it as I was.

"Yep, we're all set here. What time do you want me to set up again?"

"The fun begins at seven, so plan on being there no later than five. We don't want to send poor old Mr. Carter off into retirement on a bad note, do we? You're sure you don't want me to go with you? I could hang around for a bit just to make sure everything's okay?"

She did. I could tell from her expression, but Allie wasn't ready to admit to it and I didn't want her to lose confidence in herself.

"You're ready, Allie. You could do this in your sleep. If you need me, call me. Otherwise, tell me all about it tomorrow."

* * * *

The very first thing I did when I walked into my apartment, after I'd found Max and apologized, was to check the answering machine for messages. The bright red zero told me all I needed to know. I was never going to see Tyler Bennedict again. He'd gotten exactly what he'd wanted from me. He'd slept with me, probably spent the day with me out of some feeling of guilt — or worse — boredom.

As hard as I tried, I wasn't able to concentrate on anything, including the latest romance novel I'd been working on in my spare time. Romance was the last thing on my mind tonight. Real life now overshadowed all of my fantasies. I was beginning to wonder if anything in those happily ever after stories ever came close to reality.

After roaming the apartment and totally freaking out poor Max enough to send him retreating to his secret hiding spot, I did something I'd never been able to share with Aunt Mable because it would only worry her. I went out into the hot Austin night and walked for hours.

This was my last hope when all else failed. Growing up on a small ranch outside of Early, Texas, I'd gotten used to walking off my problems across the open pastures of Aunt Mable's place.

When I finally made my way back to my apartment, I was slightly more at peace. Exhausted and sticky, but at least I'd forgotten about Tyler for a while.

I took a quick shower, put on a pot of coffee and flipped on my computer. After slipping in my favorite CD, I turned the volume up as high as I could risk without interrupting my only neighbor, a sweet little lady who was my adopted grandmother. Mrs. Hazel Pearson.

With Elvis Presley's *Loving Arms* blaring and a cup of strong coffee next to my mouse pad, I sat staring out of the window, unable to get started on the blank page glaring back at me.

My mood was bland. Happily ever after was hard to come

by when I was in this state of mind. So instead, I sat listening to the King and singing along at the top of my lungs. It took me a full minute to realize that the ringing sound wasn't coming from the song, but from my front door.

Max gave an angry meow just to let me know visitors were most unwelcome, as far as he was concerned. "Sorry, Max!" I apologized on my way to answer the door.

When I opened the door and saw Tyler standing there, I did something I couldn't even begin to explain. I slammed it right back in his face.

Geez. I mean, I'd been missing the guy like crazy and the second he showed up, I slammed the door in his face.

"Carrie, open the door."

"Just a minute." I glanced at myself in the mirror. Oh yeah, I looked as bad as I thought, but clearly he wasn't leaving and I couldn't hide out here all night. I yanked the door open.

"Hi. What do you want?" I didn't invite him in, but he came inside just the same.

He closed the door softly and looked at me with an expression on his face that told me I wouldn't be strong tonight either.

"I'm not sleeping with you." Boy, did that really sound as childish to him as it did to me?

"Elvis?" Tyler smiled, choosing to ignore my rudeness. I hated his smile.

"I happen to love Elvis. You have a problem with Elvis?"

"Me? No way. I love Elvis too. Do I smell coffee?"

Somehow, I resisted the urge to laugh at us. Here we stood, two grown adults, unsure of each other and acting like a couple of kids.

I turned and walked back into my small kitchen, knowing he would follow. "It's just plain old Folgers. Nothing fancy."

"That's okay. I like Folgers."

The sincerity in his voice made me want to cry. What an idiot I was turning out to be. When I saw him standing there in my tiny kitchen looking so humble, I believed him.

"What are we doing here, Tyler? I mean what…" I shook my head, unable to finish. I wasn't really sure what I'd been about to ask him. *I* didn't even know what I was expecting from him.

"I don't know." This wasn't the answer I needed to hear from him right now, and it showed in my reaction. I was close to tears again and I hated him for making me cry.

Then, I did another foolish thing. I went into his arms, and he let me. Tyler held me close while I cried my foolish tears.

"Carrie, I'm sorry. I wish that I could make you promises, but I can't. I don't know where this is going."

"I don't need promises," I whispered against his chest then scrubbed at the tears before facing him with what I hoped would be some amount of self-control. God, I was behaving like a simpering idiot.

He smiled. "Yes, you do. And I'm sorry that I can't give them to you." The sincerity in his gaze was enough for the moment, I told myself. I could handle this relationship on his terms for now.

He brought his hand to my cheek, drawing my mouth to his. Every fiber of my being screamed at me to stop this before it went too far. He pressed his hand against my lower back, molding our bodies together as one. When he claimed my lips, I let go of the doubts. As I would soon discover, this would be a dangerous pattern for me. When Tyler touched me, clear-headed Carrie disappeared entirely.

I opened my eyes and found him watching me. The questions I saw in his gaze were easy to read. He wanted me. Every inch of his taut body confirmed this, but he was waiting for me. I found his lips again, silencing the voice of reason in my head. He gathered me close in his arms, crushing our bodies together. With a shake of his head, Tyler lifted me and I wrapped my legs around his waist. Each step brushed our bodies together in an erotic promise of things to come. We devoured each other with our mouths. We stumbled to the bed, the weight of his body crushing me into the mattress. For a moment, he pulled away. Something I couldn't even begin to understand flashed in his eyes, filled with heat. Fear? Hope? I tried to capture it, but his lips took mine again then we were in a race to undress each other.

When Tyler thrust inside me, our eyes locked. The world outside — the doubts, the fears — ceased to exist. My fingers intertwined with his. For a moment, neither of us moved. We watched each other in the dimness of the room, drinking in longing. Then, slowly, Tyler began to move within me, his eyes never leaving mine. I ached with emotions I'd never experienced before. I wanted this moment, this feeling of falling, to last forever, but under Tyler's skillful stroke, I lost that battle. My body arched against his thrusts as wave after wave of pleasure swept me away. Tyler held on until I grew still beneath him, then with one final push, he shuddered and lost himself within me as well.

The last thing I remember before we both collapsed into exhaustion was the seductive sound of my name coming from his lips.

It was a long time before we came up for air again. The coffee I'd made earlier had scorched in the pot. As I stood waiting for a new pot to brew, Tyler roamed aimlessly around my living room, picking up pieces of my life. He'd spotted another one of my passions — my prized Cary Grant collection.

"Elvis and Cary? You are definitely living in the wrong decade. Any more dark secrets I should know about?"

"I was named after Cary Grant. My mother was in love with him. She used to tell me if Cary had been available, she would have married him in a heartbeat. Instead, she settled for my father, a Cary Grant look-a-like. I grew up watching those old movies before I could even walk."

"I hope you don't expect any real man to live up to those standards." He gave a little shake of his head. "Where do your parents live anyway?"

"They passed away. They died in a car accident when I

was ten. I went to live with my Aunt Mable—my father's sister—after the accident."

"That must have been hard."

"It was." I handed Tyler a coffee mug, hoping to cover up the pain that was always there whenever I thought about my parents. I still missed them terribly, even though they'd been gone for many years now. "But Aunt Mable was great. She took me to live on her ranch and became like a second mother to me. Well, a very eccentric mother anyway."

"And where are you from, Carrie Sinclair? Because you're definitely not Austin material. Some place small town, I'm guessing."

"So you don't like small towns either? You really are a snob, Mr. Bennedict. I'm from Early and yes, there really is a place called Early, and yes, it's definitely tiny. My aunt has a ranch just outside the city limits."

"I think I've been through there before. Definitely small town, but it suits you. It gives you a certain innocence."

"Ha. Just because I'm from a small town doesn't mean I don't know what's going on in the world, you know, or how to deal with you, because I do."

"I don't doubt that for a second, Miss Sinclair." His little grin returned. "I think you've dealt with me pretty good so far."

Those words made me blush with embarrassment. Who was I kidding? I didn't have a clue what I was doing with him.

Tyler, on the other hand, was used to moving through different circles—fitting in. He probably had a line for all occasions. Was I crazy? I could never trust this man.

Tyler must have guessed my thoughts, because he changed the subject. "So, how exactly did you decide upon this career choice of yours? Aunt Mable is a caterer, right?"

This made me laugh. Oh, it wasn't as if my aunt couldn't cook. She knew perfectly well how to prepare all those amazing country dishes like chicken fried steak and fried chicken, but my aunt hated cooking so much that after a few years of trying to do what was best for me, she'd abandoned that line of attack altogether and we'd ended up eating out mostly.

Until I discovered the old romantic comedy *Sabrina* at the tender age of twelve. From that moment on, I was smitten with the idea of going abroad to learn how to prepare all those exotic dishes they'd talked about in the movie. For me, *Sabrina* managed to combine two of my favorite passions — romance and cooking.

Of course, I'd burned my fair share of dinners before finally getting the hang of it. Then I'd taken charge of the kitchen. I made lavish meals for my aunt and her friend Trudy.

Trudy and Aunt Mable preferred simple dishes, but were good sports about it. They never complained, even when I served them sushi or escargot. They'd simply suggested we move on to another country with a different cuisine.

I finished telling Tyler about my childhood. He ended up laughing through most of my life's story.

"Your aunt is a woman after my own heart. I like her. So after you came home from studying in Paris, you decided to try your hand at working for someone else here in Austin. What happened? It obviously didn't work out, otherwise Carrie's Creative Catering would never have taken life?"

"I don't think I'm good at working for others. There was a…falling out." That was putting it mildly. Alex Reynolds, the person I'd temped for at one of those many jobs I took while trying to make my small catering business a success, had been a huge flirt, as well as very married. I'd ended up telling him off. Eventually Alex and I had become friends. He told me once that I was the only woman who wouldn't put up with his crap.

"I decided to start my own catering service then. It was… scary."

Tyler stopped in front of my computer screen and picked up the photo of David holding Max. This was the only picture of David I hadn't torn to pieces. I kept it as a reminder not to repeat past mistakes. Apparently, my philosophy wasn't working so well.

"Fiancé—ex-fiancé, that is." At Tyler's questioning expression, I forced myself to expand. "It ended a few years back," I said and wanted to cringe at the nastiness in my tone. Still today, every time I thought about David's betrayal, I couldn't quite keep my bitterness from showing.

"Not very nicely, I take it?"

"No. David didn't really understand the whole commitment thing. You see, he thought it was okay to see other women. I didn't. We broke up. End of story."

Tyler raised an eyebrow, but he must have recognized how hard it still was for me to talk about my broken engagement. He pointed to another picture I'd taped next to my computer of the house I'd fallen in love with in Colorado.

A few years back, Steph, Ed and I had been skiing in Parrish, Colorado, for a week and we'd done a little exploring around the town.

We'd ended up driving around in a subdivision outside of town that was made up of thirty-acre parcels of land—some with houses, some still in development. The second I'd spotted the house, I'd loved it. It was set in the middle of thirty of the most beautiful acres I'd ever seen. Surrounded by mountains on all sides, the view alone would have been worth any amount of money, but the house... Well, the house was a dream.

I'd taken almost a full roll of film on the house alone. I'd even conned Ed into calling about it the next day, only to learn that the price was way beyond my modest reach, but that hadn't stopped me from checking the real estate agent's website every month, just to see if the place was still available.

"What's this?" Tyler asked

I told him about my dream house and he seemed to be torn between being enchanted and amazed at my naiveté.

I glanced at the clock, surprised to see the time. "Can it

really be two a.m.?"

"Do you want me to go?"

I did. I needed to be alone to try to regroup. Since meeting Tyler, we'd skipped over so many getting-to-know-you steps. My head told me we were moving way too fast, but my heart? Well, what I wanted and what was sensible were two very different things.

"No."

"I won't touch you again, at least. I only want to hold you while you sleep. Will you let me?"

This guy was good. I almost believed that he meant that — that he was close to feeling the same out of control way about me as I did for him.

Almost.

Then I remembered Steph's words and about all those other women in his past and Tyler Bennedict's cold, cold heart, and I steeled myself for the inevitable.

He held me for the rest of the night, even though it was a long time before either of us actually slept. We each were uncertain of the other.

Thousands of questions raced through my mind. I wanted to ask him about his life, where he grew up, what was his favorite childhood memory? Did he like cats? But I couldn't seem to find the courage to ask him about his life or where I fit into it.

I awoke to Tyler's lips against the nape of my neck. I leaned back against him and let the passion grow. Soon, kissing and touching weren't enough. I needed him inside me, needed to be as close as I could be to him. For a long time neither of us were willing to get out of bed.

* * * *

As I stood waiting impatiently for my morning eye-opener to brew the following day, I could hear Tyler whistling *Loving Arms* in my shower. Over and over, I reminded myself not to be taken in by all of Tyler Bennedict's charm.

44

David was every bit as charming as Tyler, and look where that had gotten me.

He found me staring aimlessly out my kitchen window. "What are you looking so serious about?"

I tried to smile away the little niggling of uneasiness. "Nothing. Just thinking, I guess."

"I see. What are your plans for today? Do you have to go in to work?" Tyler looked down at me in a way that made me want to tell him yes.

Instead, I shook my head. "Why?"

"I have to go to Fredericksburg today. Come with me."

"Why do you have to go to Fredericksburg?" This almost came out sounding uninterested. Surely, it would be enough to make me not seem like such a pushover in his eyes.

"I'm sure your friend must have told you my family is in real estate."

Oh yeah, Steph had told me a lot about Tyler and his family's business. I knew the Bennedicts were in real estate, just not your picket fence, two kids, one dog, middle class dream kind of real estate. Tyler's family bought and sold houses bigger than most malls, not to mention ones that cost a lot more.

"I have to go to Fredericksburg to check on a house we're thinking of listing. It's a nice drive. We could take a picnic lunch. I happen to know a great caterer. She comes very highly recommended..."

* * * *

The property in question turned out to be a three million dollar mansion situated on a hundred acres of prime riverfront. It was enormous, beautiful and shockingly over-priced.

"So, who exactly owns this little shack?" Once Tyler had finished showing me around the place, I was impressed by it and him and disgusted with myself for being so impressed. I desperately wanted to find some way to show him how unmoved I was by all this luxury around me. Sarcasm seemed to do the trick.

"A friend of my father's — some guy who made it rich in the software business, only to lose everything with the recent market bust. Do you like the place?"

We stopped to admire the view from the third-floor master suite, which seemed to go on for miles. I could fit at least two of my apartments into this room alone.

"It's beautiful if you like all this over-indulged, over-priced stuff."

Tyler laughed and I forgot I was trying not to appear impressed.

He dropped the picnic basket next to the French doors, which opened out onto a deck. "That's what I like about you, Miss Sinclair. You're just plain honest, aren't you?"

We spent the rest of the day exploring the property until the evening settled in around us and Tyler asked the question I'd known was coming from the beginning. I just didn't know how I was going to answer until this moment.

"Do you want me to take you home, Carrie? I will if that's what you want. I don't want to..."

To what? To force me into a relationship I didn't have any business being in or any idea what direction we were heading? *Too late for that.* Instead, I merely shook my head. I didn't want to leave. I wanted to spend the night with Tyler in this three million dollar house and pretend I could fit into his world.

We spread the blanket out on the deck, ate cold chicken salad and drank wine as the surrounding night made the temperature become almost bearable.

"So are you ever going to tell me anything about yourself?" Somehow, I'd finally managed to ask the question I'd been dying to know since we'd met. "I mean, you know all about me by now — all my secrets. What about you?"

Tyler was silent for so long that I wondered if he would say anything, but slowly, in little bits of conversation, he finally opened up to me.

He told me he'd been reluctant to follow his father's example in the beginning. Now, at thirty-eight, Tyler was all but running the real estate empire that his great-grandfather had founded, while Richard slowly let go of more of the responsibilities of the business. I found myself wondering about this. It didn't fit with my impression of Tyler's father. Richard Bennedict wasn't very old, according to Steph. From all the things Tyler had told me about his father, he certainly didn't strike me as the type of man to retire early. He'd probably die arguing over the price of a piece of property.

"Do you at least like what you're doing?" I couldn't help but wonder from all of Tyler's answers if maybe he was simply biding his time, waiting for something better to come along.

He turned to me and smiled. "It's a job. I guess that's all I can really say. I'm doing it for my dad. It's what he wants. It's a family tradition."

Tyler had lived a very privileged life, attended all the finest schools around, and yet he told me he still missed his mother, even though she'd walked out on them when he was only three years old.

"Do you remember very much about her? You were so young when she left. It must have been hard."

"It was, but I remember she was always laughing. I guess that's somewhat strange, considering she just walked out on us without even leaving a note. She must have been unhappy. I guess she was just good at hiding it. At times I can still remember the perfume she wore." He caught my expression and smiled. "I know. But every so often I'll pass someone wearing the same fragrance and I remember my mother laughing and holding me close."

"Your father never remarried?"

Tyler actually laughed at that. "No, Dad prefers the single life too much. My father has many girlfriends, but he'll never remarry. I guess my mother's leaving hurt him more than he'll ever admit."

"I'm sorry. I shouldn't have asked. I didn't mean to pry."

"No, it's okay. I guess it's still hard to talk about it without realizing how much I missed having a mother around growing up. My father tells me I was lucky. She wasn't much of a mother, in his opinion."

"Oh, Tyler, what a terrible thing to say!"

"Maybe, but true nonetheless. Isn't it obvious? She left me as well, didn't she?"

"Yes, I guess she did. I'm sure she had her reasons." I hesitated for a second before asking the question I needed him to answer. "What about you? You've never been married, I take it?"

He turned toward me once more, his eyes searching mine. I could feel his tension growing. This wasn't a comfortable subject for him. "No, I never married."

"Just waiting for the right girl or…let me guess. You don't believe in love, right?" I joked, secretly dreading his answer.

The seriousness in his tone should have been my first warning. "No, I don't. I'm sure that's probably not what you want to hear, but it's how I feel. I think you're only setting yourself up for failure if you believe two people are meant to spend the rest of their lives together. Either you end up hating the person you're with or you simply accept the relationship for what it is and move on when it's over. There's no such thing as soul mates. It's just a fantasy cooked up to sell romance novels."

That hurt. I mean really, really, deep down, wounded straight through to the heart hurt, but at least it brought me back to my cautious self again and if I knew what was good for me, I'd keep it that way.

* * * *

Exactly one month into my relationship with Tyler, and after enduring Stephanie's weekly grill sessions, my friend decided that either I was a glutton for punishment, or I had something Tyler just couldn't live without. Either way,

Steph decided it was time she and Tyler met for a face-to-face.

I wasn't nearly as convinced. Steph was a regular bitch when she wanted to be and it was painfully clear she and Tyler were never going to be friends—with good reason. Steph was becoming more worried about me with each passing week.

In the month I'd spent with Tyler, I still didn't have any real sense of where our relationship might be going. I couldn't seem to shake the feeling that I was one step away from the train wreck I'd been expecting from the beginning.

By this time, Tyler was pretty much living at my apartment with Max and me, although I would never be so bold as to admit this to myself, much less to Steph, or God forbid, Aunt Mable. It was true nonetheless. I'd given him a key. He spent just about every single night in my bed, with the exception of the few times we stayed at his place.

Tyler's house was located in Cat Mountain, an exclusive section of Austin. Although the house was beautiful, I'd never been quite comfortable staying there.

A designer whose name I recognized from Steph's reverent, albeit disappointed complaining of the past, had decorated the house.

Steph had desperately wanted Therese to decorate her home, but unfortunately, the waiting list was enormous. In the end, she'd given up and settled for the second best decorator in town. I didn't have the heart to tell her about Tyler's place.

I was afraid to touch anything in the house because most of the pieces cost more than I made in a year. Although Tyler tried to reassure me I was being silly, in the end, we wound up spending most of our time at my small apartment.

Even Max was warming up to Tyler's constant presence in his life. After a few initial run-ins, I actually think they were starting to like each other. On more than one occasion, I'd been surprised to find Tyler rubbing Max's tubby belly and my angry little kitty? Well, he was purring.

They were just a couple of guys trying to mark their territory and keep from losing ground. I was caught somewhere in the middle, trying to keep them both happy.

"Carrie, if you're going to keep seeing Tyler, then don't you think I need to get to know him better? I want to be supportive, but it's hard. I don't trust him with you. He's going to hurt you someday, you know?"

I did. Oh yeah, I could recount every single one of the nightmares I'd had about that hurt.

"I know you're only concerned about me, but I'm fine... really. I'm a big girl and I know the risks." Her look told me she didn't believe any of the things I'd just said.

"Then it's settled. We'll have dinner at the restaurant he's so good at getting into. You know, the one with a waiting list months in advance. Why not set it up for this Friday?" Steph was determined. This suggestion was a challenge directed straight at Tyler.

When I'd told him about it later, I'd said it in a kind of joking manner, hoping he'd tell me I was crazy. He hadn't. By this time, Tyler had heard all about Steph and he was ready for her.

"Sure, it shouldn't be a problem. Remember, I know the owner. I'll make the reservation for eight. Should we meet them at the restaurant or do you want to pick them up?" Tyler knew I wasn't looking forward to putting him and Steph together in the same room. He'd long ago guessed that Steph was my snitch. I think he was actually enjoying the whole idea of confronting her. This was definitely a bad sign.

By the time Friday rolled around, I was a nervous wreck. I'd spent most of the morning wondering what was going to be left of my friend and Tyler when the evening was over.

In the end, I was the one who was surprised. Tyler was the perfect gentleman and quite charming. Even though Steph was still determined not to like him, he did manage to win her over ever so slightly by his charm. Or maybe it was just the fact that he knew the owner of the most exclusive restaurant in town.

As Ed and I sat across from one another, we stared in amazement at our two companions. Of course, I'd cheated just a little. I'd given Tyler a clue what he would be up against tonight.

"She's very protective of me since David. Steph doesn't want to see me hurt again."

"And she thinks I'm going to hurt you?"

Yes. "No! No, of course not. I just want you to be aware of what you'll be facing tonight. If you want to back out, it's not too late."

His only answer had been to smile and tell me not to worry so much.

After I had introduced Steph to Tyler and spotted the determined look in her eye, all I could do was turn to Ed for help, not that Ed was much. He loved his wife and indulged all of her little idiosyncrasies. He'd back Steph up, no matter what.

"Actually, Carrie, Stephanie and I have met before. It was at the Guichard opening a few years back, wasn't it? You were there with your family. I wasn't sure if you remembered after all this time."

I watched a little more of Steph's anger be replaced with doubt. If Tyler Bennedict actually paid this much attention to her, then maybe he wasn't so bad after all.

"You think you have women all figured out, don't you? You read Steph like a book." I couldn't wait to confront him with this after we'd dropped my friends back at their house and were walking up the steps to my apartment.

This was not the way I'd envisioned the evening turning out. In fact, I'd been counting on Steph's help. She was going to do what I couldn't. Steph was supposed to take Tyler down a notch or two. Instead, she too was beginning to crack under all Tyler's charm. If Tyler could make someone like Steph cave so easily, what chance did I have?

Chapter Four

A Place to Run Home to When Life gets Too Tough

Even though Tyler and I were, for the most part, all but inseparable, he never once suggested introducing me to his father.

I'd long ago found out what a tough customer Richard Bennedict was through Steph, who was proving to be a virtual wealth of information. She had enough connections to the ultra-rich society world Tyler moved in, to know what went on there.

Over one of our Starbucks gossip sessions, we'd jokingly nicknamed Richard 'The Dick', because according to Steph's sources, he had a reputation for being a real ass in the business world and beyond.

Although Tyler never talked about his father, I suspected that if Richard even knew about our relationship, he certainly didn't approve. Tyler had never invited me to attend any of the social functions or dinner parties his father was constantly hosting, which Tyler didn't know I knew anything about.

One night I finally confronted him about this. I'd invited Tyler to see a movie with me the following Friday night.

"I'm sorry, but I can't. I have to attend a party my father is hosting for some business associates. I can't get out of it. Believe me I've tried. I have to be there." He glanced up from undressing in time to catch my hurt reaction. "Don't look at me like that. Trust me. You don't want to be there. *I* don't want to be there. I have to do this. Go see your movie. I'll be home as soon as I can."

"Does your father know about us? Does he even know I exist?" It hurt that he didn't care enough about me to insist that I be included in family plans, even though he was right. I didn't want to go. But that wasn't the point, was it? I wanted to be included in all aspects of his life.

"Does it matter? My father has nothing to do with us. This has nothing to do with you, Carrie. This is business — nothing more. You're not part of that, okay?"

* * * *

By the time I got up the next morning, Tyler had been gone for quite some time. He'd told me he was going to get an early start since the party he was attending was at his father's ranch near Dallas.

In the kitchen I discovered he'd made me coffee. A single white calla lily lay next to my favorite cup with a note —

I'll miss you.

As much as I wanted to believe this was really how Tyler felt, I couldn't. I still remembered our argument the night before. Tyler only wanted to include me in his life when it was convenient for him.

Even though I'd had dozens of conversations with my aunt since meeting Tyler, I hadn't once been able to tell her about him. At the prospect of spending the entire weekend alone with all of my doubts, I needed her sound advice more than ever before.

Steph was my friend, but she would have an 'I tried to warn you' look plastered all over her face and I wasn't ready to see it again.

So instead, I packed some things for Max and myself, jotted a short note to Tyler just in case he happened to return this weekend — or ever, for that matter. I let him know I'd decided to spend some time with my aunt. I hoped my note conveyed just enough 'I don't care about you and won't be missing you one little bit attitude', even if it wasn't genuine.

Unfortunately, the farther I got from Austin, the more worried I became about the ridiculous note I'd left at the apartment. Since I didn't want to have to try to explain it to him over the phone, and just to keep some amount of self-respect, I turned my cell off entirely.

My aunt's ranch is less than a three-hour drive from Austin. By lunchtime, I was turning my small compact car onto Aunt Mable's gravel drive.

The house was typical country in design. One of my ancestors built the place over a hundred years earlier. It was two stories, white and shuttered, with a nice wide porch and a swing to boot. It was country!

Aunt Mable knew exactly what time to expect me. She and Aunt Trudy, who I'd long ago adopted as my second aunt, would have lunch waiting for me by now. I'd bet they had both been standing outside on the porch waiting for me the second my car had left the blacktop.

My aunt was eighty years old and she didn't have a single strand of gray in her light brown hair. Those vibrant blue eyes I'd always been jealous of as a child were still the same deep blue I remembered. Today they reminded me of Tyler, the person I'd made this trip to forget. Mable was petite like me, barely more than five foot-two and a hundred pounds soaking wet. She was fit and trim, whereas dear old Trudy was plump and becoming more rounded with time. She and my aunt were as opposite as night and day, and just a close as sisters.

I hugged them each in turn then again because I'd missed them both terribly. Max, who had grown tired of being squished in the middle of all this hugging, let out a meow and bounded from my arms.

Aunt Mable hadn't been too thrilled the first time I'd brought Max home to meet her. She'd warmed to him slowly. Now she told me he was the only male she could tolerate being around much anymore.

"Max, there's milk by the fridge waiting on you."

He acknowledged her generous offer by rubbing between

her legs on his way to the kitchen.

"And there's lunch on the table ready for you, child. My goodness, do you ever eat anymore? I swear, for someone who cooks for a living, you're as skinny as a rake. Or has something else got you pining away to nothing?"

As always, my aunt understood the real reason behind my sudden need to visit. I didn't have to say a word, and she wouldn't ask a single question, because that's what family did for each other. They gave quiet comfort.

"I'm starving, Aunt Mable! What's for lunch?"

Trudy and Mable gave each other a knowing look. They'd get the truth out of me eventually. But they could wait.

"Well, nothing fancy for sure, not like you're accustomed to preparing, but I do seem to remember how much you like my fried chicken."

I would have recognized the delicious smell of Aunt Mable's fried chicken anywhere. No one made fried chicken like my aunt. I still didn't know what she put into the mix and she would never tell me. Only Aunt Trudy knew her secret.

"Oh, yes! Yes! I've missed your fried chicken so much! Oh, thank you, thank you, thank you!" I hugged her again.

"Well then, come sit down and let's eat. Trudy will need to take her pills soon anyway." This was my aunt. Never much on sentimentality, but always there with a good solid shoulder to lean on whenever I needed it. God, I'd missed her! She'd give me all the time in the world to tell me what was wrong.

We spent the rest of the afternoon catching up, which meant I got to hear all about the latest gossip going around Early. Apparently in the three months since I'd been home last, plenty had happened.

"You know Seth Walton—the boy you dated for a while in high school? The one we thought was such a nice boy?"

I'd never told my aunt Seth was my first lover, but I think she'd guessed as much.

Aunt Mable paused a moment for effect. "In jail!"

"No! Seth's in jail? What happened? He was always so sweet," I asked.

"Don't I know it, child, but apparently, he was only fooling. The boy was involved in a stolen car ring. Uh-huh," she confirmed when she saw my surprise. "Buying cars stolen from around the area and selling them to some people overseas. Can you imagine?" Aunt Mable shook her head and handed me another chicken breast. It didn't matter if it were my second helping. It tasted wonderful.

"Geez, I never would have guessed it. Seth's in jail. And I was going to marry him!" I could laugh about it now, but at sixteen, I was certain Seth Walton was the man of my dreams. I guess my pattern for choosing losers started young.

My aunts and I spent the rest of the day talking and gossiping. I was happier than I'd been in a long time. I'd missed them both so much.

After dinner, Aunt Trudy, who was spending the weekend with us, went up to bed and Aunt Mable and I sat in her old-fashioned kitchen with the windows opened to the gentle summer night breeze, drinking coffee. It was then that I finally got around to telling her everything— and I mean everything except about the sex—about my relationship with Tyler.

"I know you must be disappointed in me, especially after David. You always told me I needed to be stronger—not let any man get under my skin."

"Oh, honey, you're my flesh and blood and I love you, but you and I are worlds apart emotionally. I can say those things and mean them. You, on the other hand? Well, you've always worn your heart on your sleeve, just like your mother. I can't tell you how many times I wished I were more like Elizabeth. She was special. No, you just keep caring about people the way you do, Carrie. I'm willing to bet things will work out just fine with your young man in time."

My aunt had a habit of inviting some of my old high

school friends to drop over whenever I was in town, so when the doorbell interrupted our conversation, I assumed this was one of those times. The last person I was expecting to find standing on my aunt's front porch was Tyler.

"What are you doing here?" I blinked a couple of times to make sure I wasn't actually hallucinating. No way was Tyler Bennedict supposed to be here in Early. He was supposed to be at some fancy party hosted by his father, forgetting he even knew me.

"I couldn't stand being away from you. I got as far as the outskirts of Dallas before I called my father, listened to his favorite speech about how I needed to behave more responsibly, but all I could think of was how much I missed you. When I got home and found your note, I freaked. I'm sorry. I probably should have called first. I did try, but your phone must have been turned off. May I come inside?"

I stood aside and let Tyler in. He closed the door softly then reached for me. His mouth found mine, urgent, demanding—a dream come true.

"God, I've missed you," he breathed against my lips and I closed my eyes, shuddering at the raw desire in his voice.

I desperately wanted to believe him. "Me too."

He brushed my hair away from my face and the tenderness in his touch made me want to linger here with him for a while. I didn't want to break the spell.

"Carrie, who is it?" The sound of Aunt Mable's voice brought me out of my shock.

Before I could answer her, Tyler captured my lips once more. I melted against him, the world around me all but forgotten. When he ended this kiss, it was a long time before I could catch my breath.

He gave me another quick kiss. "I think you'd better answer her."

"I have a surprise visitor." We walked into the kitchen to face her together. She was smiling. She'd guessed already.

"This must be your young man?"

I glanced at Tyler. He was actually grinning. I'd been

so careful not to think about him in any other terms other than just the man I was dating at the moment. But he wasn't denying it and we'd certainly moved beyond casual acquaintances a long time ago.

"Aunt Mable, this is Tyler Bennedict, my friend from Austin. Tyler, this is my aunt."

She ignored Tyler's outstretched hand entirely. Instead, she enveloped him in one of her surprisingly strong bear hugs while winking at me over his shoulder. I tried not to laugh.

"Any friend of Carrie's is welcome in my home. I hope you'll stay with us?" This had both my aunt and me looking at him curiously. I'd been so surprised to see him I hadn't really thought beyond the fact that he was here. But Tyler didn't appear to have any baggage with him.

"Only if you're sure it isn't an imposition? I wouldn't want to be in the way. I was just planning to get a room in town...but this is awfully nice of you." While Tyler's charm might work on Steph, and it certainly did on me, it wasn't going to work on Aunt Mable.

"Now, I wouldn't have offered if it were a problem, boy, so don't try to smooth talk me."

Tyler was clearly a little taken aback by her.

"Carrie, honey, why don't you show Tyler up to your room?"

I'm sure my jaw must have dropped a mile at her little bombshell. Of course, Aunt Mable knew I wasn't a chaste virgin anymore, not at almost thirty-five, but we hadn't really talked about sex since I was younger. I certainly would never have considered sleeping in the same bed with my boyfriend while staying with her.

"Now don't look at me like that. You'd think I was dead— or worse. I know what young people do together, so there's no point in you looking so shocked. Why don't you go with Tyler and get him settled in? Then you'll both come talk to me for a little bit. Right now, I think you have things to settle between you, don't you?"

I followed Tyler outside to the rental car and waited while he retrieved his overnight bag. He dropped it at our feet then I was in his arms again.

"It's nice out here. Peaceful. Do you mind if we stay here for a bit?"

I nodded against his chest.

"I like your aunt. She's not your typical sweet, old lady though, is she?"

"Not at all. You'll meet her best friend since grade school tomorrow. Aunt Trudy is spending the weekend with us. How long are you staying?"

"As long as you want me to. I'm going to enjoy getting to know your family." He was quiet for a moment before he asked the question I'd known was coming since my aunt's outrageous remark. "How many other men have you brought home to meet Aunt Mable?"

I wished more than ever that I could tell him hundreds — make up names even — but for reasons that seemed to escape me, I couldn't seem to lie to Tyler.

"I don't make a habit of bringing men home to meet my aunt."

"Not even David?"

I hesitated. In the two years David and I had dated, he'd never once visited my aunt's home. Aunt Mable and Trudy had met him on several occasions when they'd visited me in Austin and, as always, my aunt had been direct. She'd never trusted David. She'd told me to get rid of him almost from the moment she met him. What would her opinion of Tyler be?

"Not even David, and if you recall, I didn't bring you here either, buddy. I don't know why she said those things. I'm just as surprised by it as you."

"I know. You should have seen your face." He kissed my nose. "I think we'd better go inside before she gets the wrong idea about what we're up to out here."

It was becoming a dangerous pattern for us, not talking about any of the things we needed to talk about with each other.

Tyler followed me up to my old bedroom on the second floor. Somehow, I think he sensed I was feeling a little overwhelmed by his appearance.

"Are you sure you're okay with me sleeping here with you? If not, I could always use another room or go to a hotel."

I hated this confusing way Tyler had of letting me make all the decisions about our relationship. It was as if it absolved him of any wrong-doing by making it my decision entirely. As much as it hurt to consider, I wasn't ready to send him away.

"No. No, you don't have to go. I want you to stay with me."

I opened the door to my little girl room caught somewhere in the eighties and remembered just how small my twin bed was.

"That is, unless you'd rather sleep someplace bigger."

His answer was to grin at me. "I don't think so. You can't get away from me in this bed."

Seeing Tyler in my bedroom made me all the more aware of the things that represented home to me in the past. All of my familiar teenage fantasies now made me feel vulnerable and young, not at all like the chic, in-control woman I needed him to believe I truly was.

The girl who left this room behind at seventeen was a hopeless romantic. It showed in every single piece of my past, from the frilly pink oh-dear-God-what-was-I-thinking bedspread to the tons of romance novels I'd never been concerned about before this moment.

Unfortunately, all of these worries showed on my face when Tyler glanced my way. There was a tenderness in his expression that I would never have believed him capable of possessing. He came and brushed my hair back in a gesture I would always associate with him. "So this is where little Carrie spent her nights dreaming," he teased.

Tyler spotted the picture of Aunt Mable and me taken

shortly after I'd come to live with her, back when she was still trying to be the June Cleaver mother figure.

My aunts and I had been at Six Flags for the day. It had been before I'd become settled in enough at my new school to make some friends closer to my own age. I remember vividly every detail of that day.

It had been one of those perfect late summer days, when it wasn't too hot and there was just a touch of fall in the air. Aunt Mable and I had both been soaking wet from one of the rides I'd insisted on dragging her on, my short blonde curls going in all directions, much as they still did today, my aunt's light brown hair slicked back and dripping wet. We had been smiling at the camera while Aunt Trudy had taken our picture. We'd forced her to come along, but she'd put her foot down about riding any of those "crazy rides", as she'd called them.

Tyler held the picture up. "You were cute as a bug, even back then."

I wasn't falling for all that tenderness in his eyes. I didn't believe any of the reasons he'd given me for coming here today. I couldn't. It was just too out of character for the Tyler I knew.

Instead, I fought to cover my happiness by reminding myself that my aunt was waiting patiently for us downstairs.

"Are you hungry? Because Aunt Mable made fried chicken and you haven't lived until you've tasted her chicken." Of course, I was talking too fast, trying to cover my nervousness. When Tyler looked at me the way he was right now, with nothing of the previous smile on his face, my insides did strange things and my tongue said the first thing that came to mind. There was just no censoring it.

Tyler kissed me again, thoroughly shutting me up. "You're right. We shouldn't keep Aunt Mable waiting. And no, I haven't eaten and I'm starving. Chicken sounds wonderful."

He held my hand as we walked downstairs together. Another surprise. Tyler wasn't a hand holder — at least not usually. His whole behavior just by being here right now was confusing.

The minute we walked into the kitchen, I spotted what was on my aunt's mind. She had the chicken out and waiting for him. Ice tea poured. "Come sit down and have some dinner, Tyler."

Aunt Mable was a woman on a mission. I'd given away far too much by simply being here today. She knew I cared about Tyler a great deal, just as she knew there were plenty of things I didn't know or understand about him. Aunt Mable was determined to get to the bottom of it.

She set the plate of chicken in front of Tyler but didn't give him time to pick up his napkin before she started in with her interrogation.

"So, tell me a little about yourself Tyler? What kind of work do you do?" She knew exactly what he did for a living because I'd told her Tyler was in real estate. She was simply starting him out with a few simple questions, giving him a false sense of security before working up to the more difficult stuff.

Tyler glanced from me to my aunt and smiled.

"Well, it's really not all that interesting. I'm in real estate, like my father. I joined the family firm a few years back." He threw me a slight wink to show me he'd guessed what she was up to, but she didn't intimidate him, as she was so good at doing to most of my other boyfriends. Aunt Mable had finally met her match. Tyler didn't need me to rescue him, even if I'd considered it.

"So your family's been in real estate for a while then? Have you always lived in Austin?" On and on she went with the questions until even I was ready to beg for mercy.

Tyler never once hesitated from answering any of them. He looked her straight in the eye and never wavered throughout the entire interrogation. When Aunt Mable finally decided she'd pushed enough for one night, I breathed a sigh of relief.

"Carrie, it's such a pretty night out, why don't you and

Tyler go for a little walk? I'm going to bed. It's way past my bedtime already." Aunt Mable hugged us both before leaving us alone.

An absolutely gorgeous night was in the works outside, the kind you only find in the country, outside of the intrusive city lights. I grabbed an old blanket Aunt Mable kept in the hall closet for just such occasions and walked outside into the stillness of the night.

"What's the blanket for?"

I had to smile. He was such a city boy.

"You'll see," I told him. I knew this place by heart. I'd been over every square inch of it growing up on foot and later on the back of my favorite mare, Jelly Belly. I could find my way to the lake with my eyes closed.

Tonight, the summer breeze carried the scent of Aunt Mable's lilac bushes. They'd be in full bloom by now. As a teenager, I used to pick armloads of them, but she'd never complained. Deep down, Aunt Mable was a hopeless romantic just like me. She talked tough and she'd told me more than once never to let a man break my heart, but I knew hers was once broken, even though she would never tell me the details. On more than one occasion, I'd begged Trudy to share what had happened, but she was a true friend. They'd kept each other's secrets safe through the years.

Tyler and I reached the grassy bank of my aunt's small lake. I tossed the blanket on the ground, turned to Tyler and smiled. "Don't tell me you've never been stargazing before? This is the perfect spot for it."

The sound of his laughter against the night breeze sent a shiver of something unpleasant through my body. "Stargazing, huh? I can't say that I've ever done it quite so…simply before."

He sat down next to me as I tried to read the meaning behind those words. No doubt he'd been stargazing before with dozens of women, more times than I cared to contemplate. I'm sure most of their stargazing would include the finest champagne and certainly something better than a worn out blanket handmade by Trudy.

Tyler possessed the uncanny ability to read my thoughts when I least wanted him to. He knew exactly what I was thinking right now. He glanced my way. He was trying to understand my mood. "This is nice."

"Yes." I hoped to sound uncaring, while secretly I wanted to ask him about all those other times. He leaned over me, blocking out the stars and forcing me to meet his gaze. When he kissed me, I forgot all those other past and future women in his life. The touch of his lips, the feel of his body next to mine, had the power to make me believe there was hope for us. No matter what horror stories Steph had told me, when Tyler kissed me, I believed I was the most important woman in his life.

When Tyler lay next to me again, his eyes no longer on me but the stars above us, I could speak again without fear of my voice trembling over every single word. I tried to find something to say to change the subject.

"I'm sorry about my aunt."

"What are you sorry for?" Blue eyes shifted back to mine, unsettling me for a moment.

"I'm sorry for all the questions. Aunt Mable means well, but she can be a little stubborn when it comes to me."

Tyler trailed his fingers across my cheek and I trembled in response. God help me I wanted him more than ever before.

"I like your aunt. She's straightforward and honest and she's crazy about you. She's a good woman. A little eccentric maybe, but she cares about you." He stopped for a second, his eyes searching mine in the darkness. "My father does know about you. I don't want you to think I'm keeping you secret from him."

"He just doesn't approve." I said the words for him.

"It's not you. It's…"

"It's just *who* I am?"

He didn't answer. He didn't need to. It was all there in his silence. I'm sure in his father's opinion I was as wrong for

Tyler as the plague and just as unwelcome.

We didn't do much stargazing that night. We made love right there beneath them. The cool night breeze shivered across our heated skin, a welcome relief. It was as if we'd been apart for years instead of just a few short hours. This was how it always was with Tyler and me.

I loved him and I wanted him, and because of this, my heart and head were at constant war with one another.

Chapter Five

Having the Upper Hand with Your Boyfriend

When I awoke the next day, the sun was high in the morning sky. I forced my eyes open only to find I was alone in bed.

Voices drifted up from below my bedroom window. I showered and dressed as quickly as possible, hoping to rescue Tyler from Aunt Mable. I found him sitting on the back porch next to my aunt, who was rocking in her favorite wicker chair. They were both shelling peas. Yep, my ultra-rich boyfriend was actually shelling peas. I would have given just about anything for a camera at that moment.

"Well, good morning, sunshine. I see some things never change. You're still a lazy bones in the morning. Me and this one here have been having ourselves a nice little chat about you." My aunt gave me another one of her conspiratorial winks. All of my earlier amusement over finding Tyler shelling peas disappeared the second I heard those words. I understood too well what her *nice little chats* involved. The extent of just how painful it must have been was right there on Tyler's face. He looked as if he'd just undergone an interview for a seat on the Supreme Court. I'd been in the hot seat enough times in the past to know how relentless my aunt could be.

"You know, I bet your friend over at Sangria's would love to see you right now." I hoped to lighten the moment. The second his eyes lifted to mine, I stopped feeling sorry for Tyler. He certainly didn't need my help with Aunt Mable or anything else. Tyler knew how to stand on his own.

"We'll be having these for dinner tonight, Tyler, so all

your hard work will have paid off. I'm afraid you two are on your own for lunch today, though. Carrie, you remember Trudy and I always do our garage sale-ing on Saturday morning before having lunch at Binions Steakhouse."

"Of course." I leaned down and kissed her cheek. "I don't want you and Trudy giving up your fun for us. We'll be fine."

My aunts were garage sale junkies. It didn't matter if Aunt Mable had more money than she would spend in a lifetime, she loved those little bargain items she and Trudy found at the sales around the county. They'd been garage sale-ing for years.

Aunt Trudy was clearly surprised and more than a little put out at finding Tyler there, wrecking her perfect weekend plans for me. I was the only child she'd ever known and the thought of having to share me with anyone other than Aunt Mable just didn't sit right with her.

I promised her I would take her over to her apartment later in the afternoon to get some of her things and spend some quality time alone together. She settled for that.

At this point, since things probably couldn't get much more embarrassing for me, I settled into my role as tour guide. I took Tyler to all the places I'd spent my time growing up and he did his very best not to appear bored.

He almost convinced me he enjoyed seeing where I attended high school. I barely remembered the girl I'd been back then when I believed life revolved around cheerleading.

"Do you still have that outfit? I bet you looked amazing in it."

I ignored Tyler's little comment entirely. There was just no way that I was going to tell him the outfit in question still hung in my closet.

It was late in the afternoon before my aunts returned with all their little treasures. Tyler would just have to sink or swim alone with my Aunt Mable. I needed to spend some time with Aunt Trudy.

"Go. I'll be fine. Maybe I'll talk your aunt into giving me her recipe for fried chicken. I'm sure my friend at Sangria's could increase his business by a great deal with the help of such a recipe."

"Fat chance of that happening, mister," my aunt told him before retreating to the kitchen with Tyler in tow.

Through the years, Aunt Trudy and I had worked through so many problems at the local Dairy Queen, usually over a hot-fudge sundae. Today, she didn't appear to be in any hurry to go to the apartment. There was definitely something on her mind, not that I hadn't known this since I'd introduced her to Tyler. Apparently, I possessed all the signs of someone in love with the wrong man. It must be like some disease. The people who loved you the most could spot a doomed relationship from miles away.

"Honey, I don't mean to butt into your business and you know I love you, but wake up! He's not the one for you. He'll hurt you, and I mean hurt you bad! I can see it as plain as I can see the nose on my face. Don't put yourself through that again. Get out while you still can."

I'd guessed this would be her opinion of Tyler. It was easy to read because Trudy never bothered to hide how she felt about anything.

We sat across from each other in a booth listening to bad country music on the jukebox that had been part of the décor of the restaurant forever. I wanted to deny every single one of her worries but I couldn't. I knew them all by heart, because I felt the same way.

"Aunt Trudy, Tyler isn't David..." I couldn't go on in the face of her worried expression. "You're right. I know what you're saying is true." This surprised her to no end. She was expecting me to be my usual stubborn self. "I agree with you. You're right. Tyler isn't right for me and I have no doubt whatsoever he'll end up breaking my heart someday."

"Then why are you with him, honey? Break it off! Get out before it's too late. Don't let him break your heart." When my gaze met hers, she stopped. She saw the truth before I confirmed it. It was too late already.

"Well, maybe I'm wrong. After all, what do I know about it? I never had a man want to marry me. No, you do what you feel is right in your heart, Carrie. You have a good heart, honey."

We finished the rest of our hot fudge sundaes in silence. The trip to Aunt Trudy's tiny one-bedroom apartment was strained as well. I'd always cherished our time together, but now for the first time, something stood between us. Tyler.

Tyler and I left for Austin after attending Sunday services with the aunts. After we dropped Tyler's rental car off in Brownwood, the drive back to Austin was a quiet one for both of us. Max settled into Tyler's lap while he drove and I pretended to sleep. Somehow, I couldn't shake the feeling that I was leaving something important behind, something I might never have again.

* * * *

"My father wants to meet you..."

Those words sent me scurrying out of the bathroom, toothbrush still in my mouth and a have-you-lost-your-mind expression plastered on my face.

"He wants to meet you for himself. There's this thing next week." Where Tyler was concerned, there was always a thing. Since the weekend we'd spent at my aunt's place two weeks earlier, he hadn't mentioned his father again.

"It's one of those black tie events—next Friday." Tyler yelled this part at me because I'd gone back into the bathroom and shut the door. I needed time to think. Alone. Preferably without Tyler close by, reading all of my uncertainties.

It wasn't as if I wasn't secretly dying to meet The Dick, because I was, if only for comparison purposes. It's just, well, frankly, he scared me to death.

Richard Bennedict ate little girls like me for breakfast. I

wouldn't stand a chance with him.

"Before you can come up with a good excuse in there, I've checked your schedule already."

"Damn," I muttered to the angry woman staring back at me in the mirror with toothpaste on her mouth. I was just ready to tell him about some imaginary dinner party I'd scheduled for the exact same night.

How bad could it really be? The man was nothing to me...right? Only the father of the man I was crazy about. Only the man Tyler worshiped and whose opinion meant everything to him. Only his father. No pressure there.

I came out of the bathroom. "Sure, I'm free and it sounds like fun." It sounded anything but fun. It sounded like sheer torture. If the laughter in his eyes was any indication, the man standing in front of me wasn't buying my act either. Tyler was getting a little too good at figuring me out. I'd need to work on my poker face, otherwise, *he'd* eat me alive.

"It won't be so bad. If you want, you can invite your friend Stephanie. I have extra tickets and this type of thing should be right up her alley."

At the time I'd thought, *There's no way I'm putting my best friend through that, buddy.* When Monday morning rolled around, I was singing a slightly different tune. I was now desperate.

I spotted Steph, dressed in her perfect little suit in just the right shade of green to set off her eyes. I barely waited until we took our seats before hitting her with it.

"Here's the deal. There's this thing, the annual art something or other on Friday—"

"You mean The Fine Arts Benefit Ball," she correctly supplied for me.

"Um, yeah, I think that's it. Anyway, Tyler has extra tickets and I was wondering if you and Ed would like to come?"

"*You're* invited to the Fine Arts Benefit Ball?" There was no denying the astonishment in her tone, which seemed to imply they'd be crazy to let the likes of me into such a swank

70

affair. There was just enough reverence in Steph's voice to remind me that I was way out of my league. I desperately needed her help.

"Well…yeah. I'm supposed to be going with Tyler. The Dick wants to meet me."

"You haven't met The Dick yet?" Her total shock convinced my not so big deal was now enormous.

My tone lacked any confidence at all. "No. Is this a big deal? Wait… This isn't supposed to be a big deal, Steph. Tyler told me it wasn't a big deal!" I stopped talking then when I threatened to hyperventilate.

"Carrie, calm down. Maybe it's not such a big deal after all. I'm sure it means nothing." She dismissed my panic with a wave of her elegant hand. We both knew better, and Steph's attempt at convincing me differently wasn't working any better for her than mine had done for me all weekend long.

"You don't believe that any more than I do."

"Of course I do. It won't be so bad. Stop worrying."

"Oh give me a break! I am such an idiot!"

"Oh Carrie, you are not. You're just someone who—"

"Someone who was stupid enough to fall in love with the wrong guy yet again? Someone who should have known better? Someone whose best friend tried to warn her?"

"I was going to say, someone who's falling in love."

When I'd first told Steph about Tyler's surprise visit to my aunt's house, she'd been shocked. It made her doubt some of her previous bad feelings about him. In her opinion, if Tyler cared enough about me to face those two, surely he couldn't be entirely bad.

Steph had met them both on several different occasions when the aunts came to Austin to visit me. At first, they were just abrasive enough to set her good manners on edge. By the end of their first trip she was in love with them and overlooking their less than genteel behavior at times.

Tyler had clearly gotten the all thumbs up from Aunt Mable, which was something David never accomplished.

This forced Steph to take a closer look at him. Trudy's opinion she discounted entirely.

"Oh God, what was I thinking? I'm in so much trouble here. I'm in way over my head. I can't go through this thing alone. Please, please, please, say you'll come with me. I don't even have a dress to wear. I'm not sure what type of dress is called for at this sort of thing. Please, Steph, you have to come."

"Are you kidding? I've been trying to get an invitation to this thing for years. It's *the* event of a lifetime. I'd kill to go to it."

"The event of a lifetime. Oh God, I think I'm going to be sick. There's no way."

"Oh yes there is. Because I'll be there with you to make sure everything turns out perfectly."

* * * *

The plan was for Tyler to pick Stephanie and me up at her house around seven on Friday. Since Ed had to work late, he would change at the office and meet us at the hotel where the ball took place.

I arrived at Steph's house several hours early to get fixed up. By the time Tyler arrived, I might have been a wreck on the inside, but I looked good on the outside in my strapless black gown I'd spent way too much money on because it set off my perfect—*no tan lines, thank you very much*—glow. From Tyler's expression, I could tell he was impressed as well.

So was I. This was the first time I'd actually seen him in anything other than a suit and the occasional jeans and polo. Dressed in a black tuxedo, Tyler was even more stunning.

"You look amazing."

He seemed amused by my outburst. "And you, Miss Sinclair, are breathtaking."

I gave him a little twirl so he could get the full effect. When I turned around, his expression said it all. If we weren't at

Steph's right now, we wouldn't be going anywhere.

The Wentwood Hotel is one of the oldest hotels in Austin. Built somewhere in the early eighteen hundreds when downtown Austin wasn't much more than a cattle trail, it had survived one fire, which had pretty much destroyed the place entirely then there had been a tornado that had taken off the roof along with the top floor. All that and it had made it through several recessions when the business struggled just to keep its doors open. Restored in the late nineties to its past glory, the Wentwood had never looked more beautiful, prestigious or more intimidating than it did tonight.

Steph, Tyler and I waited close to the front entrance for Ed to arrive. He showed up a short time later looking about as thrilled to be there as I felt. Ed was willing to humor his wife. Steph was in heaven. I was in hell. Ed was somewhere in between, but leaning toward my direction.

"Relax, you're doing great, and you just happen to be the prettiest girl here." When Tyler whispered those words against my ear as we danced close, I forgot all about my upcoming meeting with The Dick.

After several hours had passed without any sign of Tyler's father, I actually began to feel a little cocky. This was nothing. Why had I been so worried?

The food arrived, served buffet style, of all things. They charged a thousand dollars a plate for this? My professional caterer's mind cringed at the very thought of serving a buffet, which consisted of foods I could have thrown together in my sleep, to this caliber of guests. This was nothing. Yeah, I could survive this night.

Then I came face to face with The Dick.

"Tyler, there you are."

Tyler and I both turned at the same time to see an older, but not any less attractive, version of Tyler making his way through the crowd of people.

"You came. I was afraid you were going to stand us up once again."

"Dad. I looked for you earlier but you were…busy. Dad this is Carrie Sinclair. Carrie, my father."

You could have cut the tension between the two men with a knife. They were definitely at odds with each other. I couldn't help but believe it was all because of me.

Once Tyler had introduced his father to Steph and Ed, Richard didn't waste any time. He turned to me, took me by my arm and told his son he was stealing me away for a little while. I just caught Tyler's angry expression before Richard pulled me out onto the dance floor. It took everything inside me not to push him away.

"So, young lady, we meet at last. I was beginning to think you were just a figment of my son's imagination. Now I understand why he's been keeping you a secret. You're just as lovely as Tyler said. There's no doubt my son has excellent taste in women." Richard Bennedict was the epitome of politeness, but I couldn't help but feel as if I'd just been insulted in the worst possible way. In the space of just a few minutes, he'd managed to put me in my place very thoroughly as nothing more than some little plaything for his son.

Out of sheer desperation, I glanced around the room for help, only to see that Richard was slowly dancing me farther away from Tyler. I suspected this was deliberate. He wanted to get me away from my lifeline to have some fun with me.

I was relieved when the music finally stopped. Unfortunately, Richard didn't seem intent on taking me back to Tyler right away.

"Why don't you let me show you around a little? You're not in a hurry to go back to my son, are you?"

I tried to smile but inside I was quaking. This man scared the daylights out of me. I nodded my answer, unwilling to trust my voice not to make a bigger fool out of me.

Richard didn't bother introducing me to any of his friends, even though there were certainly enough of them stopping us along the way to wherever he was planning to take me.

Again, this was deliberate. He was sending me a message and I got it loud and clear. *Don't get too comfortable.*

After we'd wandered around the crowded room for almost half an hour — and yes, I was counting the minutes on my watch — Richard finally remembered he was there with someone.

The girl he did introduce me to was in the same boat as me — on the outside looking in. Unlike me, she was thoroughly enjoying her jaunt into the ultra-rich society world. I don't remember her name — something along the lines of Muffy or Mindy. She was a bleached-out blonde with a knockout body and definitely fake boobs. She was the flavor of the moment.

Richard excused himself by telling me, instead of Muffy or Mindy, he would be back soon. He left me there with my social equal to become better acquainted.

After listening to her awestruck chatter for another ten minutes, I was ready to call it quits. I'd just started contemplating working my way back to Tyler when Richard reappeared and took me to him.

When Steph and Ed deserted us around midnight, I had been ready to leave with them. As much as I'd enjoyed Tyler's company, I'd seen enough of Richard and the ultra-rich society for one night.

"Carrie? Carrie Sinclair? Oh my God, look at you?" I recognized Alex Reynolds' voice above the noise of the room. I turned to see Alex making his way across the crowded dance floor to my side.

In his usual fashion, Alex lifted me up off the floor and twirled me around in a gesture most people, certainly his wife, would interpret as intimate. "What are you doing here?" He finally put me down once more.

Alex Reynolds had been a learning point for me. In spite of all my travels abroad, I had been still quite green when I'd moved to Austin and had started supporting myself by working as a temp.

Alex's advertising firm had been my first stop on the road

to success. I'd almost gone out with him. He was devilishly handsome after all, but also very married—a point Alex had failed to make clear in all the times he'd asked me out. He was a big flirt and, I suspected, unfaithful to his wife, but he did love Melissa.

I'd told him off, and somehow won Alex's respect because of it. I think I was one of the few people who'd ever had the nerve to stand up to him. We'd eventually become good friends. In fact, until Tyler became a part of my life, we'd made it a point to have lunch at least once a month. Since Tyler? Well, I'd been dodging Alex's calls, hoping to keep him a secret. I wasn't sure why. It wasn't as if I'd done anything wrong, but it sure felt like it, especially now.

Once I'd opened Carrie's Creative Catering, Alex had begun throwing business my way while begging me to sell my little cooking business to him for his wife. Melissa, he told me, was good at planning parties, and she needed something to occupy her time so she wasn't constantly wondering what he was up to.

Alex was the only other man I knew who was rich enough to attend this type of affair.

"I thought you hated these pompous things, as you were always so fond of calling them."

I caught a glimpse of Tyler's stony expression and realized how my little interchange with Alex must look to him. "Alex, this is Tyler Bennedict. Tyler this is my *friend*, Alex Reynolds."

Tyler and Alex exchanged the kind of strained pleasantries that made it clear they weren't going to be friends. Thankfully, Alex left soon after. I could feel Tyler's anger growing as he led me out on the dance floor and we danced one final time. "Don't try making me jealous, Carrie. I'm not the type of man to become jealous." This was all he said. It was enough. It was too ridiculous to dignify with a response. After the song ended, Tyler practically pulled me from the hotel, handed the valet our ticket and we stood in tense silence waiting for the Range Rover.

The drive back to my apartment was a silent one, with no break in the tension between us.

"I'm not staying. I have an early appointment in the morning."

Once he'd parked the Rover, I didn't give him time to do the polite, gentlemanly thing Tyler was so good at doing.

Instead, I got out of the SUV, almost tripped over my skirt, and ran up all four flights of stairs to my apartment. Tyler didn't come after me.

By the time I reached my apartment, I was angry and hurt and would have slammed the door as hard as I could to relieve all of those things if I hadn't remembered poor Hazel sleeping next door. I settled for throwing my bag halfway across the room, followed by the clothes Tyler was so good at leaving lying on my bedroom floor.

After pacing the apartment trying to work off my temper without much success, I showered, removed the pounds of makeup Steph had insisted I needed and finally got my hair shampooed out of the French twist it had been escaping from most of the evening.

I was determined that Tyler wasn't going to keep me up, worrying about if I'd ever see him again. With a whole lot of help from Aunt Mable's cure-all, Southern Comfort, I accomplished my goal. I no longer cared *who* Tyler was, much less *if* I'd ever see him again.

* * * *

"I'm sorry." Those words were the first thing out of Tyler's mouth when he called the next morning. "I'm sorry. I don't know why I reacted the way I did last night."

"Alex is just a friend. I worked for him, and yes, he tried to make it more, but I couldn't. Alex is married. It would have been wrong. He's not a bad person really. He's just used to getting his own way."

"It's okay. You don't have to explain anything to me."

"But you believe me, don't you?" I wished those words

back the second they were out of my mouth. They sounded so needy.

"I believe you."

We talked for a little while longer but neither of us brought up the problems in our relationship, which were now growing more evident with each passing day. At least Tyler and I had one thing in common. We didn't know how to face up to our problems, much less deal with them. By the end of the call, we were almost back to our usual 'don't ask, don't tell' way of life.

* * * *

For Carrie's Creative Catering, this year's holiday season was gearing up to be one of our busiest. I had parties lined up for just about every single day through the end of the year. In my current career choice, business was booming. In my personal life, nothing could have been more confusing.

I still didn't know where I stood with Tyler any more now than I did at the beginning of our relationship. It was becoming harder to remain content with this. I was in love. I wanted to spend the rest of my life with him.

So to avoid having to face any of those problems, I threw myself into my work. I booked parties like crazy, in the hopes that I could run away from my troubles. Of course, I knew it wouldn't work for long, but for the time being, it helped to keep busy instead of worrying.

Tyler and I continued to see each other every single night, even though he'd never once mentioned his father again. He didn't need to. I knew where I stood with The Dick. He'd made this perfectly clear. From the very beginning, I'd believed Richard was trying to break us up, now I was certain of it. Oh, Tyler never said as much, but any party his father hosted never included me again. I knew.

On the occasions when Tyler couldn't get out of one of those commitments, I took advantage of the time to write. My romance novel was flourishing, even if my real life romance was at a standstill.

The Wednesday before Thanksgiving, Tyler and I sat down to dinner with Steph and Ed. This was a tradition Stephanie and I had begun years earlier. Steph's family was enormous and so was Ed's, which meant that they'd usually ended up spending Thanksgiving at her parents' house and the following day with Ed's family. Even though Steph always invited me to come along, I couldn't imagine spending the holiday with all those relatives.

So we'd made up our own Thanksgiving tradition instead. This year, I'd been determined to keep the tradition with or without Tyler. Yet here he sat, next to me, laughing at all of Ed's not-so-funny jokes.

The next morning Tyler and I left before daylight for Early. I'd been thrilled when he'd told me he wanted to spend the holiday with me instead of his father, even though there would be hell to pay with Richard.

"My father's idea of Thanksgiving usually entails inviting a few dozen of his friends over for a formal sit-down meal. It always seems so overdone and meaningless. I would really rather spend the holiday with you and your aunts, even if Trudy doesn't like me very much."

Aunt Mable wasn't at all surprised to see Tyler with me, in spite of the fact that I'd told her not to expect him. She took me aside and told me she'd known he was coming.

"Oh yeah, and just how did you know this? I didn't even know until a few days ago?"

"I knew. Whether you believe it or not, even if he can't say it to you yet, Tyler is crazy about you."

I wanted to believe in what she said so much, but I didn't. Instead, I tried to keep it together in front of my strong aunt.

"Oh, honey, now it's not so bad. Give the boy time. He'll come around. You'll see. He's crazy about you. Trust me. I know men."

Tyler never told me what his father said about his absence. I'd only heard one side of the conversation but it was enough to understand how angry Richard was.

After dinner, while Aunt Mable and Tyler watched a football game on the TV—Tyler was delighted to learn my aunt was a football fanatic from way back—Aunt Trudy took me outside to show me something.

This was Trudy's way to get me alone. I dreaded going with her because I was afraid, she would ask me why I was still with Tyler. I didn't know how to answer her. Instead, what she said shocked me.

"Have you noticed how pale your aunt is looking lately?"

I glanced at Aunt Trudy's concerned expression and tried to keep from panicking. I had noticed, but I'd thought in her usual fashion, Aunt Mable simply had overdone preparing Thanksgiving dinner. She always went all out. "Yes. Is she okay, Aunt Trudy?"

"I don't know, honey. You know your aunt—stubborn as a mule. She doesn't want to go see the doctor and she'll never admit this to you, but she's been tired an awful lot lately. I don't mind telling you, I'm starting to worry about her. She doesn't take care of herself, you know?"

Hearing Trudy's fear forced me to ask the question what I didn't want to consider. "Do you think there's something seriously wrong with her? Should I stick around—insist she go see her doctor?"

"I'd like to see you try! No, I'm just worrying too much, I guess. But you two are all I have left and I don't want anything to happen to her. She's not a kid anymore, but try telling her that."

"Do you think she would listen to me if I talked to her?"

"No, forget I mentioned it. It won't do you any good. She'll only get mad at me for telling you. I'll stay here with her for a while and try to make her slow down a little. She has too many irons in the fire, as usual. What with the Thanksgiving party she organized for her Bible study group and those dolls she's making for the sale at church next week, not to mention making a huge dinner for all of us today, she is in constant motion, and she's always worrying about you. But I'm sure it's nothing to get worked up over." Trudy patted my hand. "I'll keep a close eye on her. If anything changes, I'll give old Doc Worthy a call and have him check her out. Might give her a thrill."

At any other time, this comment coming from my slightly prudish aunt would have struck me as hilarious, but not today. I was remembering all those times recently when I'd called Aunt Mable and she'd sounded exhausted. She'd brushed it off as simply running to catch the phone. Now I wasn't so sure.

For the rest of the weekend, I kept a close eye on her. By Sunday afternoon, she looked much better. I was worrying without any reason, I told myself. My aunt was tough as nails. She just needed to slow down a little.

* * * *

Back in Austin, my life took on an intense pace. With all the parties coming up, there wasn't time for worrying about anything. I still made a point of calling my aunt every single day to check in on her as well as talking privately with Trudy every chance I got. Things seemed to be back on track for them. Soon, even Trudy wasn't worrying anymore.

Chapter Six

Taking Stock of Your Life

With just a few weeks to go before Christmas, I'd convinced Tyler that he needed to buy a Christmas tree for his house.

"Why do I need a tree when I'm always here at your place?" Tyler had told me that in the two years he'd owned the house, he'd never once put up a Christmas tree. I'd told him this was sacrilegious.

So, in spite of both of our busy schedules, we somehow managed to find time to look for the perfect tree.

I decided – mostly because Tyler seemed confused by the whole tree shopping experience – that not just any old tree would work for his house. No sir-ree. The place needed one at least fourteen feet tall to do it justice.

It ended up costing a small fortune for the artificial pre-lit blue spruce tree alone, not including all the oversized green and red frosted glass balls and rustic ornaments. Then, of course, we had to find the perfect angel to top the tree. Once the last piece of tinsel was up, it looked amazing. Even Tyler was impressed.

We sat on the floor in his living room with the lights out, admiring our handiwork, when Tyler quietly dropped a bombshell on me.

"I was thinking maybe you and I could spend Christmas together this year? I know you probably go home to be with the aunts and I'm sure my father will be expecting me as well, but I would really like us to spend this year alone, just the two of us. We could go somewhere if you'd like. How about you show me the house that you're so crazy about in Colorado?"

I almost jumped into his arms. Tyler and I had been juggling our busy schedules for weeks just to have a few moments to spend together. The thought of having him all to myself for a whole week was sheer heaven.

"We can go skiing. Just the two of us. I have some friends who have a cabin near Parrish," Tyler informed me.

"Are you sure? I mean—"

At this point, Tyler did the one thing that always shut me up when I said something foolish. He kissed me. Once he'd gained my silence, he released me.

"I'm positive. Christmas with my father usually means traveling to Europe with his friends. It's just so meaningless that I've come to hate the whole season. Even though I'd love to spend the holiday with the aunts, I'd like it to be just the two of us this year…if it's okay with you?"

Okay? *Okay?* Was he crazy? Of course, it was okay! It was more than okay. It was a sign. It must be. Tyler was actually choosing me over his father.

* * * *

If I ever believed miracles could come true, it was that Christmas with Tyler in Parrish. We spent our days on the slopes, where Tyler rescued me so many times that I eventually lost count.

On Christmas Eve, he decided it was time to check out my dream home. The real estate agent showing the house had given Tyler the access code to the key box as a professional courtesy. As we drove up to it, I could tell that time and the elements hadn't been kind. The place was definitely showing signs of having stood vacant for far too long, but none of this mattered to me. I loved it. It was as if the house were waiting for me to make it mine.

Tyler, on the other hand, wasn't nearly so impressed. He followed me through each of its rooms then out onto the upstairs balcony before saying a word.

"You love this place, don't you? You're eyes literally light up when you look at it. What is it about it? You've been in far more expensive houses, I know. What's so special about this one?"

I didn't know how to answer his question. For me, this house represented things I could never admit to Tyler—things like family and romance. "I don't know. I can't explain it, I guess. I just knew the moment I walked into this house that I would love it. I guess that sounds crazy."

Tyler didn't answer. He couldn't. He didn't understand.

We left soon after and I couldn't help but feel a little disappointed. Something important had changed between us. I wished I'd never told Tyler about the house.

We ate dinner at a small Italian restaurant in town. He seemed so preoccupied that I wondered if he was regretting spending the holiday with me. I'm sure for someone like Tyler, my foolish dreams must seem very naive.

When we returned to the cabin, Tyler handed me a small gift-wrapped box he took from his jacket pocket. My heart went into overdrive as I looked at it. Instead of opening it right away, I took my time handing him his present, the old football jersey he'd been so obsessed with finding, before slowly unwrapping my tiny box, all the while telling myself not to show any emotion.

Inside the small purple and gold jeweler's box, nestled against white cotton, were the most beautiful diamond earrings and pendant. They were lovely and perfect and no doubt cost a fortune. I wanted to cry. What had I been expecting anyway? Some promise of forever.

After Tyler was sleeping next to me, I tried not to make a sound as silent tears slipped from my eyes, and in the distance, I could almost swear I heard the whistle blow one more time for that fast-moving train of heartache.

* * * *

84

With the start of the New Year, my workload slowly began to trickle off and I found myself with more time on my hands to obsess over my future with Tyler. When Allie told me she'd landed a major benefit party for the first week of February, I was thrilled. At least I would have something to occupy my time since Tyler was spending more time than ever traveling on business.

His father was expanding the business into the Dallas-Ft. Worth area. One of Richard's oldest friends, Stan Davenport, was now considering his offer to merge the two firms into one mega agency. This meant that Tyler was away in Dallas even more, and with my crazy schedule, we rarely saw each other anymore.

At his father's request, Tyler spent long weekends in Dallas, going over all the paperwork for the merger. In addition to the trips to Dallas and the late hours spent at the Austin office, Tyler's father still expected him to attend all of the firm's social functions as well.

Our time together was now little more than a few days here and there during the week. We tried to make the most of it, even though we were both running like crazy just to have a few hours together. I kept myself busy during those long weekends alone by experimenting on new recipes for my clients.

On the day of the benefit ball that was dedicated to saving the salamander — or something equally bizarre — Allie and I were just finishing the final touches for the meal when Tyler called, canceling our dinner plans. His father had made different arrangements for him to attend some business function at the last minute. He told me not to expect him until late. When faced with spending another evening alone, I stayed to help Allie out with the serving.

Allie wasn't pleased by this news — not that I could blame her. Lately I didn't much like being around myself either. I was cranky and restless, not a good combination.

Since we'd be serving a sit-down meal for two hundred fussy rich people donating money to the salamander cause, though, I guess she figured she could use all the help she could get, even from her cranky boss.

She and I drove the van to the hotel where the event would be taking place. We got there a few hours early to set up. By six, everything was ready and the banquet hall was packed. At seven, we were serving the meal.

As I stood before my first table, my tray laden with food, who should I see seated before me but Tyler. He was my first customer and, apparently, he'd brought a date with him.

My knees threatened to desert me at the sight of them together. I dropped Tyler's plate in front of him with a loud clatter, resisting the urge to throw it at him instead. Evidently, I'd used enough force to send the gorgeous brunette seated next to Tyler into a panic, which managed to take his attention away from the conversation he was having with the gentleman seated to his right.

"Carrie?" Tyler was clearly surprised to see me.

"Do you know our server, Tyler?" Gorgeous Brunette asked ever so innocently as a frown wrinkled her perfectly smooth forehead.

"Yes, Tyler, do you know me? I think you do, or maybe you've forgotten you have a girlfriend. Perhaps you'd like to introduce me to your date?"

Unfortunately, my anger didn't manage to elicit the reaction I was expecting from Tyler. He merely smiled up at me. "I didn't realize you were hosting this benefit."

"I bet not! Otherwise I'm sure you would have thought twice about bringing a date to it," I told him sweetly before turning on my heels to leave him and the entire table staring after me.

I pushed open the swinging doors to the kitchen so hard I almost hit another server coming out with a fully loaded tray. As I turned to apologize, I realized Tyler had followed me.

I ignored him entirely and began loading another tray to take out.

"Carrie, it's not what it looks like."

"Really? Because it looks like you failed to mention you might have another date tonight. I guess I understand now why you canceled on me."

Tyler caught my hand and forced me to be still. "She's not my date. She's here with her father. The man who owns the firm in Dallas, the one we're in negotiations with. This is business, nothing more. They are both old friends of my father. That's all it is."

"Ha! Whatever, Tyler. Sorry, but I'm not buying it. If she's not your date, then why didn't you introduce me to her?"

"She and her father are business associates, nothing more. This has nothing to do with you."

"Oh, right—I forgot. It's just business. Give me a break! Either I'm part of your life—your entire life—or I'm not. Clearly, I'm not. Look, if you want to date other women, go right ahead, but could you at least tell me beforehand. As hard as this is for you to imagine, I don't like running into my boyfriend's dates."

I started to leave with another tray but Tyler took it from me and calmly set it down on the counter. "She's *not* my date, and you *are* part of my life. The only part that matters to me and you can believe that or not!"

I stood staring angrily back at him, telling myself not to be foolish enough to fall for what he'd just said, when Allie interrupted our argument.

"Are you going to take the tray out now or what? It's getting cold." Coming from anyone else, I would have taken offense, but Allie was more than just an employee and she was trying to salvage this dinner as well as save my professional butt.

"Right, Allie. I am." I picked up the tray and pushed past Tyler, who was determined to follow me. I began shoving plates in front of guests when Tyler actually started to help me serve.

"What are you doing?" I stopped to watch him with a plate of my best roasted beef au jus suspended over a gray-haired woman's head.

"I'm helping out, since it seems to be the only way I can talk to you!"

"Go back to your date."

"Carrie, she isn't my date."

"Dear, something's dripping on my hair!" the older woman yelped, getting my attention at last. My delicate au jus sauce was slowly oozing from the plate onto her perfectly coiffed hair.

"Oh," I set the plate down in front of her with a thud and grabbed the napkin out of her lap. I began quickly patting her hair dry. When Tyler had the nerve to laugh at me, I tossed the napkin at his face and stormed off before he could see my tears. What an idiot I was turning out to be.

"Sorry, Mrs. Clement. She's new here." Tyler apologized for me to the woman he obviously knew. Apparently, he said something else equally amusing because I heard the entire table join in laughing.

I'd made a huge mistake by coming here tonight. I should have gone home to my empty apartment and let myself remain blissfully ignorant of the other woman.

"Where are you going?" Allie's panic-stricken voice called after me as I walked past her and out of the back door. I couldn't answer. I needed to escape the fiasco I'd left behind. Outside, one of the parking valets was standing next to the door smoking a cigarette.

"Can I have one of those?"

He held up the half-empty pack to me. I took one out, waited for him to light it then thanked him before walking away. I found an empty spot beyond the staff parking where I could be alone with my cigarette and have a good cry without anyone having to see my childish behavior.

I hadn't smoked since experimenting with it in high school. The first initial puff made me light-headed and sent me into a coughing spell, which made my throat feel raw and gritty. Through the smoky fog gathering around me, I spotted Tyler coming my way and tried to scrub away the evidence of my tears.

"That was some show. I don't think Mrs. Clement is going to forget this night anytime soon. When did you start smoking?" he asked in amazement.

Through my tears I tried to focus on his expression. Was he...amused? "You're laughing at me?" Fresh tears stung my eyes. I'd just made the biggest fool of myself, all because of Tyler, and he was amused by this?

"Honey, I'm not laughing." His voice gentled when he spotted my tears. "Carrie, I'm sorry—"

"Oh shut up," I would have given anything to simply walk past him and leave him, but Tyler caught my arm and pulled me close. "No." I closed my eyes and tried to be strong. The moment his arms slipped around my waist and his lips claimed mine the fight was over.

"How could you think I would be dating someone else?" he whispered against my hair. "I barely have enough energy for you."

I didn't say a word. I couldn't. I'd just made a fool of myself in front of Tyler and half of Austin society. I'd probably be blacklisted after tonight.

"You believe me, don't you?" he asked with enough sincerity in his tone that I did.

"Yes, I believe you." And I did, but tonight's little breakdown went way beyond the insecurities David had left me with. Somehow I couldn't get the image of Tyler and the gorgeous brunette out of my head. They looked as if they belonged together. She fit into his world. I did not.

* * * *

After months of coaxing, Tyler finally convinced me to spend more time at his place. Once I'd gotten over my initial fear of breaking things, I immediately fell in love with his fully-equipped-with-everything-any-chef-could-possibly-want kitchen. Tyler let me try out new recipes on him without complaining. He was becoming *my* romance novel. Tyler was better than any book on love I'd ever read. I was still waiting for the disaster I was certain was inevitable. When it finally came, it wasn't anything like I was expecting.

One Monday morning as we sat in front of the fireplace reading the paper, my cell phone chirped from inside its hiding place in my purse. The second I fished it out and heard Trudy's voice, I knew it was bad news. Tyler must have realized it as well, because he came to stand close to me, watching my expression carefully.

"Oh, honey, I don't know how to tell you this but it's Mable." Her voice broke and I knew. Aunt Mable was gone. "She's dead, Carrie. Mable's dead. It was a heart attack. Last night in her sleep. I found her cold in her bed this morning. I don't know what to do."

"No, this can't be, Aunt Trudy. I just talked to her yesterday,"

"Honey, I'm sorry, but it is. You know I loved her like a sister, but I don't think I can handle this alone. Please come home soon."

"Of course I will," I tried to catch the tears that were so close. I needed to be strong for Aunt Trudy. I could almost hear Aunt Mable scolding me, telling me Trudy needed me. Stop crying and go to her.

"I'll leave right away. I'll be there as soon as I can. Are you at the house?" I wiped the stream of tears from my eyes while Trudy told me that she was. "Then I'll come there. I promise I'll be there soon." I hung up the phone and turned away from Tyler as tears flooded my eyes. Aunt Mable was gone. It wasn't possible, was it? I prayed I would wake up and find that this was just a bad dream. I didn't know how to go on without her.

"Carrie?"

At the concern in Tyler voice, I tried to gather my composure. I wanted to be strong. Tyler was the perfect man who lived in a perfect world. I didn't believe he'd want to see this weak, frightened girl who didn't know how to survive her aunt's death.

"Carrie, what is it?"

"I have to go. I have to go home." I hated the helpless tears that took away my voice. Tyler touched my arm, turning me gently to face him.

"Carrie, tell me what happened."

At the command in his voice, the last of my resolve cracked. "Aunt Mable…she passed away. Trudy said it was a heart attack. She died last night in her sleep. I have to go. I need to pack some clothes. I need to see if Hazel can keep Max for a while. I need to call Allie and make sure she can handle the schedule next week. I need…" I didn't finish. I broke down and he gathered me close.

"I'm coming with you." Tyler spoke the words I needed to hear, but I couldn't accept them coming from him.

"No, it's okay. I'll be all right."

"I'm coming with you, Carrie. Go and pack. I'll tell Steph and Allie what's happened." I didn't want to lean on him, but I couldn't get through this alone. "Go get started. I'll call Hazel and ask her to watch Max for us."

I tried to function enough to pack even the simplest of things. I could hear Tyler talking quietly on the phone. I didn't have anything to wear to a funeral, especially not to my aunt's funeral.

I sank down onto the bed Tyler and I shared and covered my mouth as the first sob came. Aunt Mable was dead. Dead. I replayed the words over and over in my head.

Please, God, please, no. Please let me wake up and find this is just a terrible dream.

"Carrie?" Somewhere during all my pleading with God, Tyler had joined me. He sat down beside me and held me close. There in his arms, I found the shelter I needed to let go. I cried until there were no more tears left in me then I became angry.

I got to my feet and paced the room. "This can't be happening. She can't be dead. How could God let this happen to her? This is so unfair. There are people out there who are evil, truly evil, and he takes *her*? What kind of God does that?"

"Carrie." Tyler came to me and tried to take me back in his arms, but I couldn't let him. Part of me wanted to blame him. How many times had I promised her I'd come see her, only to put it off because of something that was going on between Tyler and me. How many times in the past was I aware of that little 'I wish you were here' sound in her voice. I always felt guilty hearing it. Now there was good reason to feel this way. She was gone. I'd never get to hear her laugh or listen to her gossip again. *I've given up precious moments with my aunt to be with Tyler.*

The drive to Early seemed endless. Tyler kept trying to get me to sleep. I was numb inside. All I could think about was that I'd never see my aunt again.

* * * *

It was almost midnight when we arrived at my aunt's house, but Trudy was there waiting for us. She took me in her arms and started to cry. Somehow, Tyler got the two of us inside and into the kitchen, sitting us down.

"I just don't know what I'm going to do without her. She was my best friend. She was like a sister."

I shook my head. "I can't believe she's really gone."

"She didn't suffer any. That's the only good thing in all of this. Doc Worthy said she just drifted off to sleep. Somewhere in the night, her heart gave out on her. She's with God now." Aunt Trudy turned to Tyler then. I could see a new respect in her eyes for him. He'd won some of her approval today. "Thank you for bringing her, Tyler. I didn't want her to make the trip alone. I'm glad you're here with her."

Exhausted and emotionally drained, I lay next to Tyler, who held me while I tried to sleep. He soothed back the hair from my face with his gentle fingers.

"I spoke with Steph. She and Ed are coming in the

morning. She has directions to the house. I guessed you'd want her here with you, and there's plenty of room."

I fought back my tears at his tender consideration of my feelings.

"Thank you, Tyler."

"For what?"

"For being there for me when I lost it earlier. For calling Steph and Allie. For coming here with me. For taking care of Trudy the way you did tonight. Thank you." I'd started to cry again. Tyler never said a word. He just pulled me close and held me all night long.

* * * *

When I woke the next morning, it was late. The numbness inside me made it feel as if I hadn't slept at all. I went downstairs and found Tyler and Trudy in the kitchen.

Aunt Trudy was busy covering her grief by preparing an enormous breakfast no one felt like eating. Tyler at least tried to do the polite thing by accepting the plate she handed him.

He spotted me the second I walked into the kitchen. "Come have some coffee."

Tyler sat me down in his chair and poured coffee while Aunt Trudy looked at me and tried to decide what I needed. She offered me breakfast, but I couldn't even think about food.

Dozens of flowers and plants had begun arriving at the house already from people in the community who knew and loved my aunt. An enormous spray of roses came from Tyler's father, which surprised us both.

Over coffee, Tyler told me there was an appointment scheduled with the funeral director for later that same afternoon. I closed my eyes. I didn't want to think about arranging my aunt's funeral.

Steph's arrival was wonderful for me emotionally, but Tyler was the one I clung to. He and Trudy went with me to make the arrangements while Steph went shopping to find something for me to wear.

The funeral director turned out to be an old friend of my aunt's. Unbeknownst to either Trudy or me, Aunt Mable had decided long ago how she wanted her funeral organized.

She'd insisted on a closed casket because, according to the director, Mable didn't want people remembering her dead. There was not to be any viewing. She didn't want any long drawn-out service at the church either. Aunt Mable wasn't having any of it. Instead, she wanted a brief ceremony at the grave site then she'd insisted we throw the biggest party around to celebrate her reunion with God.

The director had been kind enough to get in touch with the minister at my aunt's church and arrange everything, so there really wasn't anything left for us to do except plan the party of a lifetime for Aunt Mable.

Crowds of people began stopping by the house as word of her death reached the community where she'd lived all of her life. Everyone who knew her wanted to offer their condolences, share their own story about how Aunt Mable had touched their life or simply bring food. It seemed like the house was never empty.

In spite of my aunt's wishes, the service was the worst moment of my life. I don't think I would have made it through without Tyler.

Aunt Mable had included all the details for the party as well, so on the evening that we buried her, we threw her the best sendoff party anyone could ever want. There was tons of barbecue catered by her favorite restaurant. My aunt's favorite country band played well into the night. I could almost imagine Aunt Mable smiling down at us from above.

Steph and Ed left a few days after the funeral. With their absence, the house grew quiet again. The rest of the week went by in silence. This was something I would come to associate with this time in my life. Silence. Waiting. The crowds that were once so comforting after the funeral were all gone now. It was just the three of us.

One night after Tyler was sleeping and I couldn't, I got out of bed and went out to the front porch of Aunt Mable's home to take stock of my life.

My only living relative was now dead. The woman who had taught me so much, who'd brought me up since I'd been a small, frightened child of ten, was gone from my life forever.

There was Trudy, and I loved her just as if she were my family, but the light of both our lives had gone out.

Early might be the town I called home, but it wasn't the town that brought me back time and again. It was the woman. For me, Aunt Mable had represented home. Now she was gone.

So what did I have left? Aunt Trudy of course, my best friend Stephanie, several close acquaintances — and Tyler. I'd told Aunt Mable that Tyler was my boyfriend, but was it the truth, or was it wishful thinking? Maybe were we nothing more than good in bed together? For me the answer was clear. I might have been ignoring it for months, but it was here with me tonight. I loved him. He wasn't any of those things for me. He was the man I loved and the one I would never get over.

Tyler would have to answer that question for himself someday, if he hadn't already. He'd told me once that he didn't believe in love.

In the distance, the whistle of the two a.m. train broke the stillness of the night. It was always on time and always predictable. It was nothing like the man asleep in my bed.

* * * *

The following morning I'd come to a decision. I needed to be away from Tyler for a while to think about my future. So after breakfast I took him for a walk and told him he should go home.

"I'm not leaving you here alone." He didn't have to say the words. Tyler believed I needed him. He was right. I *did* need him, but I needed to figure out some things on my own as well.

"It's okay. I'm going to spend a few days here with Trudy and settle Aunt Mable's affairs. Her attorney wants to talk to us tomorrow morning. It's okay, Tyler. I'll be fine. I just need to be alone for a little while."

He'd left me, even though he hadn't wanted to. Two weeks ago, I would have been thrilled that he was reluctant to leave my side. Now I was numb.

Trudy and I met with my aunt's attorney the following morning, where we were both somewhat surprised to learn the size of her financial estate. I knew she was comfortable. I just didn't realize how comfortable. She'd left Trudy with a sizable income, which would allow her to live without ever having to worry about money again. My aunt had told me once how difficult life had been for Trudy growing up. She'd struggled most of her life just to survive. Now she would never have to struggle again.

As for me, Aunt Mable left the remainder of her finances along with the house I couldn't bear to think of living in without her. I talked with Tyler later the same night and told him about the will and the house. He told me if I decided I wanted to sell, he would help me.

I stayed with Trudy for another week. I guess I just wasn't ready to leave the past behind just yet.

Aunt Trudy and I spent precious time together during that week. We talked about my aunt and I think we both found a certain amount of healing in each other's company. After all, we were the two people who knew her best.

By the end of the week, I'd made some decisions about my future as well. I was going to give the house to Trudy. I believed Aunt Mable would have been happy with that decision. She'd loved Trudy like a sister.

I made all the arrangements with my aunt's attorney then I broke the news to Trudy over a hot fudge sundae at our Dairy Queen. Her reaction was exactly what I'd been expecting from her.

"Oh, honey, I can't take the house. It was Mable's. She'd want you to keep it in the family. No, I won't take it."

"You are family, and it's done. I want you to have it. Since I can't talk you into moving in with me, it's the least I can do."

"Bless your heart. I'll always remember your aunt and all the good times we had together there. And you'll come home and see me every chance you get, won't you?"

"You know I will," I told her, smiling for the first time in a long time.

She held my gaze with one of those assessing looks of hers before adding, "There's something different about you, Carrie. Have you made up your mind about Tyler? You know Mable was just about convinced he was the one for you and nothing I could do or say was going to change her mind. At first? Well, I didn't like him one little bit, but now? Well, I've changed my mind about him."

I couldn't bring myself to tell her I'd made some decisions about Tyler as well. I needed to know where our relationship was going. I needed definition. I loved Tyler and I wanted to spend the rest of my life with him, but I wasn't prepared to accept this relationship on Tyler's terms any longer. I couldn't. I'd barely survived one dead-end relationship. I wasn't sure I would survive another.

In my heart I believed Tyler was trying hard with me, but it wasn't enough anymore. I needed a commitment. A future. Children. Losing my aunt had put things in perspective for me at last. I couldn't ignore what *I* needed any longer, not even for Tyler.

I couldn't tell Trudy any of those things. She deserved to be happy thinking her sweet thoughts about me. She'd lost her best friend. She'd been through enough. Trudy deserved to be happy.

"I promise I'll come back in a few weeks to check on you, and you have my number, so use it."

It was so hard to leave her behind. It was as if I were deserting her when she needed me the way I had Aunt Mable. But Aunt Trudy wouldn't have it any other way. I was young. I had my life and my man, as she called Tyler. I needed to be with him. As much as I hated leaving her, I dreaded confronting Tyler with these decisions almost as much.

Chapter Seven

Not Settling

It's strange sometimes, how parts of your life flourish, while others seem dark and desolate.

Carrie's Creative Catering continued to grow by leaps and bounds. I ended up hiring two more assistants to help with the workload, which allowed us to double our clientele. Life should have been great. I was successful at last, after all those years of struggling and scraping by.

But I wasn't happy. I was restless. I kept replaying the last conversation I'd had with my aunt over and over again in my head—the one I'd been trying to shut out since her death.

It had taken place the day before she'd passed away. Everything about the call stood out in my memory because it had all been about Tyler. I'd told her I didn't think things were going to last between us and she'd told me her beliefs in the simple way she had of getting straight to the point.

"Don't settle, Carrie. Don't you dare settle for less than you deserve. Do what you need to do for once, instead of what everyone else wants you to do." She knew this went against my nature. I was a pleaser. I didn't like to rock the boat. But Aunt Mable had told me it was time for me to take what I needed from life. Don't settle. She'd said those same words at least a dozen times that day. She'd told me she liked Tyler and she believed he was crazy about me as well, but life was just too damn short to live in doubt. "Do what you want. Get what you want. Become the person you need to be."

Those had been her last words to me before she'd said goodbye for what turned out to be the last time. Since her death, I'd taken each of those precious words to heart.

I loved Carrie's Creative Catering — loved the success I'd made of it — but it no longer made me happy. It wasn't what I wanted to do with my life. I wanted the secret passion. The dream of my childhood. I wanted romance. None of the things I possessed with Carrie's Creative Catering — or with Tyler.

* * * *

Even though I'd promised myself I was going to finally have that serious discussion with Tyler as soon as I returned home, there never seemed to be the right time for it. Unfortunately, since I'd returned to Austin, my time with Tyler was becoming virtually non-existent.

Richard continued to expand his son's responsibilities more in Dallas, which, in my opinion, was a deliberate attempt to keep us apart as much as possible. I guess Richard assumed 'out of sight, out of mind'.

Tyler and I still talked almost every day and I could tell he sensed my restlessness, but I'm sure he just attributed it to my aunt's death. Only Steph knew something else was seriously wrong with me — something that went beyond my grief.

"What's up with you lately? And don't say it's because you miss your aunt, because it's more than that. You look so unhappy."

As much as I wished I could tell Steph the truth, I couldn't say the words aloud, not even to her. "I don't know, I guess things just feel out of kilter lately. Maybe I'm still reacting to Aunt Mable's death or maybe I'm just worried about Trudy. I don't really know."

"It must be hard. I know how much you loved her. But you have Tyler and Trudy and me. You're going to be okay. It just takes time."

* * * *

I went home to see Trudy a few weekends later. I arrived shortly before lunch, only to find my dear, sweet—who I'd wanted to believe needy—aunt in the company of a gentleman caller. This just about floored me. Aunt Trudy disliked men. She'd told me on more than one occasion that men only went for pretty looks and a nice figure.

In the weeks since I'd seen her last, she was a changed woman. This wasn't the same woman I'd hated leaving. This woman was smiling—actually smiling—and giggling like a schoolgirl as she introduced me to Mr. Fred Anders, who she informed me was retired from working at a local factory in Brownwood most of his life, and who was a widower of more than twenty odd years now. Why she felt it necessary to give me the poor man's dossier, I'm not sure.

I found out they'd met at an over-fifties social at the church. When she told me this, I did a double take. *Oh, no, no, no!* This wasn't my aunt at all! Clearly, someone had replaced her with an alien. Trudy hated those 'stupid things', as she'd referred to them every single time Aunt Mable had dragged her to one. She'd preferred spending quiet time alone to parading around like a Christmas ham—also her words—for some man.

After Fred left, I turned to her with my mouth hanging open and my expression saying it all. "Okay, what's up with you?"

"Oh, Carrie, don't look at me like that! Fred's a nice man and we're just friends. Nothing wrong with being friends, now is there? Besides, he likes to go garage sale-ing just like your aunt did. We really do have a lot in common. He owns his own home and has a nice income from his pension at the factory. He's not after my money!" She was actually blushing as she said these things, which further reinforced my alien theory.

"So why are you blushing like a June bride all of a sudden? Are you in *love* with dear, sweet Fred?"

She *was*. It was there in her eyes. My sweet, old-maid aunt of almost seventy-two years, was in love, quite possibly for the first time in her life! I didn't know whether to laugh or to cry.

Trudy was moving on. She didn't need me. There was Fred now. I was the one who was alone. Restless, searching. Alone. Aunt Trudy had found someone who genuinely cared about her. I could tell this from the adoring way Fred looked at her. She'd found someone to help fill the void left by Aunt Mable's death. Me, on the other hand? Well, I was throwing myself into my work, trying to cover the unhappiness left in my life by my uncertain future with Tyler. Aunt Trudy was in love with someone who returned her feelings. I was not.

"I think it's great! No, it's wonderful, and I'm happy for you, Aunt Trudy. But how long has this been going on? You never once mentioned Fred on the phone. I was actually worried about you being alone, but now I see I don't need to be and...and I think it's great! No, it's wonderful." I continued babbling on, desperate not to show her how much her happiness hurt. *I* was the one alone, not Trudy.

"Come sit down and have some coffee and I'll tell you all about him. Oh, but first, how's your young man? He didn't come down with you this time?" At the innocent, caring, *in love* way she looked at me, I couldn't bring myself to spoil her happiness. Instead, I smiled, pushed aside my heartache and lied to my sweet aunt.

"He's fine. He's working this weekend, so he couldn't make it, but he really wanted to come." This wasn't exactly a lie, but it wasn't exactly the truth either. I didn't know if Tyler wanted to come with me or not. I hadn't asked. I'd simply run away, avoiding the inevitable. I was getting good at running away.

"You two sure do look good together. I don't know why I ever doubted Tyler was right for you. You two are perfect together. You don't know how many times Mable told me he was the one for you." Aunt Trudy finally caught sight of the tears I'd been desperately trying to blink away and stopped. "Oh, honey, what is it?"

At the sympathetic tone in her voice, I lost it. I started to cry and just couldn't stop. She came and put her arms around me, at a loss for the moment as to what to say to make it better.

"Oh, honey, I'm sorry. I should have realized it's hard for you to talk about your aunt. It's still too soon, isn't it? You were so busy trying to be strong for me and everyone else. Why, you hardly cried at all at the funeral. You go right ahead and bawl your eyes out. It'll do you a world of good."

I almost laughed out loud. Trudy assumed I was crying all these useless tears over my aunt's death, but the truth was they were all for Tyler.

Seeing Trudy happy, in love and in a normal relationship — well, as normal as any seventy-two-year-old, never-been-married-before woman, and a sixty-eight-year-old widower could be — only brought home all the things lacking in my own life.

Aunt Trudy reached inside the pocket of her dress and handed me a fresh tissue. She shoved it at my face, reminding me for the moment of the old Trudy once again, making me laugh. I didn't realize how much I'd missed her. I'd told myself she needed me, but the truth was *I* was the one who was desperate here. I wanted to be with her to forget about what waited for me back in Austin.

I'd planned to spend just the weekend with her, but now I wasn't so sure. Did I really have to rush back to an empty apartment and an empty relationship? I could stay here with this sweet woman until I was strong enough to face my future.

"So, is your garage sale-ing time exclusive to just Fred now or can I tag along?"

She looked at me as if I'd suddenly lost my mind before she smiled. She knew something was wrong, but she wasn't going to push me to tell her, the way the old Trudy would have. Being in love had smoothed away her rough edges.

She would let me come to her with it, just like Aunt Mable would have.

Aunt Trudy and I talked for a long time that day. She even went with me for a walk. I was feeling reminiscent and melancholy, all at the same time. I wanted to be around all the things that had made me happy as a child, and Aunt Trudy had played a major role in my childhood happiness.

She took me down to the barn where I'd spent so much time riding as a young girl. The stalls were empty now. I still held fond memories of Jelly Belly, my mare.

Aunt Mable hadn't blinked an eye when I'd told her what I wanted to name my horse. Jelly Belly died of old age after I'd gone abroad to study the first time. I still remember how I'd cried for weeks after hearing the news.

"Do you remember Aunt Mable's face when I told her I wanted to name my horse Jelly Belly?" I glanced at Trudy when she laughed.

"Oh, I sure do. You wouldn't believe how we used to cringe every single time you called the horse's name."

"So how are you *really* doing?" I turned to look her in the eye. "You seem happy. Are you?"

"Honey, I miss her more than I could ever have imagined. There's not a day that goes by that I don't think about her or want to share something with her. Then I remember she's gone, but I try to think about all the good times we shared together through the years. And let me tell you, after knowing each other for going on sixty-five years, the good times far outweigh the bad. I'm doing okay. How about you? You seem weighted down somehow. The world got you struggling or is it someone in particular?"

She'd given me the lead I needed. I could spill the beans, tell her everything and probably feel so much better for having done so. But even as the words formed on my lips, I just couldn't say them. I couldn't bring my fears to light. I was still afraid by doing so they'd become a self-fulfilling prophesy.

"I'm okay. It's just the business, I guess. It's growing and

I love it, but I don't know… Something about it just doesn't excite me anymore. I guess this sounds crazy, considering all the years I struggled to make it work, but it's getting harder to remember what it was about the job I found so appealing."

We'd started back toward the house just as the sun slipped from the sky and dusk settled in around us. Not that it mattered. Both of us knew every square inch of this place by heart. We could walk it in our sleep. The dry winter grass crunched beneath our feet as we walked across the pasture behind the house.

"Honey, your aunt told me a long time ago that life was too short for sticking to bad decisions. If you're not happy doing what you're doing then make some changes. Be happy! Do whatever it takes, but just be happy. Don't settle, Carrie. You're too nice a person to settle for anything less than you deserve. And you deserve to be happy."

I tried to make out her expression in the twilight but couldn't. Somehow, I suspected she knew that what I was really talking about didn't have anything to do with work.

"You know, before Mable's death I wouldn't be caught dead with Fred. But since then? Well, I don't care what any of those old gossips around town have to say about it. He makes me laugh and I'm happy for a little while when I'm with him. So let their tongues wag."

"Good for you! I'm so proud of you. You deserve to be happy, too. And if Fred can make you happy then I'm all for it."

I hadn't called Tyler at all. I was deliberately trying not to think about him. I grabbed a blanket from the hall closet and went for a walk by the lake. Tyler was there with me in the memories that we'd made here together. It was almost like a ghost following me that night.

I sat down on the bank and watched the moon slowly rise over it. As the stillness of the night closed in around me, he reached out to me.

The cell phone that I'd brought with me, hoping that

somehow he would call while praying that he wouldn't, broke the silence and sent birds scattering from their roost.

"So, you are alive. I was beginning to wonder. Were you just not going to call me at all or were you waiting for me to call you?"

How could I tell him that the answer was yes? Yes to all those things. I wanted him to be worried about me and he obviously was, but that didn't make me any happier. I wanted him to call me and he had, but the sound of his voice only reminded me that he was miles away and I would be sleeping alone and missing him tonight.

"I'm sorry. I've just been so busy with Aunt Trudy." The pause on his end told me he wasn't buying that, but he was willing to let it go.

"How is she? Is she doing okay?"

We were back to our comfortable 'don't ask don't tell' selves again, but for the moment I was glad. I didn't want to delve too deeply into emotions that I had no business feeling without him here.

"You're not going to believe it. Aunt Trudy has a boyfriend!" I took his silence as stunned amusement before going on. "Well, she doesn't call him her boyfriend. He's just a friend that she hangs out with, but you should see the way she looks at him and the way he watches her—" I stopped when I realized I was babbling like a fool. I hoped he didn't realize all the reasons behind my nervousness.

"Tell her I'm proud of her. How about you? How are you?"

Ready to cry, ready to run… Scared to death of losing you. I could tell him none of those things, so I kept quiet. I wanted to cry. That was the sum of my emotions right now. I wanted to cry.

"I'm okay. I'm glad that I came. I've been so worried about her. I needed to know she was okay and she is."

I heard a noise in the background and asked him where he was.

"We're at dinner. Dad and I are schmoozing some potential

clients. God, I hate these things. I have to go, Carrie. The old man is throwing me that look that tells me just how unhappy he is with me right now. I'll call you tomorrow. What are you doing, by the way?"

I told him about the garage sale-ing and he laughed, although I could tell from his voice that he was only half listening.

"Tyler, I'm glad you called."

"Me too. I miss you, you know. I just needed to hear your voice. You have no idea how much I miss you right now. I'm sorry baby, but I have to go." When he hung up I was able at last to let go of the breath I'd been holding so tightly inside. It was then that I lay back against the bank of the lake and let go of my tears as well.

* * * *

I left for home shortly after church services the next Sunday, refusing Aunt Trudy's offer to buy me lunch. I told her I needed to prepare for a brunch coming up the following Tuesday, but of course it was nothing but a lie. In truth, I was actually becoming physically sick at the sight of love. Being around two people who were happy in love was hard to take.

Lately it seemed that on the few occasions when Tyler and I still talked to each other anymore, we ended up arguing, mostly at my instigation. I was irritable, moody and throwing up most of the time. My allergy to love was starting to take its toll on every part of my life.

I found myself spending more time away from the things I loved. I just couldn't face all the happy people around me.

One particular morning, after managing to shower and dress—forget makeup, I wasn't leaving my apartment at all today—I was still in the planning stages of my day of hiding when my phone rang. I was sitting cross-legged on my sofa with my comforter wrapped around me. Since I wasn't up to seeing anyone, naturally I didn't jump to answer it.

When the answering machine picked up, Richard Bennedict's voice came through the line, loud and clear. I shrank a little deeper into the security of my comforter. Of course, I knew I couldn't hide from him forever. I could for a little while longer. I ignored his message entirely. Unfortunately, Richard was not giving up so easily. He knew I was home. He'd probably been searching all over Austin for me. And The Dick did not intend to go away empty-handed.

"Miss Sinclair, I know you're there..." When Richard's fourth call rang through to the answering machine, I cringed over every condescending word that came out of his mouth. I literally hated the man. If it weren't for his constantly meddling in Tyler's life, perhaps our relationship would have turned out differently. Now, here he was addressing me for the first time since the night of the ball. If I didn't answer the phone now, I feared I'd have to deal with him in person.

"Hello." I picked up the handset and tried not to sound intimidated by him and his power over Tyler, while my stomach started its usual heaving.

"I thought I would find you there, Miss Sinclair. We need to talk, wouldn't you agree?"

"No," I surprised myself by sounding almost calm. "No, I don't need to talk. I'm good."

Richard actually laughed then. "I can see why my son finds you so interesting. Well, beyond the obvious. Okay, you don't need to talk to me, but I certainly have some things to say to you."

I just bet you do, I thought. *And I just bet I don't want to hear any of them.* I didn't actually say any of those things. I couldn't because I was holding my hand over my mouth trying to keep from heaving in his ear.

"I'd like you to have lunch with me today." To anyone listening in on our conversation, this might have sounded like a request, but it was really a command. *Be there or you'll regret it for the rest of your life.*

"Uh," was all I managed to get out before he interrupted again.

"I'll be at Drakes at one. I'll expect to see you there as well." And just like that...click. Richard Bennedict had hung up on me.

I knew the restaurant he'd mentioned only by name. I'd never actually been there before. It was one of those places that is way overpriced with so-so food. It was all the rave among the ultra-rich, and, in my opinion, a deliberate move on his part.

* * * *

When I arrived half an hour late, Richard waited politely for me to take my seat before summoning the waiter, who was obviously standing in the wings waiting for his command to appear.

He filled Richard's wine glass then started to pour mine when my stomach reminded me that I was already on very shaky ground. Wine wasn't on the list of things I could get away with.

"Could I have some water instead, please?" The waiter raised an eyebrow to me before turning to Richard as if to ask his permission. While Richard gave the command to the waiter, I took advantage of the moment to study The Dick. Something seemed different about him since the last time I'd seen him. Oh, he was still just as commanding as ever, but today, it looked as if Richard had aged at least ten years since I'd last seen him. He appeared almost frail. Since frailty was a human trait, I dismissed this thought instantly as merely wishful thinking on my part. Was it strictly my imagination or did Richard's silver hair appear thinner?

"Have you been here before?"

I wanted to tell him yes, I came here all the time. Instead, I simply shook my head and ignored the sound of my knees knocking. He knew damn well I'd never been here before. That was why he'd chosen this restaurant in the first place.

"No, this type of place really isn't my style." I hated these games. I was never any good at playing them, and I certainly didn't want to try to guess what Richard was up to. I just wanted him to get it over.

"Well then, let me suggest the quail. They do it excellently here."

At the thought of those cute little birds giving their lives for lunch, my stomach heaved again.

"I'll just have the soup." At my choice of lunch items, I was rewarded with the return of his smug smile.

"Yes, well that's excellent as well and probably more to your taste." Richard gave our orders to the waiter, who had again appeared out of nowhere.

I was still trying to dissect why he'd invited me here in the first place when the waiter returned some time later with our orders. Certainly, it wasn't simply to have this little innocent chat with me.

"So how *is* your little business doing?" This brought my eyes away from the warm crusty bread, which was a godsend to my queasy stomach. What did my business have to do with him? What did he know about it?

"Good. Wonderful, in fact. Why do you care?"

He smiled again as if he found me thoroughly delightful. I knew differently. He was only trying to make polite conversation until our lunch was over and out of the way. Then he could get down to the unpleasant stuff.

"I don't. How's your soup?"

"Good." This was about the extent of the conversation during lunch. The soup hit the spot and took away most of my nausea until Richard's next words brought it all back — then some.

Once the waiter had cleared our plates away, Richard ordered coffee, which I refused. When we were alone again, The Dick didn't waste any time getting to the point.

"Carrie, where do you see this relationship between yourself and my son going? I ask because I don't want you to get your hopes up. I would hate to see you disappointed."

This was it. The moment I'd been dreading for almost a year now. Richard Bennedict was about to say the words his son couldn't say to me. This was not going to be a pleasant conversation, no matter how much Richard might be smiling.

"Surely this is Tyler's and my business, not yours?"

Again, Richard's smile resurfaced. I hated that smile. It told me I was only kidding myself. "My son will do exactly what I tell him to do. At first? Well, I can certainly understand Tyler's attraction to you. You are beautiful, after all, but you are *not* Bennedict material, nor will you ever be. You should cut your losses now and get out before you get hurt."

Tears stung my eyes, but somehow I managed to fight them back by reminding myself just how much I hated this man.

"You think Tyler will leave me because you tell him to?" Yeah, I actually threw the gauntlet out to him.

Richard smiled his smug smile again and laid the truth out for me in black and white. "You won't even be around come next year. You'll be replaced at least a half dozen times over."

Whatever else Richard might have said didn't register beyond those words. This was all it took. I'd started to cry just as my stomach started to heave.

I caught something in his expression that reminded me of Tyler, something resembling regret.

"Carrie." He grabbed my hand, preventing me from leaving.

I didn't wait to hear what he would say next. I pulled my hand out of his grasp and ran, literally ran, from the restaurant. I'm embarrassed to say I was sick, right there in those perfectly manicured shrubs next to my car.

It was hard to get through the rest of the day. I couldn't go back to my empty apartment, which was no longer my sanctuary. I couldn't turn to Steph. Couldn't call Tyler. I spent the afternoon driving around Austin until my car was almost out of gas. Then I found myself downtown, at the theater where Steph and I went to watch old movies. I spent the rest of the afternoon crying over Tyler while watching Cary Grant.

It was after midnight when I finally went back to my apartment. There I found at least half a dozen messages from Tyler and just as many from Steph. Apparently, Tyler had called her when he couldn't reach me. I would have ignored both of them had Tyler not chosen to call one more time.

"Are you all right? Where have you been all day? I've been calling for hours! I was starting to worry about you."

I could no longer trust all the concern in Tyler's voice. His father had painted a different version of his son to me. No matter how much Tyler sounded as if he cared about me, I didn't doubt Richard's influence on him. I'd be gone from Tyler's life and replaced by someone more fitting for the Bennedict name and prestige. This was fate. The past year had been all about fun for Tyler.

"I'm fine. I went to a Cary Grant marathon downtown. I needed to do some thinking."

"But you're okay?"

It took a second more for what I'd just said to register.

"Thinking about what?"

Now's your chance! Do it before you change your mind! "About us, Tyler."

"What about us?" He knew. I could tell from the slight edge that had crept into his voice he knew what was coming next.

"I'm tired of playing games with you. I want… No, I *need* to know where you and I are heading." It was hard to force those words out.

"Carrie…"

"No, Tyler, this time I'm serious! We've been practically living together for almost a year now and I still don't know what you want out of this relationship. I'm tired of living by your rules, rearranging my life to fit into your schedule!

112

I can't do this anymore! I'm sick of it!"

"Carrie, you know I care about you—"

"Yeah, well, it's not enough anymore. I want more than just to fit into your schedule when it's convenient for you. I deserve more. I *need* more."

"Can't we talk about this another time? It's late and obviously you're not in the right frame of mind to have a rational discussion…"

"No, it can't wait. I want to talk about this now. I want you to tell me where you see us going."

He was silent for so long that I believed I had my answer.

"Carrie, I *can't* tell you that, because I don't know. I'm sorry, but I won't make promises to you that I may not be able to keep. You know how demanding my father is, and how crazy my job has been lately. I have to stay entirely focused on the business. I can't do this right now."

"I think you already have, Tyler," I told him quietly. "I don't think we should see each other anymore."

"You're breaking up with me?" Tyler couldn't believe what he'd heard.

"Yes. I'm sorry, but I think it's for the best."

"You're breaking up with me? Over the phone?"

"I'm sorry."

"Carrie, no." If I didn't know the truth, I might actually believe I'd somehow managed to hurt him. He sounded hurt. Stunned. Confused. "Please, just wait until I can come home. We can talk about this then."

"No. If you really wanted to make this relationship work, you would be willing to talk about it now. No, we wouldn't even need to talk about it, because there wouldn't be any problems to talk about. If you really cared about me, you would include me in all aspects of your life, not just the convenient parts. Just be honest with me for once. We don't want the same things from each other, and you know it. I need something permanent. I can't go through another dead-end relationship. I'm ready to settle down, have a family. I guess you were only looking to have some fun."

"Fun? You think that's all this was for me? Fun? How can you believe that about me? Look, obviously we need to talk about this in person. I'm coming home tonight."

"No! No, there's nothing to talk about anymore. You gave me your answer. There's nothing left to say. You can't change the way you feel and neither can I. I don't want to see you anymore."

"Carrie, for God's sake, why now? Is this because of your aunt? Look, baby, I know you miss her, and you've been feeling lost without her. And I know I haven't been around very much to talk to, but it won't be like this forever. Please try to understand. Give me time. Don't walk away from us, not like this. Not when you're still emotional from your aunt's death."

"It's not because of my aunt's death. Losing her just made me see the truth at last. You've used your work as an excuse to keep me at a distance from the beginning. If it weren't the job, it would always be something else. You know it's true. We don't want the same things from this relationship."

"Carrie, you knew what I was like from the beginning. You knew how important my work was to me. It never bothered you before. Why the sudden change in attitude?" He was clearly frustrated by my announcement. Even now, at the end of us, Tyler still didn't have a clue what I wanted.

"You're right. I did know. But I guess I thought... Well, it doesn't matter now. I can't do this anymore. I'm sorry, but I'm done with it. I don't want to see you anymore. Please just respect my wishes."

"I don't believe you—"

"And I don't care what you believe." I hung up the phone before I lost my nerve and begged him not to listen to anything I'd just said.

I was still standing with the phone in my hand, trying to talk myself out of ringing Tyler back when Steph called.

"I'm coming over there right now," she said without so much as a hello. The dial tone replaced Steph's voice I didn't bother to call her back. She could be determined when she wanted to be.

Half an hour later, she was ringing my doorbell.

"You look terrible!" she told me before asking me what I'd been up to all day to get Tyler so worked up.

"Nothing. Who knows? You know Tyler. It's always something new with him. Maybe he and The Dick are fighting again." I tried to sound nonchalant about the whole thing but the words came out too shrill. "I went to see some old movies downtown. Cary, you know."

Steph knew something was up, but she figured I'd tell her when I was ready. "And you didn't invite me? I could just kick you."

Her company was better for me than any medicine ever could be. We talked about silly things like fashion and her in-laws until just before dawn when finally out of sheer exhaustion, I fell asleep.

Chapter Eight

Letting Go of What You Want for What You Need

When Steph called at the crack of dawn the following morning, I knew right away she'd talked to Tyler. In her usual, straight-to-the-point way, Steph asked me if I'd lost my mind.

"You broke up with Tyler? Carrie, are you crazy? You love him!"

"That's not true. I don't love him. I just loved the whole *idea* of him."

"The *idea* of him? What exactly does *that* mean? You're crazy about Tyler and you know it!"

"No, I'm not. You were right all along. Tyler isn't the one for me. I need someone who will love me for *me*, someone who wants to be with me all of the time, not just when it fits into his schedule. Someone who will put my feelings first for once, instead of always doing what his father wants, for God's sake! I want someone who isn't like Tyler Bennedict!"

"Carrie, you are so full of it. Tyler can be all of those things if you just give him time."

"We've been together a freaking year! How much time does he need? No, I'm tired of giving Tyler time, making excuses for him, expecting things to be different. I'm tired of compromising. Tyler had his chance. He had a year of chances. It's not happening, and I don't want to talk about Tyler Bennedict anymore. I don't even want to think about him. I'm moving on with my life. From here on out, I'm only dating guys for fun. I'm done with giving up parts of myself just to be with a man. I'm *so* done with it. Serious

116

relationships — you can keep them all. They don't work for me."

"You're just upset. Tyler —"

"Steph, unless you want me to hang up the phone right now, you'd better change the subject."

"Carrie —"

"I mean it. I'm done with talking about Tyler."

"All right, I can see there's no getting through to you when you're in this stubborn mindset."

Of course, I wasn't being fair, and it wasn't as if I were even angry with Steph. But hearing her defend Tyler brought all of my doubts back to the surface. Maybe I'd just made the worse mistake of my life by breaking up with him.

"You want me to come over?"

"No, I'm fine. I'll be okay."

"You want to come over here for a while? We could go shopping."

"No, I'm okay. Really, you don't have to worry."

"Ha. You are such a liar, Carrie Sinclair."

"I'm fine. I just need to be alone. I'll call you later, okay?"

For a little while, I was okay. I resisted the urge to call Tyler for the rest of the day, mostly by taking care of all the chores around the apartment I'd been neglecting forever. I even baked Hazel's favorite pie and took it over to her. She and I caught up on our girl talk for a while then watched her favorite soap together.

That night, for the first time since elementary school, I went to bed at eight o'clock. The following morning, I was almost back to my normal self — well, at least the one who was in deep denial.

When Tyler called, I refused to answer. By Friday he'd pretty much stopped calling me entirely. He'd finally gotten the message. I didn't give a damn what he wanted anymore. I certainly wasn't prepared to sit around and miss him any longer. I wouldn't waste another minute of my life waiting for Tyler or David or any other man. From here on out, I was living my life for me.

117

Unfortunately, when Tyler knocked on my door late Friday night looking more handsome than I'd remembered, most of my resolve melted at the sight of him.

"Carrie, we need to talk..." He stepped into the room uninvited. I couldn't be close to him right now and not forget all the reasons why we didn't work together.

He tried to reach for me, but I stepped away. I couldn't let him touch me and remain strong. The pain in his eyes was so real that it took my breath away.

"No, we don't need to talk. I told you, it's over. What more is there to talk about? Please, just go..." We were so over. And the worst part of it all was I'd known this moment would come from the beginning, but nothing had prepared me for the pain.

"Why?" That single word hurt so much to hear. "Tell me why. You know I care about you. You know I'm trying with you, harder than I have with any other woman. I have certain obligations to my father, as well. I can't just ignore him. I can't walk out on him. He needs me, especially now. All I'm asking from you is to be patient for just a little while longer. Just give me some time. I'll figure something out. I promise. Please, don't do this."

"It wouldn't matter. More time isn't going to fix what's wrong between us and you know it. You're right. You have to do what is best for you and your father, and I do understand. Trust me. I understand about family commitment." I certainly knew a thing or two about regrets. I was full of them over my aunt. I understood Tyler's need to stand by his father. I just didn't believe Richard Bennedict deserved his son's commitment. "Please don't make this any harder for either of us. Just go."

"I was hoping..." He didn't finish.

"What? What were you hoping? That we could go back to the way things were? It's not possible anymore. I'm sorry." I wished that I could be angry with him even but I couldn't. I understood only too well what he was going through.

"Damn it, I care about you! Don't you get that? But I can't

just walk out on my father."

"I'm not asking you to walk out on your father. But coming in second isn't good enough for me anymore. I tried being happy with second place in David's life, and it didn't work out. I can't do it again, not even for you."

"You don't know my father. There are things about him you don't understand. I have to be there for him. I'm all he has. I'm sorry."

"What things? Just tell me what are you talking about?"

"I can't. He's my father. I promised him I wouldn't discuss this with anyone. Please, try to understand. Please don't do this. I'm sorry. I never meant for you to be hurt."

"Stop saying that! Do you even care that your father wants me out of your life?"

"That's not true."

"It is. He told me so."

The caution in his tone was hard to take. "What are you talking about? When did you talk to my father?"

"The other day." I hadn't planned on mentioning Richard's call, but now that I'd started, I had to tell him everything. For us... I had to fight one last time for us.

"What did he say to you?"

"The truth for once—that I wasn't the woman he envisioned for his son. That when it came to it, you would always choose him."

The expression in Tyler's eyes confirmed everything I'd said.

"Don't do this."

"It's true, isn't it? Everything Richard said? It's all true. You don't care about me. I was just someone you slept with. You tell me you care about me, but you shut me out of most of your life. Now you expect everything to be okay. It's *not* okay. It's over."

"Carrie." I wanted him to leave me alone before my resolve shattered completely and I begged him not to go. Tyler pulled me into his arms. I let him.

Tyler lifted me up into his arms and carried me to my

bedroom. Standing me on my feet, he stepped away.

"I'm sorry," he murmured. It wasn't so much the words but the way he said them. My heart shattered into a thousand pieces when I looked at him.

"Dear God, no! No tears. I can take anything but your tears." Frustration and anger roughened his voice.

He closed the whisper of space between us and dragged me into his arms, his lips claiming mine.

God, I couldn't get close enough to him. He tasted like forever. Familiar. Warm. Sexy.

I wrestled with my conscience, even while he lifted me in his arms and carried me to bed.

So much for promises. I'd promised myself the last time would be the last time, but it wasn't enough. It would never be enough with Tyler. I'd always want more.

Tyler reached the bed, urging me gently against it.

Then we were racing, our impatient fingers fumbling to remove each other's clothes.

The sheer pleasure of being as close to Tyler as I would ever accomplish in this lifetime left me breathless.

I surrendered myself to the same desperate need inside me that drove him on, beyond future regrets.

There was no finesse. He pushed inside me and gathered his breath. Tyler slowed the deep thrusts when he tasted my tears against his lips.

"Don't..." he groaned against my mouth. "Please don't cry. Please just let me love you this one last time."

I didn't stop him because I couldn't. I wanted these last moments with him, but I couldn't stop crying either.

He understood that I was hurting. So was he.

I ached inside at the inevitable. With the end in sight, I wanted to stop time, hold onto this moment. Pray for it to go on forever.

Even though my body shook with sobs, it didn't stop me from matching Tyler's need, kiss for kiss, stroke for stroke and touch for touch.

My legs wrapped around his waist, allowing him deeper

access, but still it wasn't close enough to touch his heart.

My tongue tangled with his, my hands skimmed across the tense muscles of his back, igniting a dangerous hunger inside and weakening his will to hold on to the moment. "Tyler…" His name sounded like a sob torn from me. I just wanted to look at him, memorize every inch of him for the dark days ahead. Hold onto this feeling forever.

Under his masterful touch, I was losing the will to hold on. My treacherous body tensed, then arched closer to his. Tyler lifted his head and watched me climax beneath him.

For a long time, neither of us seemed capable of breathing, much less moving. Tyler's weight lying heavy against me never felt more welcoming. I could hear his heart racing in perfect time with mine.

We were desperate for each other. In our last goodbye, we finally got close to each other.

Throughout the long night, I hated him and loved him, all at the same time. Somewhere just before dawn, he tried once more to talk to me.

"Please don't do this. I'll work something out with Dad."

I couldn't let him finish. I couldn't settle for second best with him or any other man.

I got out of bed and closed the bathroom door. I just wanted him to leave me alone so I could fall apart in peace.

"Carrie, open the door! Are you all right?"

I'd been hiding my sickness from him for so long, and now, when I no longer cared, Tyler believed it was all because of my broken heart. In a way, I guess he was right. I wanted to laugh. Wanted to believe that all of Tyler's concern for me was real.

"Please. I need to talk to you."

Somehow, I found the courage to face him again. "Just go. What else is there to say? I think we've said it all — done it all. There's nothing you can tell me now that will change the truth and I have to go to work."

"Carrie, listen to me! I don't want it to end like this. I don't want it to end at all." He started toward me. He was going

121

to touch me again. I couldn't let him.

"No! There's nothing else to say. We want different things. I have to go to work. I have a business to run, commitments, responsibilities just like you. I have a life too. You're not the only one who has people counting on you, you know. I have a life outside of you, and I've let you waste enough of it as it is."

This time when he came to me, I didn't try to stop him. He touched my cheek gently, while his eyes, the ones I'd fallen in love with from the very start, tried to convince me he might actually feel regret.

"I'm sorry—more than you'll ever know. I never meant to hurt you. Whether you believe me or not, I do care about you. I guess, more than I could ever find the way to show you."

Now at last at the end of our tragic love affair, he'd almost said the words I needed to hear from him for so long, right before he turned and walked to my door forever.

"I am not going to cry!" I told Max when he found me still standing in the same place Tyler had left me. Apparently Max understood what was happening in his own cat-like way. I could almost imagine that the expression on his face held sympathy. "I've wasted far too much of my time and my emotions on Tyler Bennedict. I am *so* finished with him!"

For the rest of the day I threw myself into cleaning the apartment from top to bottom. I refused to be sad, refused to mourn the ending of my year-long relationship. Instead, I baked. When the flour dust finally settled around me, I'd baked more than a dozen cakes I couldn't stand to smell. I shoved them down the garbage disposal, went out on my balcony and finally let myself cry.

* * * *

It's funny how you never really notice how many happy people there are in the world until you can't stand the sight

122

of them. They were everywhere around me—at the grocers, in the bank. At work.

Apparently Allie, the one person I could always count on for a caustic remark, was in love for the first time ever. After listening to her gush on about the love of her life, I decided it was time to put myself in a week-long, self-imposed exile away from all the happy people of the world.

I locked myself away in my apartment with only Max for company. He understood my need. Together we lounged around the apartment with me in the faded T-shirt I'd slept in before Tyler came into my life, watching WWF on television—because the only alternative was soap operas and Court TV and even those were filled with happy people. I ignored Steph, Allie and even Aunt Trudy. After my week in exile was up, I emerged from my safe haven angry, sarcastic and defiant.

Screw Tyler Bennedict for making me depressed. I'd done the right thing in getting rid of him. I mean, I barely recognized the woman I'd become when I was with him. This wasn't me. I was usually so in-control of my emotions. Since meeting Tyler, I'd gone from a fairly in-charge woman to a weeping, mindless fool, to an obsessive baker, to the granddaddy of them all, paranoid recluse! I'd run the gamut of emotions.

I'd ignored my aunt, ignored Trudy, Max, my friends and myself. I'd lied to those who actually loved me for a man whose future with me had been questionable from the start. And the worst part was that I'd known better. I'd been warned. Steph had tried to tell me Tyler would make David look like a choirboy, and she'd been right.

I'd given away more to Tyler than I had with David or any other man before him—pieces of myself I could never get back again, like my secret passions, my family obligations. It was time I got the woman I'd been before Tyler back under control. The first item on my agenda was to call Steph and apologize for being such a lousy friend to her lately.

"Carrie? Oh, my God I was almost ready to call the cops!

I thought maybe you'd been kidnapped, but then I called Hazel and she told me she'd heard you talking to Max, so I figured you just needed time. Are you okay?"

"I'm fine. I just needed to figure out some stuff in my head. Do you want to have lunch today?" Okay, this came out sounding way too perky for me. I needed to tone it down before Steph ended up calling a therapist. "I mean, if you have time. I thought I'd go over to the shop later today — you know, check on things — but I'd love to see you first."

After a lengthy moment of silence, Steph agreed. "Of course. That would be great. I'll see you at one."

Over lunch at La Madeline's, I poured on the angry, sarcastic attitude. After all, Steph was familiar with this side of me. I told her I was so glad to be done with the whole drama thing with Tyler. I would start dating again. Strictly casual dating, that is.

"Carrie, you're still in love with Tyler—"

"*Was* in love. I'm all over it now. I don't much like myself in love. In fact, I suck at love. I'm definitely not in love anymore."

"Oh right, like you aren't still thinking about him. Carrie. It's okay. It's more than okay. It's normal. It would be strange if you weren't. When you love someone, you have to give yourself time to mourn them when things don't work out, otherwise you're heading for some serious trouble."

* * * *

At the time, I'd laughed off Steph's analysis, but as the weeks drifted on and Tyler had eventually stopped trying to reach me altogether, my allergy to love and happiness had returned with a far greater force, along with my cooking habit. I was sick and cranky most of the time and yet I spent hours preparing elaborate meals for no one in particular. Max tried his best to do his fair share of eating but after a while, when I walked into the kitchen, he went into hiding.

I'm not sure what other strange habits I might have

developed next had Steph not finally put her foot down and stepped in. She came to my apartment one evening and forced me to face the truth. The second I opened the door and she took a good look at me, she knew something was seriously wrong.

"Okay that's enough. I'm making an appointment for you with my doctor tomorrow! You look terrible."

"I'm fine. I'm just tired," I wasn't sure which doctor she was talking about. Steph possessed a list of them — fertility specialist, gynecologist, dermatologist, psychologist.

"Carrie, you are not fine." She took my hand and pretty much dragged me into the bathroom, sending Max scurrying. "Look at yourself. You look terrible. You are *not* fine. This is *not* normal." She pointed to my reflection.

She was right. I'd been ignoring my own reflection for a long time now. With Steph standing next to me, I was forced to face the truth, what she and probably everyone else around me had been seeing for a while. There was good reason to be concerned. My complexion was pasty-white, my eyes sunken, my cheeks drawn and there was enough baggage beneath each eye for Steph to have packed up most of her wardrobe.

As embarrassing as it was — and probably leading to my permanent removal from the sophisticated, in-control women's club — I started to cry in front of my friend once again. Steph let out a frustrated sigh before taking me back into the living room.

"I'm serious. I'm making an appointment. You aren't well and you can't go on this way. You're going to end up in a hospital if you don't take better care of yourself. I could just kick myself for letting you get involved with Tyler in the first place."

Ha! This made me laugh. As if she or anyone else watching our train wreck could have stopped it from happening. It was fate, after all. Fate in a four-letter, vulgar sense of the word. Unfortunately, Steph didn't see the humor in it so I tried to appease her.

She gave me one of her skeptical looks. "You're right, okay? You're right. Give me the number of your doctor and I'll schedule something. I promise."

"You promise? You're not just saying that to get me to back off? I'll call tomorrow and check with them, you know? I'm giving you until lunch to do it on your own then I'm dragging you to the doctor."

"I promise… Geez. You'd think I was two years old."

Steph smiled at that. She sat down beside me and hugged me tight. "You act like it sometimes."

"Do not." While I might pretend to be angry with her, this was one of those many times I was glad to have her on my side.

"Do so."

* * * *

When I awoke the following morning, it was to the return of my good friend, Mr. Nausea. It was almost noon and Steph's threat came to mind. Since my breaking up with Tyler, I'd gotten into the routine of going to bed early and sleeping late each day.

Next to my pillow was a note with the name and number of Steph's doctor. I knew if I didn't call soon, I'd chicken out. And if I didn't call, Steph would be on my case like white on rice.

As I paced my tiny apartment, I wondered how bad it could be. He'd probably tell me I was run down, give me some vitamins or something and I'd be good as new in no time.

So why was it so hard to pick up the phone and make the call? What was I really afraid of? Maybe he'd tell me there wasn't anything he could do for me. Maybe I was dying. Could a person really die from falling in love with the wrong man? Or maybe he'd simply refer me to yet another shrink, tell me I was in the process of losing my mind.

Deep inside, I knew what was wrong with me. No matter

how much I might choose to ignore the truth, it had been there with me since the very beginning. I'd wanted what Steph, and Trudy, and everyone else who was living out the fairy tale had. I'd been searching for it for years! I wanted someone to love me and be there for me through it all—the good, the bad, and the not so nice. Instead, I'd gotten a fair-weather lover. Tyler would never stand up to his father. If I stayed with him, it would only be a matter of time before he broke my heart. I wasn't prepared to let him hurt me as David had.

After tossing Steph's name out, I was able to get an appointment with the doctor for the following week. There, I'd done it. At least maybe now she could relax, even if I couldn't.

She called later the same afternoon just to make sure I'd followed through with my end of our deal.

"Have you spoken to Doctor Turner's office yet?

"Yes, Mother. I have an appointment set up for next week, in fact."

Steph ignored my sarcasm entirely. I'm sure by this point she was used to it. "You'll like Doctor Turner. He's very nice."

As hard as I tried to put on a positive front, Steph knew I was in trouble. She called every single day with some excuse or another. She took me shopping or to see a movie. But as hard as Steph tried to keep my mind off Tyler, I still missed him more than I ever believed possible.

So, it was in this gloomy state of mind that I made it to my appointment with Stephanie's doctor. I sat outside the office for a long time with my sunglasses firmly in place, doing a little recon, just in case someone who knew me showed up. Once I was satisfied the coast was clear, I stepped inside, still wearing the sunglasses, and took in my surroundings. The office, as well as the location off Great Hills Trail, had Steph written all over it, from its tasteful yet subdued modern contemporary furniture, to the choice of magazines—*Bon Appétit* and *Travel Extraordinaire*.

I gave the receptionist my name and was told that the doctor would be with me shortly. Once I'd filled out the numerous pages of medical forms, the nurse escorted me to the examining room, told me to remove my clothes and put on the hot pink robe. At least it wasn't paper.

Doctor Turner turned out to be a distinguished gent in his mid-fifties. Steph was right. I did like him. He was kind and gentle and had the best bedside manner I'd ever encountered until he diagnosed me. Turns out, being in love with the wrong man can make you sick — and so can forgetting to take your birth control pills.

I was, according to the doctor's best estimate, a little more than four weeks pregnant. I was devastated. I almost wished he'd told me I was suffering from an incurable disease.

"But that can't be! That's not possible!"

The doctor simply smiled at me. I was getting this smile a lot lately and I hated it. "It can and it is."

"But I'm on the pill!"

"It happens," he calmly informed me, "even to women on the pill. No chance you may have skipped one or two pills? Forgot to take them?"

As I looked at him as if he'd lost his mind, I was all set to put him straight when suddenly I wasn't so sure.

I hadn't, surely. I'd been taking those little pills since I was sixteen, after a nightmare year of periods. I'd never once missed a pill, especially not after Tyler and I hooked up. So this just couldn't be. Maybe I'd gotten a bad batch.

"No, of course not. It has to be the pills. They must be bad…"

Again the smile.

"I doubt it, and as I'm sure you know already, sometimes no amount of birth control is foolproof. Nothing but abstinence is one hundred percent."

After I left the doctor's office, I sat in my car staring into space for more than an hour while the little insecure voice inside my head reminded me of how scattered and restless I'd been for so long now — since my aunt's death.

Not only was it possible, it was actually probable that I'd forgotten to take one or a dozen of those little pills. But did it really matter how it had happened? That ship had sailed. The question now was what was I going to do about it?

Still, it didn't stop me from counting the remaining pills the second I got back to the apartment. The doctor had been right. I'd forgotten several of them, in fact. Probably not in a row and definitely not on purpose, but none of those things changed the truth, did it? I'd behaved irresponsibly. I'd let my relationship with Tyler and my concerns about it muddle my common sense. I was pregnant with his baby and I didn't know how to tell him about any of my mistakes.

"So what did Doctor Turner tell you?" Stephanie probably had it calculated to the second how long it should take me to get home. I glanced down at my answering machine. She'd left me several messages already.

"Oh, just the usual... You know."

"No, I don't? What did he say *exactly*?"

Suddenly I was scared. I couldn't tell Steph the truth just yet because she would insist that I tell Tyler and I wasn't ready to face him again. In fact, I wasn't sure if I would ever be ready to tell him about the baby. I was still getting used to the idea of being pregnant myself. I certainly hadn't made up my mind what I was going to do about it yet. But if I didn't tell Steph something, would she find out the truth from her doctor, even though that should be impossible?

"He said I'm just really run down, like you thought. You know almost.... What do you call it?"

"Anemic?" Steph supplied and I grabbed at it.

"Yes, that's it."

"So, what did he tell you to do?"

I didn't know what exactly was involved in being anemic. It was something blood related but I wasn't sure what exactly.

"The usual?"

"You mean iron supplements and vitamins or is he suggesting you eat more red meat?"

Now, Aunt Mable always taught me that lying was a full time job. Once you got going, it was hard to remember all the lies you needed to tell just to cover up the first one. She'd said it was God's little way of punishing a person for lying. She was right. I didn't have any idea what Doctor Turner would have recommended, so I went for overkill. After all, Steph knew how sick I'd been.

"Both, actually. Yeah, that's it... Both."

"Oh, wow. It must be serious. When does he want to see you again?"

Doctor Turner had asked me to come back the following week. Even though I'd told him I wasn't sure I was having the baby, he'd still suggested I should have several prenatal tests run—just in case. I couldn't tell Steph any of those things.

"Not for a while."

"Not for a while? That doesn't really sound like him. He's always so cautious. Are you sure you understood him correctly? I know you've been rather scattered lately. Shouldn't you confirm this with his office?"

You have no idea how scattered, I wanted to tell her, but instead I'd started to panic again. "No. No, Steph, it's fine, and I am capable of understanding simple instructions. I'll be fine. I'll just go have a cow for dinner." The very thought of it almost sent me fleeing for the restroom. At least it made her laugh.

"Why don't you have dinner with us tonight? I mean, unless you have other plans?" For more than a year now my life had revolved around Tyler and his schedule. Now that I was technically a free woman again, I guess it never occurred to her that I might actually have plans of my own.

"Are you gonna have a cow, too?" My thoughts were literally spinning. I didn't want to be alone, but I needed to...try to figure out what I was going to do about my little problem, which was even more reason why I didn't want to be alone. I had some very difficult decisions to make on my own. Tyler would not be part of any of them.

"I'm serious. We're going to the club tonight, and you are coming with us. I'm not taking no for an answer so get ready. We'll pick you up in an hour."

After I'd dressed as best I could under the circumstances, I began eating crackers and drinking Diet Sprite like it were going out of style. The sight of beef in any form would only make me sick, but I'd just lied to my friend.

In the end, I somehow managed to fool Steph and Ed into believing I was going to be okay, but it certainly wasn't easy. The sight of the T-bone steak lying on my plate was almost too much to bear.

"Carrie, you've hardly touched your steak. How do you expect to get better if you don't eat?"

I could only turn to Ed for help. Knowing his sweet, caring wife the way he did, he was more than happy to come to my aid.

"Honey, leave Carrie alone. She's going to be okay. She just needs time." Although Steph might not listen to me, she did know when to do as Ed suggested and shut up.

For a little while, with the help of my friends, I was actually able to forget all about my problems — right up until the time I said goodnight to Steph and Ed and walked into my empty apartment.

Even Max didn't want to be around me tonight. He'd obviously found himself a nice little hiding place and he wasn't giving it up to me.

And so, I sat alone on my balcony and faced the cold hard truth at last.

I'd just dumped Tyler. I wasn't prepared to have him back in my life as a boyfriend or as a partner in the decision-making process concerning this child's fate. It was too soon. Tyler still had the power to make me forget why I'd broken up with him in the first place. I couldn't have him around clouding my judgment right now.

Somehow, I couldn't even begin to imagine myself as anyone's mother right now. Weren't mothers supposed to be able to make the perfect Halloween costume from a piece of yarn and two paper clips, or know exactly what to say when you scraped your knee or got into a fight at school. Mothers were supposed to be perfect—and married. I wasn't either. I couldn't be anyone's mother, could I?

No matter how much I thought about it, I still didn't know what the right decision was going to be for me, so I didn't make any decision at all. I threw myself into my work with a new fury, while I waited for another disaster to hit.

* * * *

By the end of the following week, after picking up the phone a dozen times to tell Tyler about the baby and after driving by his house at least as many times, I was more restless than ever before. I was sick most of the time and I needed to get out of this town for a while.

I was still trying to decide where to run to when Aunt Trudy's number appeared on my caller ID. My heart went into panic mode the second I saw it. I was still remembering the last time she'd called me.

"Are you okay?" I didn't bother with hello.

She realized immediately what was going through my mind. "Oh, honey, yes. Yes, I'm fine. I'm sorry I didn't mean to scare you. I'm fine. In fact, I'm better than fine. I'm here with Fred and we have some wonderful news. Are you with Tyler? Are you sitting down?"

I still hadn't found the right time to tell her I'd broken up with Tyler several weeks earlier. "Tyler's not here, Aunt Trudy. He's…working. What's the good news?"

"We're getting married!"

At her declaration I think I had an out-of-body experience for a second. Surely I hadn't heard her correctly.

"Carrie, did you hear me?"

Then I realized I had—right before I'd dropped the phone. I barely registered my aunt's frantic voice asking me if I was okay.

I picked up the phone again. "What did you just say?"

132

At the sound of my aunt's happiness, I fought to keep from being sick. "We're getting married!"

"Who's getting married?" *Someone was getting married? Not me? Not Tyler?* Which only left my sweet-never-been-married-before aunt. Aunt Trudy was getting married? I dropped the phone again and ran for the bathroom.

By the time I returned, Trudy was gone. She was probably dialing nine-one-one by now. I called her back and tried to concentrate on what she was saying this time. Aunt Trudy was getting married. Could this really be happening?

"It's true, honey. Fred just popped the question a few minutes before I called you.

I started to cry, but it was nothing to do with her announcement. It seemed that everyone around me was married or getting married and happy in their relationships except for me. "Aunt Trudy, I'm so happy for you," I all but wailed into the receiver.

"We were thinking we'd tie the knot two weeks from Saturday? Can you and Tyler make it? If not, we'll change the day. It's only going to be Fred and me then the two of you, of course. I've already told Fred I don't want anything fancy. I'm too old for any such thing."

I crossed my fingers behind my back and lied once again to my aunt. "I don't think Tyler will be able to make that date, but I'll be there."

She was disappointed, but she was in love. No one stays disappointed for long when they're in love.

Chapter Nine

There are the Things You Think You Need...Knowing
What to Toss Aside and What to Keep

On a perfect warm spring afternoon, outside the house
I'd grown up in as a child, my adopted Aunt Trudy and my
new uncle, by default, were married.

The ceremony was simple and to the point. No-nonsense,
just like my aunt. It lasted all of ten minutes. Afterward, I
served them cake I'd prepared especially for the occasion.

The reception lasted only slightly longer than the
wedding. When the pastor left, I took Aunt Trudy and Fred
out for a celebratory dinner at their favorite steakhouse.
Then the happy couple checked into the local Holiday Inn
for their honeymoon night, and I went back to my aunt's
empty house.

I'd never seen Trudy look so happy and I was thrilled for
her, but getting through the wedding—even one as short
as theirs—had been nothing short of torture. The minute
the minister had spoken of Trudy and Fred's love and their
commitment to each other, I'd started to cry and hadn't
stopped for the rest of the evening.

Even among the people who loved me the most, I was
alone—the odd man out. I missed Tyler and what we'd
shared together. I wanted him to love me the way I loved
him. I wanted to be important enough in his life for him
to stand up to his father for me. But what I wanted would
always be impossible for Tyler.

I'd planned to stay a week with them, but ended up
extending my stay indefinitely. Trudy and Fred were

thrilled. But then, everything thrilled them lately. They were blissfully happy, but I was willing to overlook this fault just to get away from my troubles for a while.

Unfortunately, I wasn't any happier here with them than I'd been in Austin. I was restless and I couldn't talk to Trudy about my problems.

I found myself confiding in Fred after swearing him to secrecy one night after Trudy went to bed.

Fred asked me what was wrong with me lately. I tried to tell him about my break up with Tyler but it came out all wrong.

"Things aren't so good between Tyler and me."

"What's wrong, pumpkin?" He'd only recently started calling me 'pumpkin'.

"It's over between us and I don't know how to move beyond that. Pretty pathetic, isn't it?"

At this point, Fred took my hand and looked me square in the eye. "Over? Are you sure? From what Trudy tells me, Tyler's crazy about you. Maybe you two are just going through a rough patch. Every relationship has them. Don't give up on him."

"I'm not the one giving up! I'm just accepting the truth. Tyler doesn't want the same things from life that I do. How long am I supposed to keep holding on when we both want different things? There isn't any future in it, and it isn't fair to Tyler or to me."

"Who's been telling you those things?"

"No one... It's just a feeling."

"Well, I guess you would know him better than anyone. I can only tell you what Trudy told me. She says Tyler is in love with you."

* * * *

Over the next few weeks my sadness steadily grew into depression. I was miserable and I made everyone around me miserable as well. I wanted to be in Austin. God help

135

me, I wanted to call Tyler. I wanted to tell him the truth about the baby. Instead, I found myself extending my stay even longer, ignoring my commitments and lying to my friends. I did make it a point to check in on my business regularly and was pleased to see that Allie and the staff were doing a great job of keeping things running smoothly in my absence.

After another week of moping around the place, Fred took me aside one day and read me the riot act.

"Carrie, I love you, honey. You're like my own child, but you have to get your head out of your ass. What's the matter with you? Are you going to let your problems with Tyler drive you away from everything you've worked so hard to accomplish? Get yourself together and get back to Austin. Get to work. Trust me when I tell you, it might be the best thing in the world for you. I know you don't think you can do this, pumpkin, but you're strong. You'll be okay."

I wasn't as sure of this as Fred was, but I couldn't stay here forever. I shouldn't have run to them in the first place. I'd been ignoring my responsibilities and friends and poor, old Max for weeks now.

* * * *

Once I was settled back into my old routine, it wasn't long before my restlessness returned. I didn't want to stay in Austin, but I couldn't stand the thought of being alone. I was weepy and miserable and to cover up all my sadness, I hit the ground running. I worked long hours, exhausting myself mentally as well as physically even while I became more restless with each passing day.

One weekend with Steph and Ed both out of town, to keep myself from baking again, I pulled out the picture of the house in Colorado and started thinking seriously about my future. I was still young, and well…so what if I was pregnant? I wasn't tied to Austin, was I? I'd started one business. I could do it again.

Again and again my mind kept returning to my dream home in Colorado. I'd learned it was still vacant. This might be the perfect time for me to start over. I could rebuild Carrie's Creative Catering somewhere different. I could even start writing seriously.

Without realizing it, I'd made a decision about my future at last. I turned to Max, who was sitting next to me watching the city come to life around us.

"How do you feel about Colorado?"

Now Max has never been outside of Texas in his life, but he was willing to give the mountains a shot. After all, this town was dead to us.

If I was going to make my future dream a reality, I was going to need a whole lot of help accomplishing it. So, at a little past seven that same morning, I called the one person who could offer me the type of help I needed right now.

"Alex, it's Carrie. I need your help." I didn't bother with good morning, or asking him how he'd been. I just went straight to the point.

"Carrie, do you know what time it is?"

"Yes, are you going to listen to me or not?"

"What's wrong? You sound terrible. Have you been *crying*?" This was probably about as unexpected coming from me as what I was about to ask him. In Alex's opinion, I was as tough as any man.

"I'm willing to sell Carrie's Creative Catering to you."

"You are?" He sounded stunned. "But you said you'd never sell—"

"I've changed my mind," I interrupted. "It's yours and I'm not even going to ask for what you offered me the last time you begged me to sell it to you."

"Oh really? What price are you asking exactly? And before you answer, I should remind you, you're the one in need here, not me. It's a buyer's market, so to speak."

That might be, but I had a price set in my head and I wasn't going to let Alex bid me down.

"Five hundred thousand and that's not negotiable."

"No way."

"That's it, Alex. Take it or I go elsewhere. In the past, you offered seven. It's worth at least five to you for its future potential, if nothing else. The price is final." I didn't intend to go elsewhere because there weren't any other offers of interest. I needed Alex. I just didn't need him to know this.

I guess something in my voice must have gotten through to him because Alex stopped arguing at this point. "Okay, you got it, babe. I'll have my attorney draw up the papers and we'll go over them later in the week."

"That's not good enough. I need the money in my account today. Please, Alex."

He was silent a moment longer, before he came through for me, as always. "Okay, it will be there by ten. Same bank and account as before?"

When Alex had used me in the past, he'd always deposited the money directly into my account and always on time. He knew how important this was for my small business. I could always count on Alex to be fair.

"Yes, but there's more."

"Carrie, you're pushing our friendship now."

"I know, but I'm just as serious about this as the price. I won't sell without you agreeing to it."

"What do you want now?" he grumbled.

"I want to keep the name, in case I decide to start over someplace else, and I want you to keep Allie on with the promise of making her a partner one day."

Alex met these demands with silence. I knew he was trying to do the right thing and still not come off sounding like a softie.

"I'll give you the name thing, but why would I agree to make Allie a partner? She isn't *your* partner. You obviously haven't felt the need to make her one."

"That's not negotiable, Alex. This is the only way I'll sell the business to you. I'll leave the details of how you do it up to you, but I won't leave Allie hanging. She deserves this."

"Okay, all right—you win. Anything else?"

138

"No. Just…thank you."

He so wanted to sound angry. "Do you want to come by later in the week and sign the papers or not?"

"Nope, I'm leaving town tomorrow. I won't be around to sign anything. You can call my cell phone and I'll tell you where to send the documents for my signature."

"You're leaving Austin? Why?" Another pause then he'd guessed it. "It's because of him, isn't it? Don't throw away everything because of him. Men aren't worth giving up your life for, especially not Tyler Bennedict."

This made me smile at least. Alex admitting the truth about his gender must be a first. "You're right, but it has nothing to do with him really. It's time for me to move on. This just gave me a reason to do it. You'll have the money today? And you'll take care of Allie for me?"

He made a grunting sound, which told me how hard he was taking my leaving. "You want to have lunch or something? You can't just leave without saying goodbye?"

"I can't say goodbye at all. I'm just going to ride off into the sunset. I'll be fine. So if you were thinking about worrying about me, don't. But maybe you'll come see me some day? You *and* Melissa?" He didn't answer and I knew the truth. I'd never see Alex again.

After I hung up with Alex, I called Allie to tell her the good news. She was too upset to appreciate her good luck right away. She would in time.

After I hung up with Allie, I called the moving service Steph once used and booked a time for the following week. By seven-thirty, all of the arrangements were made. I just needed to break the news to my best friend.

"Are you okay?" Steph was shocked to see me standing at her front door.

"Hi, can I come in?" I stood on the front porch and simply looked at the woman I'd known for so long. For the first time that morning, I found myself having doubts about my decision to leave.

Steph led me into her perfectly decorated living room

where Ed sat reading the paper.

"You look terrible. Have you been doing what the doctor told you to do?"

"Steph, please. I can't say the things I need to say to you if you're going to lecture me. Please… Just listen to me for a second."

She plopped down onto her Italian leather sofa and stared up at me as if I'd just insulted her taste in clothes.

"This is so hard to say to you but I've made some tough decisions about my future and they're final. First, though, you need to know the truth. I'm not anemic. I'm pregnant."

"You're what? You're pregnant?" Steph looked to Ed for help. "You can't be pregnant! You aren't even trying to be pregnant!"

"It was an accident, okay. You're right. I didn't plan for this to happen."

"An accident? *An accident?* I've been trying for years to get pregnant and you manage to do it by accident?"

My heart went out to her. I knew how desperately she wanted to have a baby.

"I'm sorry."

She waved a hand at me and shook her head. I waited in silence for her to regain some of her genteel composure again.

"Have you told Tyler about the baby?"

I'd known how upset Steph was going to be by my news, just as I'd known she would ask me about Tyler. That was probably why I wasn't in any hurry to tell her the truth about the pregnancy.

"No, and I have no intention of telling him just yet, and you can't either! You have to promise me."

"He has a right to know about his child! I mean, it's his responsibility to help raise the baby as well as yours." She stopped the second I could see that she'd become aware of my options. "You are going to have the baby, aren't you?" Steph glared at me as if I'd somehow turned into Satan.

"I don't know yet. I haven't decided." She looked

devastated that I might not keep the baby. "But either way, I'm not telling Tyler about the baby until I've made up my mind what I'm doing."

"Carrie—"

"Steph, Carrie's right, so leave her alone. It's her decision to make. It's her body. She'll tell Tyler when it's time." Right there, in my friend's living room, I found an ally I hadn't been expecting. Ed—a man—was actually agreeing with me. This meant more than I could have imagined. I smiled at him over the top of his wife's head.

"I still think you need to tell him now. He has a right to know, even if you don't have the child, but I guess you have to do things your way." She was forced to concede defeat when she spotted Ed's annoyance.

"Yes, I do. I realize this is hard for you, but it is my decision. Anyway, I told you I'd made some decisions about my future. There's more. Some things you're not going to like very much. I've decided to leave Austin."

"Leave? You mean just for a little while, right. Are you going to see your aunt?"

"No, I don't mean for a little while. I mean for good. I'm moving to Colorado."

"To the house! You're buying the dream house, aren't you?" Ed said with enthusiasm.

I'd almost forgotten how much Ed had loved the house as well.

"Yes."

"You can't just leave town? What about your business? Do you realize how hard it will be running a business from so far away?"

"I sold the business—this morning—to Alex. Maybe I'll start it up again in Colorado, or maybe I'll try something totally different." I spotted her surprise. "I'm not sure yet."

"Carrie you can't do this!" She turned to her husband for help. "Ed, will you tell her she can't do this? You're not thinking clearly right now. Slow down a little. Give yourself some time to adjust to everything. You've been through so much lately. Don't go throwing your life away like this. I mean, what if…" Steph stopped and looked at me as if she was trying to guess what my reaction would be to her next words. "Well, what if you're wrong about Tyler? What if we both were? I mean, you two have been together for almost a year now. That's something, isn't it?"

I shook my head and she guessed it was useless to argue. "You know that's not true. And anyway, David and I were together for almost two years and look how *that* turned out. I'd just lasted longer with Tyler because I'd probably put up with more than the others did. I've made up my mind about this. I've been thinking about it for a long time now, even before I broke up with Tyler. You know I've been restless for a while. I've been in a rut for a long time. I needed something… Some change in my life. This is it. This is the perfect time."

"But I'm going to miss you."

When she looked at me with those sad eyes, I lost it. I started to cry once again then we were hugging and crying all over each other. I'd cried too many tears lately, all the tears I hadn't been able to shed during my year with Tyler. I was all cried out.

"I'll miss you too. You'll both come see me, won't you?"

Steph turned to Ed. "We're moving to Colorado. *You* tell my father."

"Fine by me," Ed pulled his wife into his arms. "Carrie has plenty of room."

I loved them both for trying to lighten the mood.

"When are you leaving?" Steph sounded even sadder than I felt.

"Tomorrow…"

"So soon?" She wanted to ask me not to go, but I think deep down, she knew this was what I needed right now. "What about your furniture and all your things?"

I explained how I'd given the movers Hazel's number, but told them to call Steph as a backup just in case Hazel didn't have her hearing aid on and missed the call.

"No, I'll take care of everything for you. It's the least I can do. Now, what about your mail?"

I could always count on my friend for anything I needed, including my new life.

"Have you talked to Trudy yet? About the move? About Tyler? About the baby?"

I shook my head. "No." Eventually, I'd known Steph would get around to asking me this question. It was going to be even harder telling Trudy the truth about my breakup with Tyler and about the baby, which was why I hadn't done it yet.

"But she's going to know sooner or later. You can't hide a baby for long."

I promised Steph that once I'd gotten settled into my new life I would tell my aunt everything.

When I got back to the apartment, I called the real estate agency in Colorado. The agent I spoke with was a sweet man who was happy to tell me all about the house and its history, even about the town itself.

He offered to show me the house once I arrived, but I told him I'd seen it already on two separate occasions. I didn't need to see it again. I wanted to buy it.

The poor man was so shocked that I don't think he believed me. I was forced to repeat myself several times before he finally accepted that I was serious.

"How can I be sure you won't sell the house before I get there?"

He stammered around until he finally said, "Let me make a quick call to the seller and see if they would be agreeable to accepting a small deposit to hold it for you."

"That sounds great," I told him and hung up. I only had to wait a short time before the agent called me back.

"Good news, Ms. Sinclair. The seller has agreed upon the sales price and would be happy to hold the house for you with the deposit. Once the deposit is received, the papers will be signed and waiting for you to complete when you arrive. Congratulations," he said then told me where to send the money. I did as he'd instructed then called him back to confirm when I'd be there.

After that, there was nothing left to do but pack. The movers would deliver my furniture along with most of my personal items. I was only taking Max and my clothing with me for now. Trying to decide what to keep and what things needed discarding was an almost impossible tack to perform. I was amazed at the things I'd found valuable enough to save through the years — all the little insignificant items of my life.

In the end, a fresh start required letting go of the past. I kept only a few personal items I couldn't bear to part with, mostly things Aunt Mable and Trudy had given to me. By the time I was finished, I was exhausted and my sentimental sadness had long ago turned into emotional exhaustion.

Max and I sat outside on the balcony where I'd dreamed so many dreams over the past ten years. This was our final night in the home we'd both become attached to. I believe even Max understood this. He seemed as sad and as sentimental as I did.

There was nothing holding us here any longer. After we had said goodbye to Hazel the next morning, Max and I drove around Austin for a little while, revisiting some of my favorite hangouts.

Two weeks ago, Tyler and I should have been celebrating our first anniversary together. Instead, I'd been with my aunt and Tyler had been with his father. I drove by the first restaurant he'd taken me to. I'd been so impressed by him. Then I returned to all the old places I'd taken Tyler to in my middle class world and all the expensive, trendy restaurants he'd introduced to me.

Then somewhere around midnight, on our way out of town for the last time, I found myself at Tyler's house.

His lights were on. Even though it was late, he wasn't sleeping. I couldn't help but wonder if he was there alone. Maybe he was moving on already.

I parked the car a little way down the hill and got out with

Max. "We won't be long, buddy. I have to do this." He gave another little tired meow, which told me he recognized my pain.

I walked halfway up Tyler's driveway before stopping. I wouldn't go any farther. I just needed to say goodbye in a way I'd been too angry and too upset to do before.

As I stood in the warm, muggy Austin night crying and trying to find peace in my decision to leave Tyler and Austin behind, Tyler's porch light suddenly came on. When he stepped outside, I turned away in panic but not before he'd spotted me.

"Carrie, wait! Carrie, don't go!"

I didn't listen. I couldn't. I was humiliated that he'd caught me standing in front of his house like some foolish, lovesick child. I ran all the way down the hill with Max bouncing in my arms. I didn't stop, not even to look back, because I knew he would come after me. I couldn't let him catch me.

I'd embarrassed myself for the last time with Tyler. I'd given up so much of myself to be with him that surely there must have been a hole in my heart the size of Texas.

Up until that moment, I believe, deep down inside I'd still held out hope that someday I could come back home.

As I sped away from the curb, Tyler's image appeared in my rear view mirror. I would never be able to stay here believing that someday Tyler might get married—and he would. He'd be just across town in his beautiful home with his perfect Bennedict bride, and there would always be the chance when I least expected it that I would run into Tyler, along with her, and I'd fall to pieces all over again. No, this town was more than over for me. It was finished.

The sound of the cell phone startled Max and sent me swerving on the rain-slicked road. I didn't answer it. I knew it was Tyler. I turned the phone off and left the past in the past, and Austin, the city I'd finally grown up in, in my rear view mirror.

Chapter Ten

Having a Do-over

Bright sunlight streaming through a gap in the curtains of my hotel room was my first indication that I'd overslept—a fact that Max apparently had been trying to bring to my attention for quite some time now.

"I'm sorry, buddy." I made amends by giving him breakfast. Once I'd showered and dressed, I thought about facing another day of driving with Max for company. I sank down to the bed and cried for hours. God, I just wanted to turn tail and run home to Trudy and Fred.

To keep myself strong and to resist the urge to run home, I became determined to get out of Texas that very day. I was banking all of my future happiness on leaving Texas in my dust. By early evening, when I crossed the state line into New Mexico, it had almost worked. The first bit of enthusiasm since I'd left the hotel earlier that morning emerged. I found ten heartbreaking messages from Tyler on my cell phone, begging me to call him back. I listened to the first two then started weeping again. I erased the rest without listening to them.

All my focus was now on my new home and my new life. I was going to start working on my secret passion in Colorado. Financially, I'd be okay for a while, thanks to the money Aunt Mable had left me, along with the sale of my business.

I told myself this was the great thing about moving to a new place. It allowed me to toss out the past with all the trash I'd accumulated over the years. I could just start over in a new town where no one knew about all those little mistakes of my past. It was almost like a do-over.

Starting over in a new place with only a cat to give me comfort, not to mention being pregnant... Well, I wasn't sure I could run far enough to escape those mistakes.

I kept remembering how I'd neglected my aunt for a man who didn't know how to love me. I should have been there with her in those final days. I should have known she needed me. I did know. I'd been in a love affair that was destined to fail from the beginning. I'd hurt her. I'd chosen the wrong one to spend my time with and I could never get those moments back again. I was determined not to keep thinking about Tyler any longer. Tyler was the past. Parrish and starting over was the future.

When Max and I finally arrived in Parrish the next day, I was determined to make the best of our new start, no matter what!

"This is Colorado, Max. What do you think?"

I'd booked us into a cabin at the Parrish Peak Rentals until all the paperwork was completed for me to take possession of the house. My trusty real estate agent assured me it shouldn't take long. He was as anxious as I was to get the house off the market, which should have been my first clue — beyond the fact that the place had sat vacant for more than three years — that maybe there were a few problems somewhere? The real estate agent had suggested I have a house inspector check out the place, but I just wanted to move in, so I had turned him down.

But I was still looking at the place through rose-colored glasses when we spent our first night there, sleeping on blankets in front of a wood stove because frankly, the place was freezing.

That was when I felt my first twinge of buyer's remorse. I was determined to make the most of it. After all, there was lots of firewood around, so we could survive for a while — or at least until the local furnace expert could stop by.

For reasons no one around could explain to me, in a town

as small as Parrish, the furnace repairman was booked up for weeks in advance, even though it was still technically summer.

I was not going to let this get me down. I was concentrating on my new life while still avoiding making any further bad decisions about the old one, which translated into, what was I going to do about the baby?

So I bundled up and hauled in plenty of firewood for our long nights spent camping in front of the fire in the great room.

By the time my furniture arrived, I was actually starting to feel good about my decision to move here—until the furnace repairman showed up at my door.

* * * *

Now, the funny thing about dreams is they never quite live up to their full potential. Reality has a way of scattering the smoky atmosphere away and introducing you to the truth with about as much subtlety as a slap in the face.

By the time Mr. Furnace Repairman had left me, I wanted to cry. I'd been fighting back the tears since he'd handed me his rough estimate of four thousand dollars.

"I don't understand," I told him, while really trying to understand. "What's wrong with it? It looks perfectly fine."

He gave me a smug little only-a-woman-would-say-something-like-that laugh before trying to explain in simple layman's terms for the little lady's benefit that just because it *looked* perfectly fine didn't mean it *was* perfectly fine.

Somehow I managed to keep from snapping at him. After all, he was the only game in town and I was tired of being cold. I needed him. So I wrote the not-so-nice man a fat little check and he told me he would put me on the list.

"On the list? I've waited two weeks already. Why can't you just fix it? What does 'on the list' mean? How much longer?"

He snapped his little tool box closed and headed for

my door, apparently unmoved by my pathetic questions. There was just enough speed in his step to tell me that he anticipated a womanly moment any second now.

"Shouldn't be long... Maybe another week or so."

With this, he left, and I slammed the door behind him, then opened it, smiled and thanked him again.

Once he was out of sight, I started to cry and continued crying throughout the rest of the afternoon. What was I thinking, moving to this godforsaken state in the first place? Who moved to the middle of nowhere with nothing but bears to keep them company? And poor Max. I couldn't even let him roam the countryside as I'd promised, because I was afraid he'd end up being bear food. What was wrong with me?

This was the extent of my accomplishments for the day. I cried and put more wood on the fire, then Max and I ate. We'd been doing nothing but stuffing ourselves for days.

Even though I was exhausted most of the time from all of my wood gathering, I was finding it hard to sleep with all the peace and quiet surrounding me. My nearest neighbor was a mile down the mountainside. I'd tried once to introduce myself to him, but apparently he'd come to Colorado to get away from people because, even though I was certain he was home, he wasn't answering the door — at least not for me.

The next day dawned with me determined not to spend it moping around the place feeling sorry for myself. This was my decision to move here, after all. No one had forced me into it. I left Max on guard patrol while I went into town to meet some of my fellow townsfolk and take care of a few errands.

I found the medical center in town and promised myself I would stop by to make an appointment very soon. You know, just in case I decided to keep the baby.

I stopped in front of the local diner on Main Street and looked inside. Someone had stuck a 'For Sale' sign next to the door. The last of the breakfast crowd appeared to be just clearing out. I went inside to see if I could meet some locals over coffee and a pastry.

The second I walked into the room, the place grew quiet. All eyes were now focused on me. Apparently newcomers are easy to spot. We must stand out like a sore thumb among the locals with our awestruck expression.

The place looked as if it had been around longer than I'd been alive. The faded vinyl booths were showing definite signs of aging. Someone had tried to repair a few of them with gray duct tape. By most people's standards, it would be considered a dive, but for me? Well, I saw the potential there. A little fresh paint, some sanding and varnish on the floors, perhaps a few menu changes and who knew?

I went up to the counter and tried to decide between the apple turnover and the bear claw then decided why not have one of each?

"That'll be two-fifty, miss," a woman in her mid-fifties told me as she rang up my breakfast. She looked tired. The sign said the place opened for breakfast at five. I could only imagine.

"Are you the owner?"

For a second she seemed taken aback by the question. I'm sure everyone around town who knew her, knew she was the owner. "Yes, honey, I am... Well, at least one of them. My husband is the other. He's in the back cooking. Is something wrong with your turnover?" Clearly, she'd been expecting a complaint. Was this what she'd come to expect from most tourists who visited this quaint mountain town? Maybe all those rich people who came for the skiing close by liked to gawk and complain whenever something didn't go their way.

"Oh no. No, it's fine. I was just wondering about the 'For Sale' sign in the window? How long have you been trying to sell the place?"

"For a while," she told me with a wave of her dishtowel. "We've had lots of hopefuls, mostly from tourists who came to their senses when they realized they didn't want to live in the mountains permanently, especially not in the winter months. Are you interested in the place or were you just curious?"

"Me? Oh no. No, I was just wondering." I took my pastry and coffee off to a booth to enjoy. As I sat facing the street staring at the sign, I found myself wondering, 'Why not?'. This wasn't exactly what I'd pictured doing when I'd thought about moving to Colorado. I'd planned to write full time. But I couldn't stand to think about the long, empty days ahead for me and, as much as I loved writing, I'd pretty much stopped completely when I'd broken up with Tyler. Romance was hard to come by for me anymore. Starting up a new business might be the perfect challenge to fill my empty days and keep me from running home to Aunt Trudy.

I walked out of the diner before I could go back inside and ask the woman what the asking price was. I'd already made far too many rash decisions about my future, and lately my track record for good decision-making wasn't so great. I'd moved thousands of miles away from everything and everyone I loved to a cold, empty house. My hasty decisions weren't working out too well for me so far.

Just outside of town, I found a picturesque little park, where I proceeded to zero in on the only other person who seemed to be enjoying its amenities this morning. An elderly old gentleman dressed in a brown wool suit with a matching, slightly used derby on his balding head.

I slid onto the park bench next to him and smiled.

"What are you looking at?" the old guy virtually growled at me. In the midst of recoiling to the far side of the bench from his obvious anger, I could almost swear underneath all that unpleasantness I detected a faint Texas accent.

"Are you from Texas?" I tried to remember that a smile was supposed to represent an umbrella or something equally ridiculous. However, if this was the case, clearly mine must be tattered, because this old man was certainly raining on my small amount of remaining enthusiasm.

"What's it to ya?" His very distinct southern drawl was definitely Texan.

Be nice, I told myself. *He's probably just a lonely old man.* "Well, um, no reason, really, except I'm from Texas too." I smiled at him, which made him watch me suspiciously, as if he thought I might have stopped by to take his money.

"Ya are? What in God's name are you doing in this godforsaken hellhole then? It's colder than a well-digger's butt most of the time." It was then I learned...well, after a whole lot more cursing on his part that his name was Mr. Henry Potter. I tried not to laugh as I pictured Henry in a wizard costume. Unfortunately, Henry would not see the humor in this joke and no doubt, I would know this by all the colorful ways he'd choose to express this point to me.

I learned that Henry Potter and his wife, Claudette, had moved to Parrish around twenty years earlier. Henry had been trying to get back to Texas ever since. This was Claudette's dream—to live in the mountains. It was not Henry's. In the twenty years he'd lived here, the only friend he'd made with the exception of Claudette, who'd passed away three years ago, was the passel of cats they'd accumulated over the years. Henry just wanted to go home to Texas. As I listened to his pathetic run down of how miserable this place really was, my future flashed before my eyes. This would be me in twenty years if I continued on the path I was going.

I invited Mr. Henry Potter home for dinner right then and there.

Although Henry grudgingly accepted my dinner invitation, he told me he needed to eat at precisely four o'clock. He had to be home in time to watch Wheel of Fortune at six. I didn't really mind. What did I care if I'd barely finished lunch by this time? It wasn't as if I was trying to keep my slim figure for anyone in particular. Max didn't care how fat I became just as long as I kept his kibble coming, which I did. I was trying to bribe my way back into his affections.

After I'd told Henry goodbye, I rushed off to the grocers to buy dinner. As I stood in the middle of the store, it hit me that I didn't have a clue what Henry liked to eat. What if he was deathly allergic to all those original recipes I was so good at creating? Did I really want to risk taking out my only new friend in town?

In a pinch, I choose baked chicken — well-baked chicken — rice and peas. You couldn't go wrong with anything so bland.

At exactly five minutes before four, Henry's rusty Ford pick-up truck bounced along my gravel drive. Henry emerged, still wearing the suit.

He barely acknowledged my cheerful 'good evening' — bad choice I guess, seeing as it wasn't really evening. The minute Henry stepped into my great room, he asked me for a whiskey straight. I was speechless. I disappeared into the kitchen, leaving a very disgruntled Max eyeing Henry as if he'd like to take his best shot at shredding Henry's suit. How had I'd managed to pick up the town drunk and invite him to dinner?

The only alcohol in the house had been left behind by the previous owner. I debated over it almost long enough for dinner to become ready before deciding, what did it hurt really to give Henry a well-watered down drink?

When I returned with the whiskey, I found Henry seated next to the stove with Max purring happily in his lap. Apparently, Max recognized a cat lover when he saw one.

After dinner and over Henry's second drink, he told me he'd recently acquired four new cats.

"Strays," he acknowledged while stroking Max's fur.

"That's sweet. So what else do you like to do, Henry? I mean, besides picking up strays."

"I told you. I want to go home. Back to Texas. I hate this godforsaken place! And you will too, you'll see. Mark my words. Give it time." Henry eyed me angrily as he spoke. Did he guess the truth? Did it show how much I'd already come to hate Parrish?

"Well, what's keeping you from leaving?" I was becoming a little irritated at Henry and his predications. "Do you have family here?"

"No, and none back in Texas either. The wife and I never had kids. She weren't able to. We spent every penny of our savings to pay for Claudette's medical bills. Nothing left to go home with or for, I guess."

My heart went out to Henry. I couldn't imagine having no one to care about what happened to me. I was probably Henry's only human contact in weeks. I found myself wondering what he'd been eating and recoiled at the possibility of Henry eating cat food. Was he really even capable of taking care of himself, much less all those cats?

"Well, what are you going to do about getting back to Texas?" I asked while trying to cover up my concern.

Henry eyed me as if I'd just insulted him.

"Don't know." He sighed wearily. "Get a job, I guess. I just can't go through another stinking winter here."

I tried to think of something I might do to offer Henry a paycheck and still not insult my only new friend in Parrish.

Before Henry left, I promised him I'd stop by to meet his cats the next day and to help him figure out a plan for getting back to Texas. Henry eyed me once again. This time I was almost certain I saw a glimmer of hope in those weathered old eyes—or maybe it was just too many watered-down whiskeys.

After Henry had left and I'd polished off half a carton of ice cream, it was time to tell Aunt Trudy the truth. Telling my straight-laced aunt that not only was I broken up with the man I'd been sleeping with for months, but I was now pregnant without any chance of getting married and I'd put a couple of states between us to boot. This was going to be harder than even I'd imagined.

In the end, I chose the easy way out. I typed an email to Fred asking him to please call. I'd deliberately waited until I was certain Trudy would be in bed because I just couldn't bear to hear the disappointment I would find in her voice.

Five minutes later Fred was on the phone. "Where am I calling? I don't recognize this number?"

I couldn't get anything to come out of my mouth for so long that Fred was clearly beginning to get worried.

"What is it? What's wrong, honey?"

At the gentle caring in his voice, my silent tongue broke free and the words came tumbling out. "I broke up with Tyler. I've moved to Colorado and I'm pregnant." Just like that, in one single breath, I told him everything. It was his turn to be speechless.

"Fred?" I expected well, I wasn't sure what I'd been expecting, but Fred's reaction certainly surprised me.

"Okay, let's take this one thing at a time, Carrie. You and Tyler are having problems?"

"No," I told him matter-of-factly. "No, we're not having problems anymore. The problems are all over. We're over."

"Oh, Carrie. When?" It was his understanding without judging that was my undoing. I started to cry again.

"Over a month ago."

"Oh, pumpkin, I'm so sorry. Why didn't you tell us? Why didn't you come home to be with your family?"

"I couldn't," I wailed into his ear. The poor man was probably listening with the phone in the next room with as much noise as I was making.

"Is there any chance you two can work things out?"

"No. None at all. I broke things off with him."

"Well, I can't say I'm not shocked, because frankly, I am. Trudy said you two seemed good for each other."

Good for each other? Ha! What tragedy had she been watching? We were like an addiction for each other—a bad habit you know is going to either hurt you or kill you in the end, but you just can't seem to give it up. We were terrible for each other.

"The baby... Does he know about the baby?"

That was the one question I didn't want to answer—the reason why it had been so hard to make this call in the first place.

156

"No!" I'm sure this came out sounding every bit as defensive as I felt.

"He should know. It's his responsibility as well as yours."

"No! No, he doesn't want responsibilities or attachments, or any of those things with me, Fred. Tyler only wants fun. Babies aren't fun. I'm not fun. *We're* not fun. And anyway, I haven't made up my mind about the baby yet. You know…" I couldn't actually tell him I was considering *abortion*.

Fred simply listened without interrupting until I'd finished. "Well, I know you'll make the right decision about the baby. Now, tell me about the move." That was all he said. No judging, no telling me I was acting like a child, just on to the next item on my long list of transgressions.

"I moved here! I sold my business and Max and I have moved to Colorado!"

"Well, sometimes a fresh start in a new place can be the best thing in the world for you but there's nothing saying you have to stay there forever. You can always come home. Come stay with us if you want to."

I wondered if Fred had noticed the homesickness in my voice. "I know, but I'll be fine. I'm actually thinking of buying a diner here. You know, starting a new business."

"A diner? That's a wonderful idea. Keep yourself busy, I always say. So what are we going to do about our Trudy situation?"

"Well, I was hoping you could tell her for me. I know that's asking a lot, but I don't really know how to break it to her." Of course, this wasn't fair to him. I'd gotten myself into this mess without Fred's help.

"You know I will. You should know she's going to be calling you the second she finds out. Are you ready for that?"

"No, but then I don't really have a choice, do I? If I decide to have the baby, I can't just show up on her doorstep with it, can I?"

"Probably wouldn't be a good way of getting the news out. I'll talk to her in a couple of days, once I figure out the

157

best approach. Got to see how her mood is before I spring this on her."

That night I went to bed feeling a little bit more at peace with the world. I might have taken the easy way out, but I'd told someone about my problems. I was doing something. I wasn't stuck in neutral any longer. I was almost moving forward.

Chapter Eleven

Choosing to Live, Just in Case

The next morning I became more determined than ever not to turn into another Henry. I'd just gotten off to a bad start with Parrish. After all, I'd only been here a couple of weeks. I was still adjusting. I decided to forget about my somewhat shaky beginnings and give the town another chance.

New day, new outlook on life. As I headed in the direction Henry had told me he lived, I suddenly found myself drawn once more to the small diner on Main Street. Something about the place appealed to my sense of adventure.

I walked inside and ordered the usual. As I counted out the correct change for my apple turnover and coffee, I found myself telling Margaret, the co-owner, I was thinking about buying the place.

Where did that come from?

"Well now, honey, I'm thrilled you want to buy our diner." She eyed my drab gray sweat suit. She probably figured I'd be lucky enough to pay for the turnover much less buy a diner. "But do you know how much work is involved in running a place like this?" What she really wanted to know was did I really think I could handle it.

"I do. You see, I ran my own catering business back in Texas. It was very successful."

Margaret eyed me once more as if I might be delusional. "I tell you what. My husband and I are almost finished with the breakfast crowd for the morning. If you want to stick around for say another half hour or so, we could talk about it."

Two hours later, I knew all the details behind the Jacobs' wish to sell their pride and joy. Ernie and Margaret were longtime residents of Parrish. They loved the town, but with Margaret's rheumatoid arthritis getting worse with each passing year, they'd decided it was time to move to warmer territory. They wanted to retire to Florida to be closer to Margaret's sister Ethel, but they'd been trying to sell the diner for almost three years now.

As thrilled as they both were by the possible sale, I think they were also a little worried that I'd run the place they'd started years earlier into bankruptcy. Margaret suggested I might want to spend a couple of weeks with them, learning the routine before actually making up my mind. She told me she and Ernie preferred opening the place, because it was hard to find anyone who wanted to get up so early — apparently, four a.m. was a major deterrent for most prospective employees. There were a few people who worked from lunch until the dinner crowd showed up, which was manned by four high school students and Ernie, who supervised, as well as did most of the cooking.

"So, you'd have to find someone to help you out in the mornings and, of course, at night. I don't think Scottie would want to switch to evenings." Scottie Macintyre was the former Marine sergeant who had worked for the Jacobs since the place opened. Scottie, along with two sisters, handled the mid-day crowd.

"Scottie takes care of his mother at night and the Lister sisters would quit before they'd switch schedules, so you'd definitely have to find someone else to help out with the night shift. You can't leave the kids alone."

"Right. Why exactly is this again?"

"They're teenagers, honey," Margaret glanced at Ernie as if to say, *we're trusting her with our precious baby?* "They don't care if the place is opened or closed as long as they get their paychecks." Margaret shook her head. Clearly, she was regretting telling me the place was still for sale.

"What Margaret means is, they're good kids but they're still kids, and they need supervising." Ernie reached for his wife's hand and tried to reassure her. "You could put an ad in the local paper, maybe in some of the surrounding communities as well. Oh, and there's the employment agency a couple of blocks over. I'd try to see if you could find someone a bit older though. If you do decide to buy the place, that is."

I left the Jacobs with a promise that I would consider everything they had told me very carefully before making my decision. On my way home, I stopped by Henry's little house on Lake Parrish.

The tiny two-bedroom cabin held Claudette's influence everywhere—from the handmade afghan wrapped around Henry's bony knees, to crocheted doilies on every possible table around, to the odd assortment of silk flower arrangements. It was just as obvious that Henry missed his wife terribly.

It occurred to me then that if I went through with buying the diner, I could offer Henry a job helping out around the place. Not that I was sure Henry was qualified to work at a diner, but surely I could find something for him to do to earn his paycheck back to Texas.

"Henry, do you know how to cook?"

I realized I'd woke Henry with my question. "You want me to fix you something to eat?" He glared at me. I was finally coming to accept the glare as Henry's normal expression.

"No, that's okay. I'm not hungry. I was just wondering if you'd like to work for me at the diner someday."

"Why, you got yourself a job?"

"No. No, I'm thinking of buying the diner downtown— Jacobs Diner. But I'll need to hire some additional help in the mornings as well as in the evenings. It might be fun for us both if you helped out?" Fun was not really the word I would have chosen to describe anything Henry-related.

"Got yourself a real honey there." Henry clearly didn't

mean this in a nice way. "That place is a dump!"

I let Henry's grumpiness go for the moment, because there was something about Henry that reminded me of Aunt Mable—in a slightly nasty and definitely angrier way. Then, of course, there was the fact that grumpiness was the one thing, beyond a fondness for cats, we both had in common.

"It's not a dump. In fact, the place is doing great business."

"Then why have they been trying to sell it for ten years!"

"They haven't been trying to sell it for ten years. It's only been on the market for three. The Jacobs want to move closer to Margaret's sister." I told Henry as patiently as possible, while trying to remember that he was an old man and a fellow Texan. "So what do you think? You could start earning some real money toward Texas?"

I knew I had him the second I mentioned Texas. "When do I start?" Henry sat up a little straighter in his chair.

"Oh, probably not for a few more weeks. So, can you cook?" I yelled this to him from Henry's tiny kitchen while on the pretext of getting water. I was actually trying to be inconspicuous about checking his refrigerator and pantry for food. Along the way, I counted twelve cats. Henry believed there were only ten.

When our conversation reached a lull, it was time to go. I told Henry I would stop by later in the afternoon. Secretly I'd made a grocery list of things he needed, like toilet paper, milk and of course, cat food. Henry woke up long enough to demand that I take him back to Texas when I got sick and tired of living in this blasted hellhole.

I promised him I would.

* * * *

That night, with pen and paper in hand, I started making a list of possible names for my new diner. You know, just in case I actually went through with this crazy idea.

Carrie's Creative Diner

Carrie's Creative Disaster

Carrie's Crazy Idea

Somehow, I couldn't see leaving the place as Jacobs Diner, even though it was what the locals had called it for years and probably would for a long time after I bought the place. In my mind, it would always feel like I was only borrowing it for a little while. In the end, I kept it simple and unpretentious.

Carrie's Creative Café

Nice and simple. Nothing fancy, just like me.

The following morning, bolstered by my possible new career move as well as my burgeoning friendship with Henry, I was feeling confident enough to look for a new doctor. You know, just in case I actually kept the baby.

So far, my life consisted of 'just in case' decisions. Nothing permanent—just in case I ended up making another huge mistake. 'Just in case' was less overwhelming and easier to deal with for me right now.

In Parrish, the small medical center was located adjacent to the hospital. This was where all the doctors had their offices.

As I wandered into the center, trying to appear as nonchalant about the whole thing as possible, a curious older woman at the scheduling desk told me that one of the doctors could see me in about half an hour if I cared to wait. I didn't. I told her I would return in half an hour. Instead, I strolled down the hallway connecting the small hospital to the medical center.

Now, in the past, I'd always been a little scattered. Lately, since my life had been pretty much in shreds, this had seemed to increase by about a hundred times over. I was constantly forgetting things or losing track of time—just generally being absent-minded. This was why I didn't want to get too far away from the doctor's office. You know, just in case, I forgot the appointment I was trying so hard to keep secret.

I was engrossed in reading the bulletin board flyers when

I glanced at my watch. I'd done it again. I turned in a panic and almost ran over some poor man walking down the hallway.

Somehow he managed to keep from losing the stack of files he was carrying in his arms, while keeping me from flying down the corridor like a bowling ball. How, I'm not sure.

He placed the files on a nearby chair and looked at me. "Are you okay? I'm sorry. I didn't see that coming."

What in the world is he talking about? What didn't he see coming? Then it dawned on me. He's talking about me!

"Oh — sorry. I didn't mean to plow into you like that." I glanced at my watch again. I was getting dangerously close to being late. "I'm sorry. I have to go. I'm late."

"For what?"

Now, if there wasn't a Tyler in my past, it would have hit me hard that this man was definitely cute, and he was wearing a lab coat with a nametag attached, which proclaimed that his name was Doctor Kincaid. If this had been before my train wreck with love, I would have noticed right away just how attractive the good Doctor Kincaid truly was, but in my current state of mind, all I saw was another man. I didn't much care for men anymore.

"Huh?"

"What?" He looked at me with a comical expression on his face, like someone trapped in some strange comedy routine. Then Doctor Kincaid shook his head and tried again. "You're late for what?"

"For an appointment down the hall. Shit, I have to go."

Doctor Kincaid caught my arm and stopped me. I turned back to stare at him with the full force of my grouchy self. Henry would have been so proud of me.

"Sorry, I was just wondering if... Well, do you need me to show you where the office is?"

Somehow, through all of these crazy thoughts going round in my head, it dawned on me that he was actually trying to convey something to me. When it finally hit me, it was so unexpected that my jaw dropped.

Clearly I'd been out of the game for a while now. This man was actually smiling at me in a way that reminded me of something...something from my past? What was it? Oh yes, now I remember...flirting!

This nice looking doctor standing in front of me now was actually flirting with me. I'd been so out of touch that I hadn't even noticed those subtle hints he was tossing my way.

No way. Uh-uh. Not going there again for anyone. That was a terrible, terrible place to be — dark and cold and lonely.

"Uh, no, I think I can find it, but thanks anyway." I turned away from the terrible reminder of my past mistakes. In fact, I started walking as fast as I could away from them. If I hadn't been in a public place, I would have run like crazy.

"Okay, but maybe you'd consider having coffee with me once you're finished? I have patients scheduled for another hour but then I'm free for a while."

The good doctor glanced down at me then he began walking alongside me. At this point, I needed to do something and fast if I didn't want him knowing the truth.

"Yes that's a good idea. Sure. Where?" I blurted out the first thing to come to mind, never really intending to go through with it. *Not going down that path again*, I silently chanted.

"There's a coffee shop around the corner. Will you meet me there in an hour?"

"Good. That's good. Fine. Wonderful." I was still walking as fast as I could, with Doctor Kincaid managing to keep pace with me somehow. This was turning into one of my nightmares. "Okay, you really don't have to keep doing this! I'm sure I can find my way."

"Doing what? Oh... No, this is my office actually."

I stopped walking then. Even before I turned to read the name on the door, it dawned on me that Doctor Kincaid here was going to be my new obstetrician.

165

"Shit." Not very ladylike, but I wasn't feeling very ladylike at the moment.

"What? Oh no, you're not…?"

"Yes. Apparently, I'm you're next patient."

He picked up the clipboard. "Carrie Sinclair?"

"That's me. Well, it looks as if we're going to get even better acquainted than I thought."

"Looks like it… Sorry, I didn't realize. Look, I do have a partner, if you'd feel more comfortable seeing someone else. I could have Zack do the exam. It might be better this way."

Doctor Kincaid was looking at me with a lost little expression on his face I vaguely remembered from my past. Should I tell him I wasn't interested?

Before the words were out of my mouth, I remembered my vow to move on. Forget about Tyler. Make some new friends. I kept my mouth shut.

"Maybe it would be best."

"My name is Jake, by the way."

Oh geez. Now he was telling me his name. I didn't want to know his name. I certainly didn't want to have coffee with him.

"Carrie. But then, you already know my name, don't you?"

Jake Kincaid laughed as if I'd said something amazingly funny, not poignantly stupid.

"Why don't you follow me? I'll show you to the exam room then get Zack for you."

"Thank you, Doct—"

"Jake. Technically, I'm not your doctor anymore."

"Okay, you got me there." Another stupid remark, another laugh. Surely Tyler had never found me this funny. I don't remember him laughing at any of my jokes quite the way Jake Kincaid was. But then, maybe it was just the final farewell scene. It was stuck in my mind, erasing all of the other happier times we'd spent together.

"Don't forget…coffee, or whatever you want, at the coffee

shop around the corner in one hour. Don't stand me up, Carrie Sinclair." He pointed in the direction of the coffee shop as if he was talking to an idiot. From where he stood, it probably appeared that way.

By the time I left Doctor Zack, I wasn't much in the mood for coffee or anything else. I simply wanted to run back home to my big empty house and be with my cat, who still hadn't forgiven me for moving him to this cold, unfriendly place.

With a handful of brochures, laying out all of my future baby options—abortion, adoption, having a child after thirty-five—I was almost out of the door and home free when Doctor Kincaid caught up with me.

"You're going the wrong direction. It's this way." The sound of the good doctor's voice stopped me dead in my tracks. I wished I'd been just a little faster with my escape. "That is where you were heading, right?"

I smiled in spite of my crankiness and followed Jake outside into the perfect summer morning. *New day, new outlook on life, remember?*

I didn't have coffee, although it took everything inside me to resist the rich smell of it. Instead, I opted for juice and a donut.

Jake and I found a couple of empty seats at a table by the window and sat with the awkward, first-time-alone-together silence hanging between us.

"So tell me, how long have you been in town now, Carrie? It can't have been very long, because I just happen to know every pretty woman around these parts, and I haven't seen you before."

Pre-Tyler, this would have swept me off my feet. Now, my only response was to give him one of my not-so-nice looks. I wasn't flattered.

"I just moved here three weeks ago. I bought the old Swenson place outside of town. I've been getting settled in."

"Wow, that's a big place for just you? Or is it just you?"

Now, how to answer this without revealing to the good doctor more than I wanted him to know right now? Doctor Kincaid was on a fishing expedition. He was looking to find out if there was any competition out there somewhere waiting to kick his butt.

"No, there's just me and Max."

"I'm sorry. I didn't realize you were—"

"Max is my cat."

"Your cat?"

Although I might be a long way from romance at this point in my life, even with someone as charming as the good doctor here, I was tired of trying to carry on a conversation with only Max and Henry. I could use a friend closer to my age, not to mention my own species.

"Yes. Max is my main man. We've been together for years now."

"I see. And how did you and Max end up here alone?"

"Bad judgment. Stupidity. All of the above. Take your pick."

"In other words, you don't want to talk about it?"

"I don't want to *think* about it. But unfortunately, since I'm pregnant, I can't really ignore it, can I?"

"You're pregnant? I see." The ever so slight pause here told me he hadn't expected this bit of news. "And the baby's father? No chance of fixing the relationship?"

If I lied right now and told him maybe, then no doubt this would be it as far as Jake Kincaid was concerned but then it hit me. This man knew I was pregnant and now understood the extent of my failed relationship with Tyler. Maybe I'd better play it smart and not be in such a hurry to get rid of him. I might not be in the market for another serious relationship, but so far, I was finding Colorado pretty cold and lonely.

"None whatsoever," I told him honestly. "I broke up with him, you see. We weren't right for each other. So no, there's absolutely no chance of fixing it."

"I see."

I smiled. Was this Doctor Kincaid's best bedside manner talking? It was certainly working on me. I actually found myself opening up to him a little.

"So does he even know about the baby?"

"No, and don't give me that look. I will tell him when I'm ready and not before. Anyway, I still haven't made up my mind about the baby just yet."

The good doctor's opinion of this statement was easy to see.

"You don't agree?" I countered with the force of all the anger and resentment I'd bottled up inside over my failed relationship with Tyler.

"Doesn't matter. It's not my decision to make. I'm certainly not in a position to judge you. I've made enough mistakes in my own life, and I have one ex-wife to prove it. Just ask her if you have any doubts. She'll tell you how imperfect I am."

I didn't believe a word of it. If Jake's marriage had ended in divorce, it wasn't because of him. He had stick-with-it-to-the-bitter-end type written all over him. "How long have you been divorced?" I was happy to have the subject off me and my failures.

"Five years. The usual story. She got tired of the long hours of a doctor, not to mention always being alone. I guess I couldn't really blame her. She found someone else and I threw myself into my work. That's when I came back home to Parrish and set up shop with my friend Zack. It's worked out pretty well so far."

"So you're from Parrish? Well then, maybe you can answer a question for me?"

Jake looked as if he was trying to figure out what was coming next.

"Are people from Colorado always so standoffish? I mean, I've been here a little over three weeks now and the only people I've gotten to know are my Realtor, the couple at the diner and Henry Potter, the old man who hangs out on the park bench."

This sent him laughing so hard that he almost lost his coffee. "We're not so bad, surely?"

"Oh yeah? Trust me. You're bad."

"Well, maybe it's because you're from Texas. You people have a reputation of being overly abrasive at times."

"How did you know I'm from Texas?"

"Your accent, of course. It's very distinctive."

Accent? What the heck was he talking about? "I don't have an accent. I don't know what you mean."

"Oh please! If you talked any slower, I'd be aging right now before your eyes."

It was my turn to look uncertain. Was he serious or just teasing me? I couldn't tell until he laughed.

"I'm joking, Carrie. I think your accent is lovely, but definitely pronounced — and definitely Texan."

Against my will, I thought about another time when Tyler had said pretty much the same thing. He'd asked me where I was from, pointing out that no native Austinite possessed such a drawl, even though Early wasn't that far from Austin. Something of the memory must have shown in my eyes because Jake grew serious.

"Are you okay? Did I say something…wrong?"

It was so hard letting go of that memory. I remembered everything about the conversation, because it had taken place after we'd spent our first night together. We'd still been awkward with each other. I shook my head and tried as hard as I could to block Tyler out of my head. He might be in my heart to stay, but I wouldn't spend every single second of the day remembering all the things we'd shared. I was moving on, remember?

I shook my head. "I'm fine. I'm sorry, just a ghost from the past."

Jake and I spent quite some time talking. We probably would have been there even longer had his not assistant paged him with a nine-one-one. Apparently, his next appointment was waiting for him back at the office, and he was running late for it already.

"Come on. A few more minutes won't matter. Let me walk you to your car."

After our first awkward beginning, I'd actually found myself enjoying the time I'd spent with him until we reached my car.

"Carrie, look. I don't believe in playing games, and I'm certainly not good at reading signals from a woman, so I'm just going to be straight with you. I like you—a lot. I've enjoyed spending time with you today. But I know you've just ended a serious relationship and I know how hard it can be to move beyond that point. What I'm trying to say is, I don't want to get my hopes up if there's no chance. But I don't want to walk away from a good thing either. You're going to have to tell me what you want."

I was literally shaking all over. I was going to cry and I couldn't bite my cheek or clench my hands hard enough to stop the tears. I tried to turn away, to open my car door and simply leave him standing there, but he stopped me.

"Hey, it's okay," he told me gently before taking me in his arms. "It's okay. I didn't mean to rush you."

Everything about Jake Kincaid was foreign to me. So unlike the familiar arms of the man I loved, yet so much like Tyler that I started to cry even harder before I pushed him away.

"I have to go. And you have an appointment to keep."

I didn't say anything else but I'm sure my lack of words said enough. I hated this. I hated not being able to get over Tyler. Hated that every single memory I possessed seemed to have fused itself with him. He was branded on my heart. I hadn't been able to move beyond Tyler no matter how much I tried to convince myself that I no longer cared about him.

But I couldn't stand to think about being alone for the rest of my life, or becoming like Henry. I didn't know what to do anymore. I was more lost and confused than ever before.

The only thing I was certain about was that I'd probably succeeded in scaring Doctor Jake Kincaid away forever.

Chapter Twelve

Going Home for Your Birthday

After the embarrassing way I'd left things between Jake and me, I began seriously contemplating looking for another doctor in one of the neighboring towns. I was sitting with the phone book open in my lap, searching through the Yellow Pages when Aunt Trudy called.

"Honey, why didn't you tell me?"

It was a long time before I could control my emotions enough to answer her. "I wanted to. It's just...I was embarrassed and upset, and I'm sorry I let you down."

"Let you down? Carrie Leanne Sinclair! I couldn't be more proud of you. You have never once let me down, so don't you let me hear you say such a thing again. You've accomplished so much with your life." As a child growing up with my two aunts, I had known whenever either of them used my full name it meant I was in big trouble. Now it had never sounded so sweet.

"Oh yeah, I'm pregnant, single and I don't have a job. There's a lot to be proud of."

"Stop it right this minute! You have so much life in you, child. You literally shine, and you have more spunk than anyone I've ever met, except for Mable. You've traveled all over the world by yourself, learned how to prepare all those exotic dishes and started your own business. You have absolutely *nothing* to be ashamed of."

I was virtually grinning from ear to ear at those words. I'd been dreading her call for days because I was so sure she would be ashamed of me. Trudy was a wonderful woman.

"I'm still not sure I'm going to have the baby."

"I know… Fred told me, but Carrie, the right answer will come to you. You just take your time. Pray about it. You always come to the right decision when you pray, even if it doesn't seem like it at first."

"But if I have the baby, I'll be a single mom. What will you tell all your friends?"

"Why the truth, that's what! I'll tell them my beautiful, intelligent niece is having a baby. Let them top that. Now, honey, how are you feeling? Have you got yourself a good doctor up there?"

I couldn't tell her about my little fiasco with Jake, or the fact that I'd been searching for another doctor when she'd called, so I simply crossed my fingers and lied. I was getting so good at lying to the people I loved.

"I sure do wish you could come home for your birthday next week. I miss you so much."

The thought of my upcoming thirty-sixth birthday only made me sad. The last one I'd spent with Tyler. We'd been together for only a short time then. It was hard not to compare where I'd been just one year earlier with where I was right now. My life was so different from the woman I'd been a year ago.

"I wish I could as well, but I'm not sure if it will be possible. I'll have to get back with you." This would be my first birthday without Aunt Mable. The thought of celebrating it alone with Max and Henry was hard to contemplate.

* * * *

After seeing the terrible state of affairs in Henry's kitchen, I took it upon myself to prepare some simple meals that he could reheat in the microwave without burning the place down. Today I placed a plate of my original recipe for meatloaf in front of him and took my usual seat across from him.

"Why don't you ever eat anything?" Henry barked at me

when he noticed I was still fighting to keep from being sick at the sight of food.

"I'm not hungry, and I do eat."

"Are you having a baby or something?"

I almost fell out of my chair at Henry's astute observation. How he'd guessed this truth, I wasn't so sure.

"Yes. Maybe... I haven't decided yet. I am pregnant, but I'm not sure I'm having it yet."

"I figured as much. Where's the daddy?"

"He's not part of the picture anymore. Eat your meatloaf while it's still hot."

"He even know about it?" Henry pointed to my belly with his fork.

"No, and he's not going to for a while." I gave him a look to rival one of his own glares while daring him to object. "At least, not until I decide what I'm doing about it."

Henry simply nodded and resumed eating his meatloaf.

I left him soon after with instructions for how long to heat up dinner and promised to stop by again tomorrow. What an unusual pair we must make—me, a thirty-five-year-old pregnant woman with a knack for making all the wrong decisions, and Henry, a seventy-eight-year-old widower with a penchant for whiskey and cats.

That night I got the phone book once more and tried to make a serious commitment. I didn't quite understand why I could uproot my life, seriously consider buying a new business and dump my boyfriend, but I couldn't bring myself to face Jake Kincaid again.

I was still staring at the Yellow Pages when Doctor Jake Kincaid paid me a house call.

"Jake...what are you doing here?" I was so shocked at seeing him again—much less standing on my front porch—that I'm sure this didn't come out sounding very nice. I was still remembering my earlier breakdown in front of him.

"I made you cry. I never intended to hurt you. I came to apologize."

I was just ready to deny everything he'd said when Max

jumped out from behind the door and made a break for it between Jake's legs.

"No, Max! Jake, don't let him get away! I don't want him to end up bear food."

Jake caught Max just before he cleared the door, much to my pudgy kitty's distaste. Max's anger was evident by the nasty little hiss he threw Jake's way when he handed my cat back to me.

"Fussy little devil, isn't he?"

I could have argued the point by telling Jake how I'd uprooted Max from everything and everyone he knew and loved, but suddenly I was feeling a little awkward. I wasn't sure what to say to the man standing before me now, looking so apologetic. This was a first for me.

"Why don't you come inside?"

He followed me into the great room where my trusty stove burned at its usual full capacity. I'd become quite skilled at gathering wood since moving to Parrish.

"It's freezing in here. Is something wrong with your furnace?"

"I know its freezing, but I can't seem to get the furnace guy to come fix the darn thing, even though he certainly didn't have a problem taking my money."

Jake had no idea what I was talking about. "Who?"

"The furnace repairman. You know, the only one in town! I can't remember his name."

"Oh him! Well, he's probably got you pegged as a part-timer since you're new and he's taking his time, getting the locals out of the way first. If you'd like, I could talk with him. I have some pull. You shouldn't be staying in this cold."

"Sit down, Jake...and thank you," I was trying to amend some of my grouchy ways. My disposition was starting to match Max's and Henry's more every day. "I would appreciate it if you could do me that favor."

Once again, there was the awkward silence of two people who didn't know each other well enough to know what to say next.

"Carrie, I'm sorry I upset you. I wasn't considering your feelings. I can only imagine how I must have come across to you. But you see, it's rare these days for me to meet a woman I find interesting, much less attractive. I guess I got a little carried away. I should have realized it was too soon for you. I hope we can still be friends. What do you say?"

Faced with the road I'd stood before once more, I didn't have the strength to take a single step down that path again. I couldn't, not even for this man. There wasn't enough left inside me to survive another bad relationship.

"I'd say, how do you feel about cats?"

"Cats? You mean Max here? Well, I love cats, but why do you ask?"

"How do you feel about *babysitting* cats?" Hearing Aunt Trudy's voice earlier had made me so homesick. I needed to find some way to make it home for my birthday.

"You want me to babysit Max?"

I smiled and watched Jake's uncertainty melt away.

"Yes. You see, my birthday is next week and I want to go home to see my aunt, but I'm not up to driving. Can you take Max over to your place and watch him for a few days? You can say no if you want. It's okay. I know I'm asking a lot, seeing as we've just met, but I really would appreciate it."

Right on cue and almost as if I'd coached him, Max went to work on Jake. He rubbed against his legs and meowed up at him in a way that no human being could resist. Jake picked him up and held him in his lap rubbing Max's belly. It was love at first stroke.

"Is he always this easy?"

"No. But you're rubbing his soft spot, so you've got a friend for life."

"What about his owner? Does *she* have a soft spot?"

I had at one time, but not anymore. Mine was back in Texas, probably forgetting I ever existed.

"Sorry, forget I said that. I'd love to babysit Max for you.

I'll even throw in a ride to the airport in Denver."

After Jake left, I closed the Yellow Pages and forgot about finding another doctor.

"Max, you like Jake, don't you?"

My best friend's only answer was a tired little meow and a flick of his tail. This was all the approval I needed.

The next morning, I stopped by to see the Jacobs to tell them I would give them my decision on the diner when I returned to Parrish. Then, I went to see Henry and told him I was going to be out of town for a few days. I didn't have the heart to tell my friend I was going home to Texas, because he would insist that I take him with me. As much as I loved him, I couldn't even begin to imagine that trip.

"Where you going? You taking care of the baby thing?" Henry watched my stomach as if expecting it to explode. As strange as Henry was at times, he was also good at offering me the perfect alibi.

"Something like that, yes. I'll make sure you have plenty of meals in the freezer before I go, though, and I was thinking I'd have my friend Jake stop by to check on you every once in a while."

Henry's displeasure was apparent. "Is he a Texan?"

I shook my head.

"Then you can just tell him to stay home."

* * * *

I was so excited to be going home that I called Steph the night before I left and told her. She was thrilled as well and wanted me to stop by and see her before I went back to Colorado. I really wanted to, but the prospect of being that close to Tyler was hard to consider. I told her I'd think about it.

The following morning, I said goodbye to Max and my new friend Jake on one of those gorgeous Colorado days you hear so much about on the Travel Channel.

As hard as it was for me to accept in the beginning,

especially with Jake being a man and me having sworn off men for the time being, Jake was turning out to be something of a saint.

On several different occasions, he'd stopped by just to check in on me. When I'd told Jake I was thinking about buying the diner, he was thrilled. Of course, I think he was just happy to see me making plans to stick around Parrish for a while.

While I was definitely blown away by Jake's kindness, I didn't feel any of the fireworks I'd felt for Tyler after our first meeting. Maybe you only get one of those displays in your life? Everything after that was just a small whimper. Was a whimper so bad though? You might not have the fireworks, but maybe there wouldn't be any of the pain either.

As I boarded the plane bound for Texas, I wasn't thinking about past loves or future heartaches. My thoughts were all on Aunt Trudy and Fred—and home.

I hadn't told them I was coming yet. I was just planning to show up the day before my birthday to surprise them. I was so excited and so homesick that I couldn't wait to be there.

As I drove along the familiar two-lane blacktop outside of Early, old memories of all the other times I'd been down this same road came flooding back, chocking me with emotion.

How many times in the past I had returned here through all the different stages of my life? The time I'd come home after Aunt Mable's death hurt to remember, but that last trip still stood out dark and painful in my heart. It was the time I'd come alone without Tyler, after our breakup.

I parked the car along the side of the road and tried to stop my tears. I couldn't show my aunt how unhappy I truly was. I wanted her to believe that my life was back on track in spite of the pregnancy. I wanted this to be a happy visit for all of us.

Trudy and Fred must have realized it was me coming down the gravel road long before my car came to a stop in front of the house. They were out the door and hugging me in an instant.

This was home. This was what I'd been missing for so long. This was what no dream house could ever replace in my heart—the love and acceptance you got from people who loved you unconditionally.

"Carrie, as I live and breathe! I'd just about given up on seeing you this year. Even though I told Fred, we were going to bake a cake for you, just in case. I'm so happy you came! Come inside, honey. You look tired."

I let her pull me along, while Fred retrieved my bag from the trunk.

"Where's the cat?" How did he even remember Max? They'd never actually met. But then in all the times I'd talked to him lately, Max and Henry had been the main topics of my conversation.

"I left him with Jake."

"That nice doctor friend of yours?" Aunt Trudy, bless her heart, I could almost see her mind working. She'd want to know just how *involved* I was with the good doctor.

"Yes. He's a nice man, but just a friend, so don't go getting any ideas."

"I'm not saying a word." This was so totally unlike Trudy that I found myself studying her closely. She'd changed a lot since marrying Fred. She was softer now.

The second I walked into the house, memories of my aunt overwhelmed me. How many times had I run through the door, screen door banging behind me, only to hear Aunt Mable tell me not to slam it. I'd been excited from my day at school and so anxious to tell her all about it. I smiled even though tears were close. Trudy guessed as much.

"I miss her too, honey." She patted my arm. "More than you can know. There are times when I can almost picture her sitting right there in the chair she used to rock in, humming one of those old church songs she loved so much."

I nodded, smiling at the memory. That was the perfect description of Aunt Mable. She'd never once taken a piano lesson, but she could play it by ear. And sing! She'd loved to sing.

"Sit down, Carrie. Tell us all about your new life. How's the weather up in Colorado?"

I could see right through her motives. She was trying to distract me from those painful memories.

"Fred, take Carrie's things up to her room for her."

I wasn't able to tell my aunt I couldn't even think about spending the night in my old room. Too many memories of Tyler were there.

"It's cold. But you know how much I've always loved the snow. Now I get to see it for several months during the year. It's...fun."

"Uh huh, I remember how you used to freeze to death whenever the temperature dropped below seventy-five, as well. You're not fooling me one little bit, honey. I know the real reason you're up there. Have you talked to him?"

I didn't need to ask who she was talking about. I shook my head. Like it or not, Tyler was right here with me once again.

"You still love him, don't you?"

I couldn't meet her eyes because there would be sympathy there. I was still trying to be strong. I didn't want to lose it in front of her.

"No, I don't. That's over. I told you. I don't want to talk about Tyler anymore. He's in the past."

Her reaction was easy to read. She didn't believe me, but she let the subject drop.

"Have you been doing much cooking since you sold your business?"

I was grateful she'd chosen to move beyond Tyler for the moment. "Oh, did I tell you I'm thinking of buying a diner?" I gave her the run down on the diner and Henry, but I couldn't tell her how I spend a great deal of my time feeling sorry for myself. I'd drifted through my days, refusing to think about the past, while my sadness had grown with each passing day. I hadn't dealt with my feelings for Tyler after the breakup. I'd simply run away.

I hadn't had any idea if he was seeing anyone new yet or not. I'd fished around for answers from Steph, who still talked to Tyler. She'd finally told me straight out that Tyler wasn't seeing anyone. Steph had been very quick to point out that I'd left Tyler a wreck, and if I wanted to know any more than that I should just pick up the phone and call him myself.

This of course had sent me into a deeper depression. I was in trouble. Steph knew it as well. She'd suggested that I needed to talk to someone about my losses.

"So, I've been keeping busy," I lied to my aunt.

"I'm not surprised. I told Fred you'd be going and blowing and probably starting another business up there before we knew it."

For a little while, as we prepared lunch together, I was happy. I was with the people who loved me and would never desert me. I was going to be okay.

Aunt Trudy spent most of the afternoon touching my tummy and talking to the baby.

After lunch, Fred left us to ourselves. Trudy told me he'd converted my aunt's old sitting room into an office.

"Mostly he likes to have his own space. That man loves his computer. He can spend hours piddling around on that thing. You feel up to a short walk? The weather is nice. It must seem different from Colorado."

I'd never missed the Texas humidity more. The warmth of the afternoon would normally have been overpowering. Today it was wonderful. I'd been freezing since I'd arrived in Colorado.

We walked across the pasture once again as we'd done long ago after Aunt Mable's death. Today, there were two ghosts here beside us. My Aunt Mable's memory was there in every inch of this place, but it was the memories of Tyler I couldn't seem to get out of my head.

"Tell me what's new here? What's the latest gossip?" I turned to her, desperate to forget Tyler.

"Oh, Carrie, that was always your aunt's job, but okay...

I'll try. I hear things too, you know. Well, let's see. Oh, you know old Mr. Amos, the one who used to run the hardware store downtown?"

I nodded, completely captivated.

"Well, guess who's been stepping out on his wife?" She gave me her best impression of my aunt and I burst out laughing.

"No! With who? How did she find out? Oh wait, has she found out?"

"Oh, yes, ma'am! And let me tell you, there was hell to pay when it came about. The man was messing around with his wife's best friend. Uh huh," she replied to my shocked expression. "And the old fool had been for years!"

"Oh, Aunt Trudy, I don't believe it! What happened?"

"Well, poor Mrs. Amos, she filed for divorce. She was determined she was going to make him pay big! But the old fool didn't seem to mind. He was in love with that hoosy. Was he ever wrong!"

"What happened?"

"Well, Mrs. Amos… She pretty much cleaned the old fool out in the settlement, but him being the fool he was, agreed to it. He just wanted to be free to be with his new woman. Well, when that hoosy woman found out there wasn't any more money left and all she's getting was a tired old man, she ran just as fast as she could."

I was laughing so hard I was crying. It was good to be happy again, if only for a little while.

"Oh, you haven't heard the best part yet."

I couldn't believe it. "There's more?"

"Oh yes! The old fool went crawling back to Mrs. Amos, and you know what? That woman took him back! I would have kicked his butt so hard he'd be bouncing for days, but she welcomed him home with loving arms. They've been acting like a couple of teenagers ever since."

Aunt Trudy and I spent the rest of the afternoon gossiping while Fred worked on his computer. In the past, I'd always loved those times with Aunt Mable. Trudy was doing her best to fill the void.

After dinner, Jake called with the excuse of telling me about something Max had been up to. He was really making sure I was okay. He was such a good man. What was wrong with me? Why was I so determined to fall in love with the worst possible man for me instead of someone sweet like Jake?

When I tried Henry's number, it took him so long to answer the phone I began to worry that maybe he'd fallen in the kitchen and hurt himself or set the house on fire while heating up his dinner.

"I couldn't find the blasted thing." It was good to hear Henry's voice, crankiness and all. In some weird way, I actually missed him.

I was still smiling when I went back into the living room to join my aunt and Fred. I'd been sitting curled up next to her while Fred sat in his favorite lounge chair brought in especially from his home in Brownwood.

"You two seem close?" Aunt Trudy whispered patting my arm.

"Who? You mean Jake? He's just a friend."

"Honey, when a man calls you when you've gone home to be with your family, he's not thinking about just friendship. Remember this before things get too serious."

By the time the ten o'clock news came on, I'd been dozing for a while. I kissed Trudy and Fred goodnight and went up to my old bedroom for the first time since I'd arrived. I couldn't bear to be in the room, much less sleep in the same bed I'd shared with Tyler.

Instead, I walked out on the balcony and into the warm, sultry Texas night. I stayed outside until I was certain that Trudy and Fred were sleeping. Then, I tiptoed to the spare room like a thief in the night.

Chapter Thirteen

Admitting Your Mistakes to Yourself

You'd think turning thirty-six would have given me some sort of foresight to be up and out of bed before my aunt could come looking for me. But there I was, sleeping like a baby, completely unaware of the world around me until Trudy poked her head in and whispered, "Happy birthday!"

I tried to come up with some plausible excuse as to why I'd spent the night here instead of in my own bed, but she knew the truth.

"Don't give me that. I know exactly why you didn't want to sleep in your old room. But never mind. I'll have Fred move your stuff in here for tonight."

"No! I mean…couldn't it just be our little secret?"

She patted my hand and gave me a peck on the cheek. "Of course it can. Fred's outside feeding his chickens anyway. Can you believe of all the farm animals around, he wanted chickens? Come downstairs when you're ready, honey. Let's have some quiet time, just the two of us. He'll be out there talking to those chickens for ages."

I dressed as fast as I could and followed her downstairs where I indulged myself—it was my birthday after all—in a cup of coffee. Since discovering I was pregnant, giving up my six-plus-cup-of-coffee-a-day habit had been next to impossible.

"He actually talks to the chickens?" I took a sip of the delicious brew and sighed. "Has he named them yet?"

"Every last one of them! The man keeps telling me he's

going to eat them one day, but that's an out and out lie. He can't eat them when he's busy making friends with them. He loves pretending to be a farmer and I love him, so if he wants chickens, he can have chickens. Oh, something came for you this morning."

She went out to the living room and brought back a huge bouquet of white calla lilies. My heart began to race at the sight of them. White calla lilies were my favorite. I still remembered the last time I'd gotten them from Tyler after we'd been apart for a few days.

"They're from that nice friend of yours in Austin—Stephanie. She's such a sweet girl—and so is her husband. I remember how wonderful they were at the funeral. You should call her later."

"Yes, they're beautiful, and I will."

Aunt Trudy turned to me with a wistful expression on her face. "I never asked you yesterday—I was just so excited to see you—but how long are you staying? I hope it's more than just a few days?"

"I wish I could, but unfortunately I have to leave tomorrow. I hadn't planned on it, but I want to stop by and surprise Steph before I return home. But I'm definitely coming home for Thanksgiving. If it's okay with you and Fred, I'd like to drive down so I can bring Max—if he's still speaking to me by then. I don't think he's ever going to forgive me for moving him to Colorado."

"That cat's spoiled. What's he going to do when the baby comes? It's been just the two of you for so long. That's going to be one angry cat." Aunt Trudy had made up her mind about the baby, even if I was still undecided. But she was right about Max. I'd been worried about what poor Max's reaction would be if I brought a crying baby into his world. Would this be the last straw as far as he was concerned?

Trudy went to the pantry and brought out one of her beautifully decorated white cakes. I could smell the sugary frosting from where I was sitting and my eyes lit up.

"Oh thank you, thank you, thank you! I love your

homemade cakes! Can I have a piece now?"

She looked at me as if she thought I might be kidding then she went to the cupboard and took out two plates. "I don't see why not. It's your birthday, after all. If you want to have cake for breakfast, lunch and dinner, it's your choice."

* * * *

After Trudy and Fred had gone to sleep that night, I forced myself to do what I needed to do. Being home again had brought back some painful memories of Tyler. He was everywhere around me and I was in desperate need of exorcising some of those ghosts. I couldn't do it with Trudy constantly fussing over me.

So I took myself down to the first ghost's home to confront him face-to-face — the ghost by the lake, where Tyler and I had made love underneath the stars on a night much like tonight. I forced myself to remember every minute of the time I'd spent here with him as I lay on the very same blanket and cried silent tears.

* * * *

It was so hard saying goodbye to my aunt and Fred. Thanksgiving seemed light years away when contemplating the cold empty house waiting for me back in Colorado.

When I reached the outskirts of Austin, I phoned Steph to let her know I was coming. "I'm in town and I want to see you, but I don't want to talk about Tyler. Do we have a deal?" Of course, Steph would agree just to get me there, but I suspected she wasn't going to stick with the plan.

"It's a deal. Where can I meet you? Do you want to come here?"

I did. "Yes. I'll be there soon." The second she opened the door and I got a good look at her, I saw the truth. She'd spoken to Tyler already.

"You've talked to him? Did you call him? Did you tell him I was here?" I blurted all this out before I even got through the door. Steph didn't answer right away. She simply hugged me and told me she'd missed me terribly. I'd missed her and Ed and the town I still called home, even though it had kicked my butt and sent me packing in that final farewell scene of our love-hate relationship.

"Yes, I've talked to him, and no, of course I didn't tell him you were coming here." Steph stopped when the sound of the phone came between us

"Don't answer it!"

She threw me a look that told me I was behaving like a child.

Steph ignored my demands and picked up the receiver. I watched her expression closely and realized immediately that she was talking to Tyler.

"Yes, she's here." A slight pause then, "I'll ask her, but don't hold your breath." Steph held the phone away and mouthed, *He wants to talk to you!*

I was busily waving both hands in the air and walking away.

"Sorry, Tyler. She's being her usual stubborn self."

I glared at Steph who looked at me as if she were watching a child throw a tantrum.

"No—not a good idea." A small giggle at this point made me wonder what Tyler could possibly be saying that Steph was finding so amusing. "Exactly. I'll call you later, okay? Bye."

"You two sure are becoming awfully chummy lately. What was that all about?" I snapped, only to hear her laugh at my grumpiness.

"I thought you didn't want to talk about Tyler?"

"I don't. But you keep throwing him in my face."

"Okay, my friend—enough."

She took me by my arm and all but forced me into the kitchen. "Wait, Steph. This isn't some trick, is it? Tyler's not going to accidentally drop by, is he?"

"Sit. I'm going to let you indulge just this once in a cup of coffee, but only because you're upset and you're grouchy.

187

I think a nice cup of Starbucks will do you more good than harm right about now. Since you've been gone, I buy the coffee and brew it here. It's hard to go back to the place where we used to hang out," she added when I arched an eyebrow at her response.

I went willingly into the chair she held out for me. One sip of the best coffee around and I was smiling again. I could feel my frustration and anger fading to nothing with every sip I took.

"Better?" Steph spotted my euphoric smile and laughed.

"Much. I can almost forgive you for just telling Tyler I was here!"

Steph wasn't put off by my show of anger. "Why didn't you tell him yourself? And why haven't you told him about the baby?"

"I told you I would when I'm good and ready. Whose side are you on here anyway? You're supposed to be *my* friend."

"Well lately, since I *am* your friend, I can't seem to get rid of the guy. He's mad about you and all he wants to do is talk about you. I'm telling you, Carrie. He's driving me crazy — not to mention Ed. But I can't help but feel sorry for him, the poor, lovesick fool. It's kind of sweet."

"Sweet? That's not what you were saying in the beginning. You were the one who warned me not to go out with him, remember?"

"Yes, but that was before. He's changed. He's crazy about you." Steph dismissed my only real argument with a polite wave of her hand.

"Well, he's a little late. Don't you think?"

"No, he's not. You just want your pound of flesh."

Was that true? Was this the real reason why I'd been in such a hurry to end things with Tyler? I had wanted to hurt him the way I imagined he would hurt me? I didn't want to think about this right now because, frankly, it scared the daylights out of me. I was still trying to convince myself that I was sick to death of talking about Tyler.

"Can we please stop talking about him?" I implored, not really fooling my friend at all.

"Oh, by all means. It's only your future happiness we're talking about here! The only man you're ever going to love, and I hate to be the one to point this out, but the father of your child! Do you even plan on telling him he's going to be a father?"

"I haven't decided if I'm having the baby yet, remember? He may not be a father! I'm not telling Tyler anything until I decide what I'm doing. And you promised you wouldn't tell him either! You didn't, did you?"

"No, I didn't. But just for the record, I think what you're doing is wrong. Tyler needs to know. It's his right to know. Don't you think he would want to be a part of the decision?"

With that little incriminatory remark, she let the subject drop, but it hung between us for the rest of my visit.

Steph and I went shopping later in the day and we hit all of our usual haunts. It almost felt like old times.

By the time we'd finished, I was exhausted. This was as much work as I'd done in a long time. Steph made a bed up for me in the guest room where I lay down for a short nap before we went out to dinner.

When she knocked on my door, I'd just drifted off to sleep.

"Carrie, it's your aunt. Do you want to talk to her?"

I looked at the clock thinking I'd just fallen asleep only to realize I'd been out for almost an hour.

"Yes, it's okay. Thanks, I'll take it." She handed me the phone and left me alone.

"Aunt Trudy? Is everything okay there?"

"Yes, honey, we're fine. I just wanted to tell you Tyler called. He was asking about you. He knows you're in town."

"I know. It's okay. Steph told him."

"Now, don't you worry. He doesn't know anything about Colorado and we certainly won't tell him. But I was hoping maybe the two of you would have time to talk things over at least?"

I bit my tongue to keep my opinion of her remark to

myself. "Aunt Trudy, it's not so simple."

"Not so simple? Now listen to me, Carrie Leanne Sinclair! There isn't too much you can't fix when you love someone, and I do believe you love him. I'm certain Tyler loves you. Love just isn't that complicated. You work things out because what other choice do you have? Now, I'm going to let you go. Your secrets are safe with us, but I hope you'll think about what I've said and remember what's important to you. The hurt goes away in time, but the love doesn't."

* * * *

It was almost as if nothing had changed. Ed still treated me like his kid sister, while he and Steph fussed over me during dinner at my favorite restaurant.

"Okay, since this is officially *your* birthday dinner, Carrie, I think you should probably have some dessert," Ed offered, which really meant that Steph would let him have a piece of the best Italian cream cake in town if, and only if, I said yes.

"You know, you're right! I may even have two! Why don't you get yourself a little something as well, Ed?"

Steph rolled her eyes when the waiter came around to ask us if we'd saved room for dessert. I'm pretty much convinced that nothing ever really seems so bad if you're discussing it over a piece of Italian cream cake.

After dinner, my two best friends took me on a reminiscent tour of the city I loved so much. We drove past all the old familiar places where we'd spent so many years hanging out. By the time we finally got home, I was ready to cry all over again.

Steph decided that she and I needed to have some quality girl talk, which was Ed's cue to get lost. He'd just kissed us both goodnight when Jake called.

Hearing the voice of the man I shouldn't be leaning on — the person who was busy bonding with my cat — brought back all the problems in my life I'd been trying to forget.

"How's Texas?"

I had to be the biggest louse in the world. Jake was ready to love again. I wasn't sure I'd ever be.

"Good. Wonderful in fact. How's Max? Is he behaving himself for you?"

"Max is great. He and I have become very good friends. Did you have a nice birthday with your aunt?"

"Yes, it was." By this time, Steph was openly glowering at me. It was time to get rid of Jake.

"Look, I have to let you go now, Jake. Give Max a hug for me and I'll see you both sometime tomorrow."

"You want me to pick you up at the airport?"

"No, no, that's okay. I'll find my own way back. I'll give you a call and arrange a time to pick up Max." At this point, I hung up on Jake without giving him a chance to say anything further. I'd pushed my luck long enough.

"Jake is just a friend. He's keeping Max for me. I've told you about him before, so why are you so angry with me now?"

"Why? Because you have one man crazy in love with you already. Do you really want this one falling for you as well? Don't lead him on if you're not interested. That's not fair to anyone, you know?"

"I'm not leading anyone on. I told you he's my friend. That's it. And besides, there's nothing between Tyler and me. That's over."

"You still love him and you know it. You're just being stubborn. You've changed, and not in a nice way. You never used to be so mean."

Although we still talked for a little while longer, the visit we'd both been looking forward to had turned ugly. It was hard saying goodbye to her the next morning. I hated the way we'd left things between us.

I was almost at the airport when she called and we were both stumbling over each other to apologize.

"I'm sorry, Carrie! I have no right to be so judgmental. I don't know what's wrong with me. I wish you didn't have to go so soon."

191

"No, I'm the one who should be apologizing. I know I've been a real bitch lately. Maybe by Thanksgiving I'll be in a better mood. I'm sorry too."

I boarded the plane for my flight back to Colorado feeling slightly better about my visit and even more determined to leave Tyler behind me in Texas. Unfortunately, my heart wasn't so willing to go along with the plan.

Tyler was like a bad habit for me. I loved him. I didn't need Steph or Trudy or anyone one else to tell me as much. My foolish heart had certainly been screaming it to me since the first time I'd met him. We were still worlds apart in terms of what we wanted out of life, and not even love could overcome those obstacles. That should have been my first warning. As bad as I hated to admit it, though, it wouldn't have mattered. I had fallen in love the second I saw him. Nothing would have stopped me—not even the truth. And if I could do it all over again, would I? In a New York minute!

When my plane landed in Denver, I found Jake waiting for me, along with Max. "You look like you could use a lift, pretty lady."

He gave me a hug before handing me back my cat. Max's only response at seeing me again was an angry flick of his tail. "He's mad at me, isn't he?"

"Maybe a little, but he'll get over it. Just give him his new favorite treat and he'll forgive you in a second."

I turned to look at the man who should have been sending my heart soaring with excitement. Instead, all I could think about was Tyler.

"His *new favorite treat*? What have you two been up to while I've been away?"

"Not much. We both missed you though."

I almost didn't catch the words. His expression when he looked at me held much more than friendship.

"So what's the new treat? Please don't tell me you're been feeding my cat caviar."

"No, nothing quite so extravagant—just tuna."

Whether I liked it or not, Jake wasn't thinking about friendship anymore. I'd seen this coming from the start, but I'd chosen to ignore it, brush it aside. Hoping it would simply go away. I couldn't ignore it much longer. Jake was so close to love and I was such a fool for not returning his feelings.

When we arrived at my house, Jake took my suitcase upstairs while I flipped through the usual assortment of bills and junk mail.

"I was going to ask you if you wanted to have dinner with me tonight, but you look tired."

"I am. I think I'll just hang out here, catch up on some stuff then make it an early night. But thank you for everything. For spoiling my cat, for getting him addicted to tuna. You know…everything."

I couldn't shake the sadness. I'd once believed this house would be my dream come true. But there wasn't anything warm or welcoming here, just the emptiness of a house too big for Max and me. Every single room seemed to remind me of just how alone I truly was.

"No problem. I can spoil him for you whenever you like. We'll have dinner another time. You can tell me about your birthday, okay?"

"Sure, that sounds nice." I think I would have said anything to get rid of him. I needed to be alone before I started to cry again.

After Jake had left, I made myself a sandwich and opened up one of the dozen or so cans of tuna Jake had bought for Max. He'd gone shopping for me, as well, in my absence. Jake was the kind of man most women only dreamed of meeting. Handsome. Kind. Caring. And a doctor, to boot! What was wrong with me? Why couldn't I return Jake's feelings?

I walked through the empty rooms of the house I'd spent so much time dreaming about. How could I still call it a dream house when everything about it reminded me of the worst emotional time in my life?

Since I'd gotten my furnace fixed, thanks to Jake, at least half a dozen different things had started going wrong with the place. Not to mention that the furnace never quite worked the way it should. Half the time the house was either too hot or freezing cold.

Mr. Furnace Guy told me my problem wasn't the furnace or his work. It was my dream home. The house had been poorly constructed by someone who, in his opinion, didn't have a clue what they were doing.

I found myself seated in front of the computer reading Fred's latest email. During one of our previous heart to hearts, I'd discovered that Fred possessed a dark secret not even Trudy knew about. Fred was an avid romance reader.

He told me he hid them under a loose board in his computer room because he was afraid Trudy would laugh at him. I could almost picture Fred crouched in some corner with a flashlight in hand reading his romances.

It was during one of our talks that I spilled the truth about my little writing passion to him. At his request, I'd sent my current manuscript to him to read. Since then, he'd been after me to try to get it published.

Now, in Fred's usual, subtle-as-a-train-wreck manner, he'd listed several publishing houses that, in his opinion, would be a perfect fit for my book. He'd typed it at the end of the list —

Do it, Carrie, before I do it for you…

I loved him for pushing me, but I couldn't tell him that my secret passion had now dwindled into almost nonexistence. I no longer believed in romance. I guess that was something Tyler and I now had in common.

By morning some of my old determination had returned. I'd just been through a bad run of luck lately. Everything was bound to turn around soon. After all, what else could possibly go wrong?

The first thing I did that morning was go to the diner

and tell Margaret and Ernie that I'd made my decision. I was buying the place. They were shocked. I'm sure they'd figured once I took the time to think about it, I would change my mind. They were even further shocked when I presented them with a crisp bank check for the full asking price.

Once we'd signed the papers and the diner was officially mine, Margaret said, "Come back through to the kitchen and let's go over everything. Oh, and why don't you come by in the morning and we'll start the training again?" In Margaret's mind, I needed all the help I could get.

Chapter Fourteen

Hot Sex on the Lunch Counter...Just Because

I threw myself into my new job with a fury, learning everything I could from the Jacobs before they left town. Without realizing it, I was moving forward. I'd made a decision. I was working on a new career. I'd made some new friends. I was going to be okay. I was actually feeling good about my decision to move to Colorado for the first time. And when I went to my next appointment with Dr. Zack, I'd made my decision about the baby as well. I was keeping it.

With another big decision behind me, I stopped by the local employment office to put in a request for help. The woman who ran the place told me she would send some qualified candidates by the following morning for me to interview. With this done, I went by Henry's to give him an update on all my plans. As I was quickly learning, when Henry faked indifference, it really meant that he was interested.

The agency sent three people the following day.

The first person I talked to was a middle-aged man who told me he'd never been married. His only experience in the restaurant field was eating in one, and oh yes...he'd been fixing his own meals for almost fifty years. I learned he'd lived in Parrish almost all of his adult life. He had a place way on the other side of Parrish Mountain. He told me he preferred it that way because, frankly, he couldn't stand people. When I looked him in the eye, I could have been looking into the eyes of a serial killer.

The next young man, although slightly more encouraging, posed an entirely different problem—one I'd been hoping I'd left in my past. After Tyler, I had never expected to feel desire again. Maybe it was just the hormones talking, but I had a case of the hots from the moment I set eyes on him.

His name was Cameron Colts, and he was a fresh-off-the-bus real New York rocker. Cameron was just a musician looking for a gig to pay the bills until he made it big. He told me working at my diner would do nicely. He was twenty-five, with a body that put most of the men I'd known, including Tyler, to shame. I dismissed him completely from my list of possible candidates, because, frankly, I couldn't look him in the eye and not think about having sex with him.

Cameron was a long-haired Adonis. He was hot in a not-a-care-in-the-world, wild kind of way. He reminded me of how fond I was of sex every single time I looked at him, which was even more of a reason why I couldn't hire him. I could almost envision us making out on the lunch counter after hours. I smiled, told Cameron's Adam's apple I would be in touch, and prayed that the next person on my list would be even remotely qualified, because I couldn't hire Cameron and not have sex with him. It was as simple as that.

Luckily, Prudence Allen was somewhat more qualified, at least to my sex-crazed mind, and I didn't find myself fantasizing about her. Pru, as she insisted I call her, was thirty-two years old, the daughter of a Baptist minister, recently divorced and had just moved to Parrish two months earlier. We took an instant liking to each other through our general resentment of men. Ten minutes and one husband horror story later, I hired her.

I was beginning to feel somewhat more in control of my world. I'd moved out of the 'just in case' phase of my life, and into the 'just because'.

* * * *

With Pru's help, I managed to survive my first morning without Margaret and Ernie to lean on. We only screwed up a handful of orders. By the time the lunch help arrived, I was exhausted and definitely too tired to drive back to my lonely house just yet. I stopped in to see Henry for a while and told him I'd pick him up the next morning for his first day of work. He told me he was ready to start today. He was more than eager to start earning some real Texas money. While I admired Henry's enthusiasm, I told him he'd still have to wait until the morning.

Once I'd left Henry and the twelve cats, it was time for me to do some personal shopping. Most of my clothes no longer fit—not due to my pregnancy as much as to my overactive appetite—but since I wasn't showing enough to look for maternity items just yet, I put my vanity aside and move up another dress size.

Unfortunately, the shopping options in Parrish left a lot to be desired. There was the local Thrift Mart, which carried your basics—jeans, sweaters, and if you were lucky, bras and underwear. If you were in the market for hunting supplies, this was your place. If you were looking for something to wear to a fancy event, then you'd best move on to the next town.

I was there for the basics. I wasn't trying to impress anyone anymore, especially now that I was pregnant. I felt fat and unattractive and about as plain as the plaid shirt I'd just purchased.

Since moving to Parrish, I'd avoided the house where Tyler and I had stayed last Christmas. I refused to go in the same direction most of the time. Today, for reasons unknown to me, I was feeling sentimental again. I parked my little car just down the road and got out. The house hadn't changed. I didn't get too close, even though Tyler wasn't there. He was miles away in Texas. I hadn't heard from him in ages. Steph told me Tyler was giving me some space, but the next move was definitely mine to make.

Over the next few weeks, Pru and I settled into our routine

of working the morning shift together while alternating the evening cooking schedule. I even tried out several of my new menu items on the dinner crowd only to have them met with a lukewarm reaction. Apparently, people in Parrish didn't like to have their dinner options screwed around with. The only person to order my quiche was a man who told me he had imagined it to be some kind of new dessert.

After several more failed attempts, I finally added a few authentic Texas recipes to the menu. They received a slightly more positive response. Baby steps, I told myself.

Henry turned out to be the biggest surprise of all. He actually had the makings of being a pretty good busboy, in spite of his somewhat shaky start. In the beginning, I actually allowed Henry to have contact with the customers. Unfortunately, he made more than a few of them angry enough to walk out without paying their tabs. I discovered it was best to keep Henry in the background as much as possible. When he was allowed back into the dining area, he couldn't talk to any of the customers or make eye contact with them. So far, knock on wood, it was working out okay.

After almost a month of relatively smooth sailing, where Pru and I had managed not to screw up a single order and Henry hadn't pissed off anymore of the customers, we ran into our first major bump. For the first time in its history, the diner was robbed. I was just glad Margaret and Ernie weren't around to see it happen.

Pru had worked the night shift with the kids the evening before, so it was just Henry and me opening up on this particular morning. When we arrived at the diner, we found what little cash I kept in the register overnight was gone. I searched the place from top to bottom, but nothing else seemed to be missing except the money from the register — not even a single sugar packet — and there were no visible signs of a break in.

"Henry, call Marshal Brown," I told him while I tried to reach Pru on my cell phone. There was no answer.

The marshal arrived and confirmed my worst fears. This

appeared to have all the makings of an inside job. Someone I'd trusted had betrayed me. I immediately cleared Henry and the three high school students. Scottie and the two sisters' alibis checked out, which left only Pru.

Marshal Brown told me he would drive over to Pru's house and have a little chat with her. He called from there to say that the place was empty. Apparently, Pru had packed up and left town in the middle of the night without a word to anyone. I talked with Lacy, Seth and Brittney, the kids who worked the evening shift and learned that Pru had not been the sweet minister's daughter I had believed her to be. They told me she'd been mean to them, as well as to the customers, and she'd looked like she was stoned most of the time. When I called the employment agency the next morning, I was told that it could take weeks before another suitable candidate became available. Suitable? If Pru was their idea of suitable, I'd better rethink the whole serial killer thing.

After several weeks of working the morning shift alone with only Henry's limited help, as well as doing all the cooking for the dinner crowd, I was almost desperate enough to hire the serial killer. I would have done it, too, had he not been gainfully employed elsewhere. So I dug out the number for Cameron Colts to see if he might still be available. I would find a way to control my lust, mostly because I was too tired and I felt entirely too fat and unattractive to consider sex with someone as young and hot as Cameron.

Cameron arrived right on time the following morning. He smiled. I blushed. He asked me where I wanted him to start. I lost my train of thought. Then the first customer arrived and I reminded myself that this was a diner. There could be no sex on the lunch counter or anywhere else if I wanted to make it through the breakfast crowd.

After Cameron's first week — during which I'd somehow managed to keep my thoughts in line — he was proving to be working out pretty good. Maybe this wasn't such a bad idea after all, although I still made it a point of counting the cash in the register every morning.

Cameron caught on quickly and the customers loved him — especially the girls — and the evening shift had never run more smoothly. After another month without any further incidents, I was actually congratulating myself on my decision to hire Cameron until one night after the kids left and he and I got a little too familiar with each other.

Cameron was a constant flirt, but I was willing to overlook this fault in him because one, I enjoyed the attention, and two, my life was actually back on track again. I knew Cameron was interested in me, but so far, I hadn't found the nerve to tell him about the whole pregnancy thing.

You see, for me, Cameron was just a fantasy. I never intended to step beyond those few flirtatious moments or late night fantasies.

Unfortunately, for reasons I could only later explain away as hormones, on this particular night I threw caution to the wind. Cameron and I were quietly cleaning the grill when his arm brushed mine. My reaction to his touch went all the way down to my toes. I'd been warned that being pregnant would increase my sex drive by quite a lot, but this was ridiculous!

Cameron leaned in and kissed my lips softly. As hard as I tried to do the right thing, I really needed to be touched. I'd spent so many nights missing Tyler and denying my feelings for him. I'd been alone and scared, and before I knew what hit me, I was living out all of my f desires with Cameron. We ended up having hot, passionate sex — twice — on the lunch counter. It was everything I needed, everything I'd imagined, and I promised myself it could never happen again.

"Are you okay?" He watched me put as much space as possible between us. I tried to button my shirt, but my fingers were shaking so badly I ended up giving up and stuffing it inside my jeans instead.

"This was such a mistake!" I all but yelled at him. "This

can never happen again, Cameron."

"Why? You know I dig you, and you dig me. So what's the problem?"

I glared at him. *I dig you?* Was he like lost in the sixties or something? "The problem is, I'm pregnant. I can't be having causal sex with you or any other man who comes along, especially not on my lunch counter! People eat there, for God's sake!"

This at least wiped that sexy smile off his face. "You're pregnant? Oh God, I'm sorry. I didn't know. I mean...I would never have guessed. Did I hurt you?"

Cameron's apology made me feel even worse. "I'm okay. It just can't ever happen again. Do you understand?"

"Why? Is it just because you're pregnant?"

"No. No, it's just—"

"Carrie, I really like being with you. Why don't we slow things down a bit and get to know each other better."

"I have to think about my baby now. What you and I did was just sex, great sex, but sex and nothing more. And we can't do it anymore, okay?" When he smiled again, I knew this was not going to be the end of it. In fact, if I hadn't been turning off the lights and locking the door, if I hadn't had my keys in hand, I would have been having sex again with Cameron, right here where I stood.

Whether or not I chose to give him credit for it or not, Cameron was interested in more than just good sex. But wasn't this the very thing that was responsible for getting me in this position in the first place? Had I not learned anything from Tyler? Cameron might be out of this world sexy, but I couldn't be sleeping with him and further confusing my head.

He sensed my wavering and kissed me again. "Let's just take it slow, and see what happens. What about the baby's father?"

"What about him?" I countered.

"You don't want to talk about him?"

"No, I don't."

"Is he still in the picture?"

Now, how to answer this? I hadn't talked to Tyler in ages, but I guess technically he was still in the picture. I mean, he was the baby's father and since the first time I'd felt the baby kick, I knew I was having the child. Someday I'd have to share the news with him. It took me so long in deciding on the right answer Cameron eventually gave up and dropped the subject for the moment.

"Come on. We can talk about the ex some other time. You're tired. You want me to drive you home?"

I did, but if I let him, Cameron wouldn't be leaving tonight.

"No, it's okay. I'll be fine."

"It's late, so be careful. At least let me walk you to your car."

* * * *

Over the next few weeks, Cameron and I tried to keep our relationship under control during normal working hours, but it was next to impossible. I couldn't look at him — or my lunch counter, for that matter — and not remember how explosive we were together.

Cameron proved to be tremendously talented in bed, and he was sweet to me as well. I just couldn't quite fit myself into his free spirit lifestyle. Cameron was all energy. For a pregnant woman like me, it was hard keeping up the pace for long. All that stamina constantly amazed me. Cameron could work the evening shift, spend half the night practicing his music, and still be ready for an all-night love fest with me. After a couple of weeks of trying to keep up with him, I needed a break from Cameron's stamina for a while.

"You're dumping me?" Cameron was shocked when I finally admitted that I needed to take a breather from him — aka sex with him — over lunch one day.

Yes! My exhausted, second trimester body virtually screamed. *Do it before he kills you!* Unfortunately, Cameron was great in bed and I couldn't let go of that just yet.

"No! No, I'm not dumping you. I'm just saying I need to slow things down a bit. I can barely get out of bed anymore." This was certainly true enough. After spending an all-night session with Cameron, I'd been late to work more times than I could remember. I slept through my alarm clock as well as Max's angry meows.

"Okay." He grinned in relief. I didn't have the heart to tell him that for me, this was it. "Sure babe, whatever you need. You know it's cool with me. I dig you." This was Cameron's favorite saying. Another reason why I was years removed from him. Cameron and his gang were into the whole hippy retro thing.

During my hiatus from Cameron the rocker, Jake the doctor called. I'd been ignoring Jake during my love fest with Cameron. For obvious reasons, I could never quite bring myself to tell Jake about Cameron.

"What's been going on in your world lately? I haven't talked to you in a while."

"Nothing. I haven't been up to anything. Why? What have you heard?" This sounded a little too guilty, so I tried to tone things down. "You know, just work. Absolutely nothing but work. And you?"

Jake laughed indulgently at my babbling. Even his laughter made me feel guilty.

"Are you free for dinner tomorrow night or are you still working the evening shift?"

When Jake asked me out to dinner, I eagerly agreed. Guilt has a way of making you forget all the things you should be doing, like reminding the good doctor we were just friends and not confusing the issue any further. For the moment, I chose to push aside all of those ugly details. I'd deal with them later, after I had worked through my feelings for Cameron.

Jake took me out to the local steakhouse the following night, where he indulged me in one of my more recent obsessions. Since becoming pregnant, and after the first few months of morning sickness, I'd become obsessed with beef. I couldn't seem to get enough of it.

Jake watched in amazement as I finished off a nice-sized rib eye with all the works. "You know, this kid's going to be a cowboy if you keep this up."

While I ate, Jake entertained me with stories about his day at the office. I loved hearing about all the other pregnant women in town. For some odd reason, listening to all their horror stories made my little problems seem less overwhelming.

Once we reached my house, I could tell he wasn't ready to say goodnight just yet, which, of course, should have been my cue to be open with him. Instead, I invited him inside for coffee.

"Why don't you come inside for a little bit? I'll make you some coffee. You're always pampering me. I think I owe you one."

He didn't argue.

When my doorbell rang later, I'd been dozing for quite some time, not that Jake seemed to mind. I didn't have a clue who could possibly be stopping by at this hour of the night. The only person who came to see me here anymore was Cameron. As I went to answer the door, I prayed that Cameron hadn't forgotten about our hiatus.

Richard Bennedict was the last person I ever expected to see again, but there he stood, looking almost humble, on my front porch.

"May I come in, Carrie?" Even in the darkness, I could tell something was different about him. Richard didn't look nearly as impressive or as intimidating as in the past. He was so thin and haggard that I almost didn't recognize him.

Taken aback, I stepped aside instinctively, my gaze sliding in Jake's direction. I was still trying to decide how to explain to Jake what my ex-boyfriend's father was doing here. Luckily, Jake saved me any awkward explanation. He introduced himself to Richard then turned to me.

"I think I should go and leave you two alone. Obviously,

you have things to discuss."

"No, Jake you don't have to go."

"I do. I really think I do." He gave me that sad little smile of his. It seemed like every time Jake left me, I ended up disappointing him in some way. "I'll call you tomorrow, okay?" With those polite Jake-like words, he left us alone.

I found myself face to face with Richard for the first time since I'd run from him the time in Austin. It was a strange feeling.

"He seems nice," Richard commented politely.

"He is nice. He's also just a friend. What are you doing here, Richard?" It was hard to grasp the fact that Richard Bennedict was here, in Colorado — even harder to keep my resentment from showing.

"I wanted to talk to you about my son." There was none of the previous authority in his tone.

"We've already had this conversation, Richard. And anyway, Tyler and I aren't together anymore, remember? Your son is safe from me."

That there was definitely something wrong with him became even more apparent when Richard stepped into the light. His six-foot plus frame looked as if any strong wind might blow him away. For the first time I found myself feeling something akin to sympathy for Richard Bennedict.

"Come sit down," I walked back inside the great room and pointed to the chair closest to the warmth of the stove. "Did Tyler send you here?" Had Aunt Trudy caved and told Tyler where to find me after all?

"No, Tyler doesn't know I'm here." He took a seat. "My son told me about what happened between you two."

"I see." It took me a minute to come to terms with the fact Tyler actually discussed our relationship with his father. Somehow, this surprised me. "So then you must know it's truly over between us. You don't have to worry about me ruining your son's life anymore."

Richard flinched at the bitterness in those words. "Carrie, I've come to ask you to reconsider. Tyler loves you, you know."

At this point, I started to laugh. I'd waited more than a year to hear his son tell me he loved me. So far, it hadn't happened. If Tyler really loved me, would he let a little thing like me telling him I didn't want to see him ever again stand in his way?

It must be some sort of irony—having Tyler's father actually be the one to say those words to me. "Oh please! Tyler doesn't love me or anyone else. Well, other than you. I know he loves you. *I* was just a little bit of fun for him."

"That's not true. My son loves you. He hasn't been himself since you left him."

"Sorry, Richard, but I don't happen to believe you."

"It's true. I know you don't trust me. I don't blame you, but what I'm telling you is the truth. Tyler loves you."

"Oh please! Don't. Look, I can't pretend to know why you felt it necessary to come all this way today, but you can't convince me you care anything about my feelings. You did everything within your power to split us up when we *were* together. Well, you got your wish."

"I won't deny it, because it was true. You were not the woman I imagined my son needed in his life, and yes, it was for all the reasons you believed," he finished before I could interrupt him. "I was a snob. I admit that. I was so sure I knew what was best for my son, but I was wrong. I got my wish and I've regretted it ever since. I thought I wanted my son to take over the business for me one day, but now that he has, Tyler works eighteen-hour days, and when he's not working, he's thinking about work. I thought I wanted him to be just like me, but now that he is, I see a little bit more of his spirit disappear with each passing day. I thought I was doing Tyler a favor by not having him make the same mistakes I made with his mother. I married someone from a different class than me."

I winced at Richard's directness, and he saw it.

"I'm sorry. I know how this must sound, but please try to understand. I thought you would hurt my son the way his mother hurt me — us. Now I see I was wrong about all those things. Tyler loves you. Please, just talk to him. That's all I'm asking. Look beyond my mistakes and just talk to him."

"Richard, it's too late. He and I are not the same people we were back then. I've changed." I dug my nails into my palms to keep from crying. I needed to remain strong in front of this man. Needed to resist the urge to pick up the phone right now and call Tyler. I desperately wanted to hear him tell me all the things his father said were true, but I wasn't ready to face Tyler and tell him about our baby just yet.

"It's never too late, not as long as you're alive. You have to try. He loves you. I know you love him."

I needed time to think. I'd rushed into so many decisions in my life, screwed up so many important things. "Where are you staying tonight?"

Richard's smile suddenly reminded me of his son. I think he understood this need inside me. "I'm not really sure. I just got into town. Perhaps you could recommend someplace?"

It was late — almost midnight. I couldn't let him drive all the way back to town at this hour. "Why don't you stay here tonight? I have plenty of room." I was just as shocked by my offer as Richard

"Are you sure? I wouldn't want to be in the way."

I simply rolled my eyes, which elicited a laugh from him. "Would you like some coffee?"

He nodded and I headed for the kitchen just as Max put in an appearance to check out our newest visitor.

"Is this Max?"

How did he know about Max?

"Tyler told me," he answered my unasked question.

"Figures. The one thing he did tell his father about." I grumbled under my breath. "Yep, that's him. You'd better watch out for Max, though. I'm not sure how well he takes to strangers." What I really meant was how many of those terrible things I'd told Max about Richard, he still might be remembering. When I returned with the coffee, Max and Richard had apparently become friends.

"So, exactly how long are you planning on staying in Parrish?" The silence between us had threatened to become a little too companionable. I still couldn't let myself think of Richard Bennedict as anything but the enemy.

"Depends. As I've said, I came here to see you and to talk to you about Tyler. To ask... Well, you know."

I cleared my throat, ignoring this. "So won't Tyler be wondering where you've disappeared to? And I'm sure you'll be missing the rat race as well."

"No, not really. I told my son I'd be taking some vacation time. Again, he doesn't know I'm here. Since the illness, well, Tyler understands I need to get away by myself from time to time. It helps me deal with things. Tyler is quite capable of taking care of the business without me."

"What illness?" As hard as I tried, I couldn't stop myself from asking the question, even though by doing so, I would be opening myself up to the possibility of being hurt by this man again.

"I have cancer — lung cancer. I found out about a year and a half ago. I'm dying, Carrie."

"Oh God! I'm sorry! Richard, I'm sorry. I didn't know." I couldn't imagine Richard ever being sick, much less terminally ill. He'd always seemed so commanding, as if he were capable of kicking death's butt with a single well-placed word.

"Don't be sorry, Carrie. Very few people do know about it — just my son and, of course, my doctors."

"Are you okay now?" I hated the ridiculousness of the question the second I had asked it. Clearly, he wasn't.

"I've been in remission for several months now, so, my doctors are hopeful I might still have some time left.

"I'm so sorry." I took one look into blue eyes that reminded me so much of his son's, and I buried my face in my hands. I was sobbing so hard I didn't hear Richard's reaction to my tears. I wanted to hate him, wanted to say that this was justice, but the truth was, the man sitting here with me now was just a tired old man, worried about his son.

"Please, I don't deserve your tears." Richard knelt next to me, patting my shoulder. It was hard not to laugh at the awkwardness of his attempt at comforting me.

"You're right. You don't. But I'm still sorry. I'm sorry I never took the time to understand you better. I never really tried, even though Tyler wanted me to." I scrubbed the last of the tears away and tried to smile. "I guess you and I are more alike than we want to believe, huh?"

"That's very generous of you, but certainly more than I deserve."

Richard and I talked for hours that night. It was well after two in the morning when I stifled a yawn and told him I needed to get to bed, otherwise, I'd never be up in time to cook breakfast.

"Would you mind if I stopped by the diner in the morning? I'd like to see it."

I showed him to one of the guest rooms downstairs then we went back to the great room where I left Richard sitting on the sofa, talking to Max.

Chapter Fifteen

What Really Matters...Forgiving and Forgetting

At Max's usual time, my kitty jumped on my bed and woke me from the deep sleep I'd fallen into. It was well past time for his breakfast and the alarm, which I'd apparently been oblivious to, had been going off for at least fifteen minutes. Max was annoyed with me and he was clearly finding my laziness irritating. He stood next to my ear and meowed in a manner that told me he'd been trying to get my attention for quite some time now.

I opened one eye and found him watching me. "Did you have a nice chat with Richard last night? Just a few more minutes, okay, Max?"

None of my little spiel deterred him from his pursuit of food. He meowed a little bit louder this time and I gave up on sleep entirely.

"Okay, okay, I'm coming."

The house was toasty warm for the first time in weeks. It took me a minute or two to realize that Richard must have somehow managed to get my cranky furnace working properly at last.

I left Max eating his breakfast and picked up Henry on my way to the diner. Luckily, the morning crowd was bigger than usual, which didn't leave me any free time to think about what Richard had said to me the night before. I'd been trying to bury Tyler's memory for a long time. I wouldn't even let myself think about him anymore. I'd been making excuses for not telling him about the baby. Now, his father had showed up on my doorstep reminding me I still loved his son. I didn't know what I was going to do about Tyler.

The last of the breakfast crowd was just finishing when Richard arrived. I made him French toast and poured coffee before sliding into the booth across from him.

"So, what have you been doing this morning?"

"I went for a walk with Max. I had no idea how beautiful it is up here. Tyler told me how much you loved Parrish. Now I can understand why." It surprised me to learn Tyler had shared this little detail with his father.

"Yes, it's great." I couldn't tell him about all the problems the house developed since I'd bought it. "Thanks for fixing the furnace. I'd all but given up on it ever working properly again."

"Just a little trick of the trade I picked up years ago. These are good." He pointed to the French toast. "You need an extra cook? I could get used to living here, surrounded by all this beauty."

Somehow, I couldn't quite picture Richard Bennedict slaving over a hot stove. Richard saw my smile. "Don't laugh. I can cook."

"And don't offer unless you mean it. I can always use the help."

"I'm all yours." He glanced around the place. "So it's just you in the mornings?"

"No, there's Henry. He helps out and keeps me company."

Henry emerged from the kitchen right then, as if on cue. He spotted Richard immediately and decided to come check him out.

"Who's this?" Henry, in his usual cranky way, demanded rather than asked. "This the baby's father?"

I was still running through the possible scenarios in my mind as to how I might tell Richard as well as Tyler about the baby when Henry had solved the problem for me.

"Baby?" Richard's eyes locked with mine. "You're pregnant." He appeared to be visibly shaken. I nodded. "Is it Tyler's?"

"Yes." I didn't look away. I watched Richard struggle with this piece of information.

"He doesn't know, does he?"

"No, he doesn't." I'd almost forgotten Henry standing there with his little plastic busboy bin poised for cleanup.

"Henry, this is Richard Bennedict—Tyler Bennedict's father. Tyler is the baby's father. Richard, this is my friend Henry Potter."

Richard somehow managed to look away from me long enough to meet Henry's stern expression. He stuck out his hand but Henry in his usual manner stood stock still, refusing it.

"Henry's not much on socializing," I attempted to explain to Richard. "Henry, could you clear away tables five and seven for me, please?"

Henry left us alone, but I could see him glancing our way ever so often as he cleared off the tables across the diner.

Richard finally managed to clear his throat. "How far along are you?"

"Almost four months now." I told him quietly. "Richard, I know what you're going to say and I *will* tell Tyler. I just need more time."

He simply stared at his plate. When I spotted his quaking shoulders, it dawned on me Richard Bennedict was really crying.

"You're crying?" Geez, I'd made him cry without even trying.

"I'm just so sorry, Carrie," he told me glancing up. The sight of those two trickles of tears running down his weary face had me sobbing as well. I squeezed his hand.

"It's not your fault I'm pregnant."

"No, but if I hadn't gotten in the way, then you two would be happy, and together, with the baby on the way. You wouldn't have left Austin. My son wouldn't be turning into another me. I wouldn't be this miserable. I'm sorry for all those things."

Henry was nosily clanging around at the table close by.

He'd spotted my tears. "It's okay, Henry. I'm fine. It's just hormones." This always did the trick. Henry hated hearing about women's problems, as he called them, almost as much as he hated Colorado. Once he'd disappeared to the kitchen again, I turned my attention back to Richard.

"Look, why don't you stay for a while? You can help me out with the diner and you and I can really get to know each other. I promise, I'll tell Tyler about the baby soon. I just need a little time, okay."

"Okay — and yes, I'd like that. Is there a hotel around you can recommend?"

"You're staying with me, so don't argue. I have plenty of room and Max would love the company."

"You'll let me earn my keep? I want to help out."

"Are you kidding? I can't wait to see you in the kitchen!"

* * * *

It had been hard enough explaining to everyone around that I was an unmarried pregnant woman. Explaining that the father of my child's father was now living with me, as well as working for me... Well, I finally gave up and just introduced Richard as a friend.

Cameron was a little perplexed by the whole affair in the beginning. Henry eventually accepted Richard into our lives, and Richard turned out to be a pretty good cook.

After two weeks of supervising Richard while he worked the morning shift with me, it was time to hire a brand new waitress to help out, since I was finding it hard to keep up with the pace of the diner in my current pregnant state.

Suzie Miller was a forty-something brunette who was plain and sensible. She was nothing like the women Richard Bennedict was accustomed to dating. Richard was smitten with her from day one. It was fun watching their romance grow.

I called Steph at the first opportunity to tell her all the latest gossip. Steph was floored.

"The Dick is living with you?" She couldn't disguise her disbelief. I filled her in with the details of his arrival in town, leaving out the illness part. I owed as much to my new friend.

"You think he'll tell Tyler about the baby?"

"I don't think so. Richard is really trying his best not to meddle in our lives anymore."

"So, when are *you* going to tell Tyler?"

"Soon," I hedged. I couldn't tell Steph that each time I picked up the phone to make the call I wasn't able to do it. I guess I just wasn't ready to admit I'd screwed things up by not telling him sooner. It seemed easier just to promise myself that I'd call him soon, even if time was running out. If I didn't tell him about the baby soon, would Tyler ever forgive me?

Richard and I slipped into a routine of alternating the morning shift. This way each of us got a day off every other day. Richard did this mostly for my benefit. He loved working at the diner and being with Suzie. I think he would have been happy working seven days a week as long as Suzie was there. When I'd first told Jake that Richard was staying on with me, I could tell he wasn't pleased. But Jake wasn't prepared to ask where he stood with me just yet. He was still trying to give me time.

One morning as I sat catching up on my reading with Max in my lap, Cameron dropped by for a little visit. Since we'd agreed to take time off from each other, Cameron told me he was working more on his music. He'd found several gigs in Denver, which kept him busy.

"Hi, can I come in for a bit?" Today, in contrast to me, who was still dressed for bed at almost midday, my hair going in all directions, Cameron looked even more inviting than ever. And—likely a first for him—he was nervous.

"Sure, want some coffee?" I waited for him to take his usual seat on the couch.

"No. Look, Carrie, I have something important to tell you."

"Okay, shoot." I tried to remember the last thing we'd said to each other. It was weeks since we'd really talked about us. Mostly when we talked at all, it was about the diner or his music.

"I've been offered a job in L.A.," he told me solemnly. Definitely not the usual Cameron.

"Really? In the music industry?"

"Yes."

I think Cameron was a little insulted that I'd asked such a question.

"I'm handing in my notice. I'm sorry I can't give you two weeks."

It hit me then. Cameron was leaving me. "It's okay," I blurted out. I wasn't sure how I felt about Cameron's departure from my life. Of course, I'd known from the beginning that we weren't permanent. Our relationship was based solely on great sex, but still, I'd shared part of myself with him. "I'm happy for you, Cameron. I know how much this means to you. And don't worry about the diner. I have a couple of candidates in mind to fill your space. It will be okay." God, I was babbling.

He smiled a little sadly. "You could come with me? You'd love L.A. You could find someone to run the diner for you easily enough, couldn't you? Come with me, Carrie! This could be a new start for us."

I watched the old exuberant Cameron return for a second, reminding me of all the things I adored about him. But I didn't love him. And I was too old to become his groupie.

"I can't. You're a wonderful guy, but I can't. I have the baby to consider now. I couldn't saddle you with someone else's child."

"I wouldn't mind." He didn't quite convince either of us.

"You would. Not for a while maybe, but you would in time. You'll find your match someday. And when you do, you won't have to wonder."

"Like you found yours? This Tyler person?"

I couldn't answer. Was Tyler my match? If so, had I

216

screwed things up beyond repair by dumping him and running away?

"I should go. I'm really sorry about leaving you this way." I kissed Cameron goodbye and closed the door on our love affair at last. As I sat in front of the fire, I was actually happy for him and only a little sad to see him leave. He wasn't my forever. He had just been the one to remind me I was still alive. I still possessed needs, even though I'd been determined to shut that side of my life away. In a way, Cameron had brought me back to life and helped me realize what I truly wanted. *Who* I truly wanted.

Now, at last there were no more doubts. I knew what I needed to do. What I wanted to do. I just didn't have the courage to do it yet.

* * * *

Fortunately, fate sometimes has a way of stepping in and taking control when you least expect it.

As the temperature began to drop with the changing season, Richard developed a cold that wouldn't seem to go away. I tried to talk him into seeing a doctor in Denver, but Richard insisted it was nothing.

By this time, Henry and Richard had become good friends, much to everyone at the diner's surprise. Henry did his best to pretend indifference, but I could tell he really looked forward to their weekly night out at the community center to play bingo. Richard was even making friends with most of Henry's cats, at least the sociable ones.

In addition to working at the diner and babysitting Henry, Richard was also seeing Suzie on a regular basis. I tried to get him to slow down, take some time off even, but I guess for someone so close to death, time is precious. Richard didn't want to miss a moment of living.

Once, I'd asked him how he'd explained his disappearance to Tyler. He told me Tyler knew exactly where to find him.

Suzie called one morning to ask if Richard had left for the

diner yet. "He's not there?" I hadn't seen any of the telltale signs of his usual activity. I'd just assumed Richard was waiting to eat breakfast until he got to the diner to have it with Suzie, as he sometimes did. Richard's car still sat outside in the drive. The sight of it scared me to death.

I took the steps downstairs two at a time and knocked as hard as I could on his door. I barely waited for Richard's response. He was still in bed and burning up with fever!

It seemed like an eternity before the EMS team finally arrived. I rode with Richard to the hospital, holding his hand, even though he was unconscious for most of the trip. I gave the hospital all the information on his illness that I could and once Richard was admitted, it wasn't long before a doctor came by to explain his condition to me. He told me Richard had developed pneumonia.

"Are you his daughter?" the attending doctor asked before giving me any further details.

"I'm his daughter-in-law," I told him firmly with my fingers crossed behind my back.

"I'm afraid this is quite serious, Ms. Sinclair. I suggest you call your husband and any other family members. The next forty-eight hours will be critical. With his type of cancer, any illness can be potentially life threatening. We'll do what we can to build his strength up and help his body fight the pneumonia, but I think you should call the family in, just in case. Is your husband on his way?"

"He's in Texas, but I'll call him right away. Can I see Richard now?"

"Yes, but he's sleeping, so try not to wake him, okay? He needs to rest."

I barely recognized Richard. He looked so fragile. It was hard seeing him like this. After reassuring myself Richard was stable enough to be alone for a second, I stepped out into the hallway and made the call to Tyler that I'd been putting off for months.

Hearing his voice threw me for a moment. It was like stepping back into the past. I pushed those memories aside and forced myself to tell him what was happening to Richard.

"Tyler, it's your father. He's in the hospital here in Parrish. He has pneumonia. Tyler, his doctors aren't sure..." My voice broke for a moment. "Please come."

"I'll be on the next flight out." He didn't even hesitate. "I'll be there as soon as possible. Carrie, don't let him die, okay? Please, don't let him die."

"I won't. I promise. Please hurry."

Once I could speak again without crying, I called Suzie and told her about Richard. I asked her if she could stop by Henry's and let him know.

"Do you think I could come see him for a little while?" Suzie's voice sounded choked with emotion.

"I don't know. I'll ask his doctor and let you know soon, okay? I know you want to be with him, but right now, the best thing for him is rest."

I sat quietly next to Richard's bedside, watching as he drifted in and out of consciousness, hanging onto the life he found so precious. For the first time in longer than I could remember, I found myself praying. I could almost hear Aunt Mable chiding me for not remembering how much God loved hearing our prayers. She'd told me once it was like having a little one-on-one time with our maker. Just thinking about my aunt made me smile.

"If you're up there, Aunt Mable, please talk to God for me. Please, not yet. Don't take him yet."

By late evening, Richard began showing a small improvement. I said another prayer and thanked my aunt for watching out for him.

When Tyler walked into the hospital room, it was almost midnight. It surprised me to realize I wasn't nervous any longer. I'd had the day to consider what I'd say to him and to dread these first few awkward moments. But when he stepped into the room and his eyes found mine, I wasn't nervous any longer. I went into his arms without hesitating. If Tyler wondered about the difference in me, he never asked. His thoughts were all on his father.

"He's better." We went to his father's bedside together. "His doctor thinks he's showing some improvement."

"Yeah? That's good, right?"

"That's great!" Tyler's arm still held me close, but somehow it felt right.

He touched his father's hand, but Richard didn't awake. "Oh God, Carrie, he looks so…"

"Yes, but he's going to be okay. I just know it. I talked to Aunt Mable. She told me not to worry."

Tyler looked down at me and smiled. "You know, I miss her too. If anyone can get God's ear, it's your aunt. You look tired. You should go home. Get some rest. I'll stay with Dad."

"No, I'm not leaving him. I'll be okay."

Throughout the night, Tyler and I didn't really talk at all. The next morning, much to everyone's surprise, Richard was sitting up in bed and grinning from ear to ear. He was so excited to see his son. He kept winking at me and urging me to take Tyler home to get some rest. Our talk could wait. Neither of us was ready to leave him just yet.

Chapter Sixteen

Finally Realizing Love isn't about Fairy Tales

Once Suzie and Henry stopped by for a visit late that evening and Tyler was convinced it was okay to leave his father in their care for a little while, I talked him into getting some rest.

"Where are you parked?" Tyler asked.

I stopped walking and stared at him. It had been a little more than twenty-four hours since I'd ridden in the ambulance with Richard. It seemed like a lifetime. I'd been so worried, I'd been shivering most of the day, even through my heavy coat.

"I almost forgot. I came in the ambulance with your father."

"I'll take you home. I'm just over here."

I nodded, suddenly nervous again. We'd both been concentrating so hard on Richard that there hadn't been any time to worry about what we were going to say to each other once we were alone. Tyler and I still had unfinished business to settle.

We made the twenty-minute ride to my house in silence.

"Where are you staying?"

"To be honest with you, I haven't really thought about it. All I could think about was getting here for Dad and for you. I guess at my friends' place. You remember—where we spent last Christmas." Oh yeah, I hadn't forgotten a thing about that Christmas.

"Tyler, this is silly. It's late and you must be exhausted. You haven't slept in hours. Why don't you stay here? In

221

your father's room."

We stood in the great room facing each other in silence. Neither of us seemed to know what to say anymore. What had we talked about all those times when we couldn't get enough of each other's company? Mostly we hadn't talked. We'd touched.

Think of something else fast! I chanted in my head. I couldn't think about those times spent touching Tyler with him standing this close to me.

"Would you like something to drink, or do you want to go to bed now?"

Tyler came slowly toward me, too slow for my frazzled nerves. Somehow, I resisted the urge to back away from him. He touched my cheek, letting his hand drift down to my throat. His fingers stroked the skin there, forcing my eyes closed. I couldn't look at him and not reveal just how much I wanted him.

"Aren't you going to take your coat off?"

Suddenly I was more nervous than I'd ever imagined. By now, I'd just begun to show. Would Tyler guess? I wasn't ready to have that discussion just yet. "Um, no, I'm fine."

"Then why don't you show me around this dream home of yours?"

It took me several minutes to realize Tyler was no longer standing close. In fact, he'd moved away from me entirely. Here I stood, like some foolish schoolgirl, with her eyes closed.

"Huh?"

He smiled at my confusion, before taking my hand and repeating the question a little more slowly for the slightly frustrated lady.

For the first time in a long time, I was afraid of looking foolish in his eyes. After all, I'd bought this house without really having anyone check it out and Tyler was a professional. Would he see all the little flaws in it and wonder how I'd survived this long without being duped ages ago?

Whatever Tyler might have thought, he didn't say a single bad thing about my dream house. I certainly wasn't going to tell him it had long ago become my nightmare.

On the third floor, standing just outside the French doors leading to my bedroom, I hesitated. This was dangerous ground for me. This was the last place I needed to be alone with him.

I opened the door a little ways to allow him to peek inside before we moved on to the other end of the house and to safer territory.

I'd forgotten about all the stacks of baby literature next to my computer that I'd been intending to read. Tyler wasn't looking at the books on my desk. He glanced at my computer and saw the usual assortment of pictures there. My dream house, Max, Stephanie and me together—and him.

They were all still there, even the picture of Tyler. I was so embarrassed he'd seen it. He didn't comment on it but the grin was back in place.

Downstairs in the great room I asked again if he wanted coffee, mostly because I needed the opportunity to get away from him for a second to break the spell that made me think things I didn't have any business thinking.

I poured the coffee—black, the way he always took it—and turned to realize he'd followed me.

Max heard us talking and came to see who might be calling. He recognized Tyler immediately and rubbed against his legs.

"I think he remembers me. Don't you, Max? It's good to see someone in this family still likes me."

Okay, that was it. One of us needed to leave and since Tyler apparently wasn't planning to do so. I would have to be the one to go. I started past him at the same time he realized what I was about to do.

Tyler set his cup down and reached for me.

"No." That single word tore from me. I closed my eyes. I couldn't look at him, but in the end, it really wouldn't have mattered. He was so warm and he smelled so good, and I wanted him so badly. I'd only been fooling myself, believing my life would ever be the same without Tyler.

He put his arms around my waist, drawing me close. Only a whisper of space lay between us, but there were mountains of unanswered questions there. I could hear every beat of his heart. His warm breath brushed across my face soft and gentle as a caress.

"God, I've missed you so much." This wasn't the man I'd expected to find. Tyler sounded so lost.

The moment his lips brushed mine, I was lost as well — lost and drowning in emotions and familiar memories, consumed by a passion that would never be quenched, no matter how many times we made love to each other.

He picked me up and carried me to my bedroom, laying me down on the bed. I wasn't sure which of us was faster at undressing the other, but we took our time on things that mattered.

In the semi darkness, the fire of passion burned in his eyes. "I've thought of nothing but this since the last time I touched you."

His kiss had the power to bring me back to life. It was as if I'd been sleeping like Snow White, waiting for his touch. Not even Cameron's frenzied lovemaking could come close to touching the part of me that just a single kiss from Tyler could.

He touched my breast. My heart responded beneath his stroke.

"Is that because of me?" he whispered in wonder against my lips.

"It's all you. It's always been you." I struggled to get the words out.

Tyler stopped for a second and looked into my eyes. "I want you. I just don't want to screw this up again." This new uncertainty in him tore at my heart.

"It's okay. You won't screw it up. You could never do that. I want you too."

224

His mouth claimed mine again and all the worries just slipped away. This was familiar ground.

This was what we did best.

This was love.

When I awoke sometime just before dawn I was confused and exhausted. Every inch of me was languid and aching blissfully. I was alone again. Next to me on the pillow, Tyler had left me a note —

I went back to the hospital. I couldn't sleep and I didn't have the heart to wake you. We'll talk later.

As I drifted back to sleep, I realized once again we hadn't said any of the things we needed to say to each other. The past still lay between us. And no amount of lovemaking — not even this crazy, can't get enough of each other kind — could hide the truth. Eventually, many things would need to be settled between us.

* * * *

When I awoke again, it was mid-afternoon. I dressed as quickly as possible and drove back into town, wondering how I could ever bring myself to face Tyler again.

I found Richard sitting up in bed, looking remarkably close to his old self once more. Tyler was there as well, but he didn't have much to say and I wondered what was responsible for this change in him.

"Dad, since Carrie's here, I think I'm going to check in with the office. I was thinking I should stay at my friends' place after all," he told me without actually looking at me.

"Tyler, you don't have to do that."

"I think it's for the best." He couldn't make eye contact with me. Tyler left shortly, leaving Richard and me alone.

"You two didn't talk, I take it?"

"No, not really."

"Carrie, talk to him before it's too late."

"I will. I'll try. I promise I'll try."

225

I couldn't seem to find the right moment, and Tyler was clearly avoiding being alone with me entirely.

Richard remained in the hospital for another week. I saw Tyler only a handful of times and never alone.

By Friday, Richard's doctor was so pleased with his recovery progress that he was releasing him the following afternoon.

When I arrived at the hospital, Tyler was there. In his usual manner, he didn't stay long and Richard spent the rest of the time staring out the window, barely answering my questions. Something was wrong between them, but every time I asked, Richard simply told me to talk to Tyler before it was too late.

For the rest of the day, I fought with my heart and somehow won out. I wanted to call Tyler and ask him if he'd still be here tomorrow. I was afraid I knew the answer to the question already. So instead, I threw myself into cleaning the house from top to bottom. I didn't stop until every single inch of the place was sparkling. I was still miserable and still missing Tyler, and still terrified that I'd thrown away the best thing to happen to me.

I spent the evening wondering if I got in my car and drove over to his house would he still be there? If so, would I find the man I loved, or had Tyler and I become nothing more than strangers with a past?

By late evening, I was sick, literally throwing up from fear and worry when Tyler knocked on my door.

The second I opened it, I believed it was finished for him. Everything — from the cold unemotional sound in his voice, to the emptiness in his eyes — told me he'd reached his limit with me.

"What are you doing here?" I just managed to get the words out over the bitter lump forming in my throat.

"Carrie — just listen. I didn't come here tonight to argue with you or to try to change your mind about anything. I see this is impossible now. I came here to tell you I love you. With all my heart, I love you. I can't erase my past mistakes, and I don't believe you can ever forgive them. So where does this leave us? I can't make you forget the past, no matter how many times I make love to you. I can't wipe it out. I came here tonight to give you this and to tell you I won't bother you anymore. I'm leaving tomorrow afternoon. Now that I know Dad will be okay for a while, there's really no reason for me to stay. I have a one o'clock flight back to Austin. I just wanted you to have these." He held out a brightly wrapped package for me. I took it because I was too stunned to do anything else.

Tyler kissed me once, then touched my hair and looked at me as if he were storing up images for darker days.

Then, just like the horrible night in Austin, he left me standing alone.

Somehow, I managed to close the door. I stood rooted in place, unable to move a single step while I listened to the sound of his car leaving me for the last time.

I tossed his package angrily into the trash and walked away from it. I was determined to let go of it and him forever. This was it, wasn't it? He'd just told me so. Tyler was finished with me. Yet something wouldn't let me walk away from Tyler or that package. I turned back to look at it lying there in the trash as broken and as lost as my dreams, and I sank to the floor and cried.

Somewhere amid all my tears at last it hit me what he'd just said to me. Tyler Bennedict had just told me he loved me for the first time. He'd actually said those words — left me without a doubt as to what his feelings were, and I'd been too angry to hear them.

He'd said, "I love you."

I'd been so determined to blame him for everything that had gone wrong between us that I hadn't been able to see he was trying to change for me. He wasn't like the man I'd believed him to be. Tyler wasn't David any more than he was his father.

Slowly I walked over to the package and stared down at it just as Max reached my side and rubbed against my legs urging me to do it. Do what I wanted to do! Max was giving me his permission.

I took the package out of the trash. It was heavy. Then I sat down on the floor with Max by my side and ripped the paper from it.

Inside was something I still wasn't convinced I could trust. My old collection of Cary Grant videos. Every single one of the movies I'd angrily tossed aside and left outside the apartment in Austin—the collection I'd spent a lifetime gathering. Next to them was a jeweler's box, which held a ring.

Tyler was giving me his ring. He'd given me his heart as well, and he'd given me Cary back. Maybe if I was really lucky, he'd given me back my secret passion as well. Maybe it still wasn't too late for love.

"He's not leaving until tomorrow." My sweet little kitty knew what I was thinking as he walked to the door.

"Yeah? Are you sure? Because this is it, Max. This is our last chance. I can't keep stringing him along." I don't know which of us I was trying to convince the most, but my only answer from Max was his usual when I asked something stupid—a single flick of his tail.

I found my keys and grabbed the jeweler's box, not even caring if I still wore my pajamas. I tossed my coat on over them. I needed to reach Tyler before it was too late.

"Wish me luck, Max." He didn't bother, which gave me hope. Maybe I didn't need luck. Maybe I just needed to tell Tyler what I should have told him long ago.

First, there was another stop to make. I needed to settle things with Jake, make it clear to both of us where we stood with each other and to ask for his forgiveness.

When he opened the door, it occurred to me Jake wasn't surprised to see me standing there, even in my pajamas. "Carrie, come inside."

"I'm sorry. I'm sorry if I've led you on about our relationship. That was never my intention. I know I've been giving you mixed signals since the beginning, and I'm sorry. I really did hope…"

"I know. And it's okay. Believe me, I understand. I know how hard it is to give up on love. But you do still love Tyler. Even I can see that. So, don't throw it away because of some hurt feelings in the past. Love is too hard to come by these days."

"You're right, I know. I'm on my way there now to talk to him. I just pray it's not too late. But I wanted to talk to you first."

"It's never too late, as long as you're honest with him. Don't worry about me. I'll always be your friend. But you'd better go. I think your future might be waiting for you."

As I turned off the main street onto the little drive leading up to the house, I prayed Jake was right – that I would still find my future there with Tyler.

What would I do if Tyler couldn't forgive me for hurting him or for not telling him about our child? What if he didn't want our baby? How could I survive so much hurt again? The answer was simple. I couldn't *not* try. I needed to do this because I loved him.

The place was dark. *Please, God. This is Carrie again. Please don't let it be too late.*

The porch light switched on, followed by another one inside the entrance and I held my breath.

Tyler opened the door slowly. It was clear he'd been sleeping. I'd awakened him with my unexpected arrival on his doorstep. Another something to be sorry for.

"Carrie?"

He looked surprised and not one little bit welcoming, and I lost it. "Don't go! Don't leave me, Tyler! Please, don't give up on me!"

As I watched, the sadness, which had become part of him, melted away. I went into his arms as if I'd never left them and he held me tightly, then he carried me to the sofa in front of the fireplace.

"I'll never give up on you. Not as long as you give me hope."

When I looked at him with tears streaming down my face, I struggled to say the words I needed to say to him. "I love you, Tyler."

"I love you too. And I'm not going anywhere. I'm sorry I made such a mess of things between us, but I do love you. I've always loved you. I waited too long to say it. If you still love me, then not everything can be bad, right? We'll figure the rest of it out. We have the rest of our lives, don't we?" I wasn't sure which of us was trying to convince the other the most. It didn't matter anymore. I now believed it was possible.

I touched his cheek and realized I still clutched the ring I'd brought with me in my hand.

Tyler took the box from me, opened it, took the ring out and held it out to me. "You didn't read the inscription, did you? I got the jeweler, a friend of mine, out of bed to put this inscription on the inside just for you, and you haven't even read the thing!"

He was trying to sound angry, but there was an uncertainty about Tyler I'd never seen before, not once in the months we'd loved each other undercover. I took the ring from him and held it up to the light.

Inscribed in the band of the most beautiful diamond ring I'd ever seen, were these words—

To Carrie, the love of my life. Now, always, forever…Tyler.

The date inscribed there was a few weeks after Tyler had met my aunts for the first time. I'd known back then that he was going to be different from any other man.

I handed him back the ring and shook my head. I loved him, but I wasn't taking any more chances. I needed to hear Tyler say the words to me. "You're going to have to tell me what this means."

His expression said it all. I'd surprised him, but I'd also hurt him. Even now, after he'd told me he loved me, I still couldn't let myself believe. .

"You never told me you loved me. I needed to hear those words from you so many times, Tyler. You never told me."

"I know, and I'm so sorry. I should have. I knew how badly David hurt you. I should have told you how I felt about you from the beginning. You never told me either. I guess we were both scared of being the first to say it. I'm sorry for not saying it all those times in the past when I wanted to tell you how I felt about you, when I wanted you to trust me not to be like David. I want to marry you. I love you and want to spend the rest of my life with you. I never want to go through again what these past few months have felt like without you in my life. It scares the hell out of me to think I almost lost the most important person in my life. And just to make it clear for you, this is an engagement ring. Will you marry me?"

I couldn't say a single word, but he understood. Tyler had given up so much for me. What more could a girl ask for from the man she loved? Except he tells her that he loves her. Tyler had said those words at last.

Chapter Seventeen

Confessing Your Sins and Having Them Forgiven

It was a long time before I finally forced myself to tell Tyler the truth about the baby and about Cameron. I wasn't sure how he would react to hearing either of those things, but he needed to know.

"Tyler, I have to tell you something — two things actually — but I can't do it when you're looking at me. I need you to go over there by the fire and don't look at me."

"Carrie, that's ridiculous. You can tell me anything. Just tell me."

"I can't. Not when you're looking at me like that. I'm serious! I need you not to look at me."

He stood and walked away from me, staring down at the fire instead, accepting my eccentricity even though he didn't understand it, simply because he loved me.

"I'll start with the easy one first."

While he still hadn't looked at me, I could tell he was trying very hard not to laugh. "There's a more difficult one?"

"Yes. First, I wrote a book." When faced with confessing all my sins, I found I couldn't actually get the words out, so I said the first thing that came to mind. Unfortunately, this was the last thing I wanted Tyler to know about me. Clearly, I couldn't have caught him more off guard if I'd punched him.

"You what?" Tyler forgot that he wasn't supposed to be looking at me. He came back to me and knelt in front of me. "What type of book did you write, Miss Sinclair?"

"Fiction. Okay, so it was a romance. It's not very good." Admitting this to him hadn't been quite as embarrassing as I'd anticipated it might be.

"I see. Well, sometimes, it just takes practice. You should keep trying. Don't give up on your dreams."

"Yeah." Suddenly we weren't talking about my story any longer.

"So does this mean you still believe in romance?" It was his turn to catch me off guard.

"Yes...maybe. I hope so."

"I hope so, too. I guess I'm going to have to work awfully hard at making you believe again."

"You're supposed to be listening to me." I didn't really mind, though. I loved what he was saying.

"Are you ever going to trust me to read it?"

How could I tell him that I'd already trusted him with so much? My heart. My happiness...our future.

"Yes. But I have something else to tell you still, so go back over by the fire. Please, Tyler."

He obeyed me even though he didn't want to. He turned his back to me again and I fought the fear inside me. I owed him this truth, even if this was the hardest thing in the world to get out. Even if he didn't want our child.

"I've slept with someone else and I'm pregnant. It's yours! I was pregnant before I left Austin. I just couldn't tell you. I'm so sorry."

His expression frightened me more than I could have imagined. Tyler seemed to be struggling to grasp what I'd just blurted out so cruelly. "You're what?" Apparently, he hadn't heard the part about me sleeping with someone else.

"I'm pregnant—a little more than four months. I know it was wrong. I know I should have told you, but things were so bad between us, and you were always gone, and when you weren't, we were fighting, and I was so angry and hurt, and mad...and...and I was scared!" My words tumbled out in a rush because he was coming toward me very purposefully now.

"We're having a baby? I'm going to be a father?" For the first time since I'd known him, I watched Tyler Bennedict cry. The sight of his tears took my breath away.

"Tyler...you're crying... Oh no! Please don't cry. I'm so sorry I didn't tell you sooner. I know it was unfair to you, but you have to understand. I was scared. I was so scared. I believed the last thing you'd want to have with me was a baby... Wait. Are you crying because you're happy about the baby? Please say you're happy."

He started to laugh before he took me back into his arms once more. "Happy? Oh God, I'm more than happy! I'm... I'm beyond words. I'm ecstatic! I just wish..." He shook his head. Not that he needed to say the words. He wished that I could have been strong enough to tell him the truth. "I wish I hadn't made it so impossible for you to be honest with me. I wish I'd caught you before you left. I wish I'd ignored my father's wishes and never let you go. I wish so many things could have been different between us. I can't blame you for not telling me about the baby. I certainly didn't give you any real reason to trust me or let you believe I would be there for you to lean on. I'm sorry for all of those things, my love. But mostly, I'm sorry for not telling you how much you mean to me."

"I was so afraid you'd guess. I mean...after the other night. You couldn't tell I'd put on a few extra pounds?" For the first time it occurred to me, there was no way Tyler could have seen the difference in me.

"No, I just thought..." Suddenly he couldn't look at me.

"What? What did you think? You thought that I was fat, didn't you?"

"No! I mean, no, I'd never think you were fat. You know you're beautiful to me, even pregnant."

"You did. You thought I was fat! What did you think? I spent all my time here eating? I'm not fat, Tyler—I'm pregnant!"

"I know, baby. I know." He pulled me closer, ignoring my anger. I couldn't stay mad at him for long, even if he hadn't said a single word about my other confession.

"I'm sorry about sleeping with someone else. I don't know what came over me. It didn't mean anything."

He closed his eyes for a second and I held my breath. "Is it over? I mean, you aren't still seeing him?"

"Oh no—God no! It's been over for a while. It never really started. It was just sex. It didn't mean anything. You believe me, don't you?" I'm sure for any other man, hearing this confession from the woman he loved would probably have been hard to take. Tyler tried his best.

"I believe you, and I'll be okay with it in time. I just don't think I can talk about it right now."

"I understand. And you know you can tell me if you've been seeing someone else, you know? I wouldn't mind. I certainly don't expect you to have been living the life of a saint. I know I hurt you terribly by ending things the way I did."

"There's no one else. There hasn't been anyone else since you broke up with me. It's always been you. Only you."

I was shocked to hear him say those things, but I believed him just the same. "Do you need to go back to Austin right away or can you stay for a little while?"

"You're not getting rid of me again...ever."

"You mean you want to stay here with me? In Colorado"

"I would stay with you wherever you want to be. Here, Early, Austin...the moon. It doesn't much matter to me, just as long as I'm with you. I won't let you go again. I can't. I love you too much to ever let that happen. This is your home now. The house is your dream."

There in his arms, I finally accepted the truth. The house hadn't been my dream at all. Just the whole idea of sharing it with someone I loved—with Tyler.

"The house is a wreck! It has a bad furnace, which doesn't work right most of the time. It's drafty and the plumbing is bad." This little piece of information came out in a hurried rush of words because I was crying again.

Tyler smiled at my tears before brushing them away.

"Those are just things. We can fix them. This is *your* dream and you're *my* dream. We'll fix whatever's wrong with the house. Don't worry."

"Maybe, but would you do me a favor in the meantime?"

"Anything, baby. Just tell me what you want."

"Would you take me back to Texas for a little while — once your father's up to being on his own again? I want to see Aunt Trudy and Fred. I miss them so much, and I want to see Steph and Ed. I think I owe everyone a huge apology. I'd like to go home for a little while. Your father can look after the diner once he's strong enough. He loves the place and it's good for him. And he and Suzie are becoming quite an item."

"I know. Dad's told me all about her. He wants to marry her." This didn't really come as any great surprise. Richard had changed so much since moving to Colorado. Or maybe it was just I'd finally gotten to know the real Richard Bennedict. He wasn't the same man I'd believed I hated.

"I'm going to be a father! You can't imagine how happy that makes me."

I could see he still wasn't able to grasp it all just yet. I pulled him closer. The poor man needed my support. After all, I'd had almost four months to prepare for this.

Just before we drifted off to sleep that night, Henry came to mind. I'd made him a promise. I sat up in bed, knowing I couldn't let my friend down. I needed to take Henry back to Texas with me.

Tyler was freaked out by my sudden revelation. "What is it?"

"I can't go back to Texas without Henry, even for a visit," I blurted out, clearly surprising Tyler.

"Henry? The old guy Dad is always talking about playing bingo with? The guy with all the cats?"

I quickly explained my rather odd meeting with Henry, which led to our friendship. "I won't leave him behind. I know what it feels like to be in a place you don't want to be. I have to take him with us."

236

"All right, we'll tell him the good news in the morning. Now…come here."

When I awoke the next morning, the room around me was toasty warm. As I sat up in bed, I spotted Tyler's suitcases sitting next to the door. "You're leaving?

"No… No, I'm not going anywhere. Well, only over to your place. I was hoping you'd let me stay with you for a while. Do you mind having a roommate?"

"Mind? Are you crazy? Just try getting away again. But we'll have to clear it with Max first, you know?"

"Then I'm definitely in. Max is my buddy."

I smiled before I kissed him. "I wouldn't be so sure about that, Mr. Bennedict. Max has been a grouch since I moved him to Colorado. You see, I don't think he much likes the cold. And far be it from me to point this out to you, but you haven't exactly kept in touch with him since the move. So, you're going to have to work hard at convincing him you're worthy of his love again."

"Why don't I just take the both of you back to Texas where it's warm for a little while?"

"It's worth a try, and it just might work."

"So" — he held the phone out to me and grinned — "who do we share the good news with first?"

I laughed at the little boy expression of delight written all over his face. I'd never seen him look so happy.

"Why don't you call Steph? I dare you." He dialed her number then held the phone out to me. I took it, but the second Steph answered, I couldn't do it. I handed it back to him.

"Steph, hang on just a second, will you?" Tyler put the phone down and looked at me with so much love in his eyes before he kissed me back against the pillows. "Put some clothes on, woman, or your friend here is going to realize the embarrassing way just how back together we really are."

He let me go, but I didn't do as he'd asked. At least not, right away. I sat quietly listening while the man I loved told my best friend our good news. I was so happy.

For the first time there were no secrets left between us — none at all. Only the truth and a future that held love — the same love I'd been so convinced that I no longer believed existed for me.

Chapter Eighteen

Friends Who Won't Desert You When You Need Them Most

Henry surprised the heck out of the both of us. Just a few months earlier, all he had been able to talk about was leaving this Godforsaken land. Today when Tyler and I told him about our plans to take him back to Texas with us for a visit, Henry had other ideas.

"I can't leave now. I have to stay with my friend. You don't desert your friends when they need you, you know."

I could tell Tyler was trying to work all of this out in his head. I was sure he couldn't understand what someone like his father had in common with Henry.

"But, Henry, I thought you couldn't wait to go home to Texas?"

"There's plenty of time for that. I'm staying. You and *that one*—" Henry was fond of referring to Tyler as *that one*—"go on and have your little visit. Besides I've got bingo Tuesday night."

Although Henry didn't say it, he would be there for Richard through it all—the good, the bad, right up to the end, until death. Because you don't desert your friends when they need you, you know. Not even for Texas.

While Henry tried to explain the finer points of bingo to Tyler, I took a moment to look back on my life through the eyes of someone a little bit wiser. I'd learned so many valuable lessons about life. The most important one was that it is precious and fleeting. Death is final. Life is to be lived without regrets.

And love? Well, love is nothing like the fairy tale. Love takes lots of hard work. When it's with the right person, it can be truly wonderful.

Love for me was Tyler. Not perfect, but once you realize none of us are perfect, then the rest is easy to figure out.

Because you see, there are the things you think you want from life and the things you think you need — then there's what really matters. Things like family. Love. Learning from your mistakes. Forgiving. Forgetting. Growing up. Henry. Tyler. Richard. Our baby. Max. Jake. Even Cameron.

And having friends who won't desert you when you need them most.

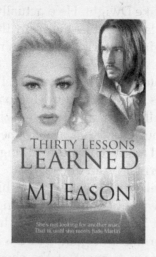

She's not looking for another man. That is until she meets Jude Martin.

Thirty Lessons Learned

Excerpt

Chapter One

It's been said that life is just a series of events with consequences.

On their own, they wouldn't add up to much, but when you put them together, you never know where they'll end up taking you or what the outcome will be once you're there.

For me, the first event with the most unbelievable consequences had been my decision to move to New York City. That decision had come with the disastrous breakup of my marriage to a guy who I'd thought I wanted to spend the rest of my days with.

Dwight Taylor. You know the type. High school football hero and all-around ladies' man—a fact that I hadn't been aware of until after I'd married the guy.

Through high school, I hadn't believed how lucky I was

someone like Dwight. He'd actually picked me, out ...ne other girls in school—me, a shy thing who'd lived ..tly in an imaginary world of her own making.

I was so lucky.

After I'd graduated from the university, I'd come home to Sweetwater, Texas, and married my football player.

But it hadn't really been until five years into our ten-year marriage that I found out that, unlike me, Dwight hadn't been quite as good at keeping our wedding vows. He'd had a fling with the former prom queen.

After I'd been all set to walk out on him, Dwight had promised me it was a one-time only thing. Me, being the innocent wife that I'd been, had believed him.

Too late I'd learned that good old Dwight had moved past the prom queen to most of the cheering squad and beyond. Truth was, Dwight had pretty much run out of likely candidates in Sweetwater by the end of our marriage and had been forced to branch out to the neighboring town.

At the time, I hadn't realized what a stroke of good luck I'd had getting out of that marriage.

I'd only seen myself alone at thirty-two and living back home with my parents.

After I'd cried for two weeks solid without consolation, I'd finally come to a decision about my future. I needed a whole new attitude—one that I wouldn't find in Sweetwater. I'd needed to get out of this town and soon. Sweetwater had been just too small. I couldn't have thrown a rock without hitting one of Dwight's women.

It had been then that I'd told my parents, John and Rebecca Wilder, that I was moving to New York City to pursue a new career path.

Secretly I'd thought my parents were thrilled. Oh, don't get me wrong. They'd been right there, supporting me through the whole ugly Dwight thing. But I'd thought they were ready for some changes as well.

The second I'd packed and had moved out once more, the For Sale sign had gone up on their little ranch-style house on Cedar Street, and they were planning their own move. Sell the house, buy an RV and see the world, starting with Galveston Island. It had been simple.

But for me it had been anything but. As a small-town girl, even a thirty-two year old, moving to New York City had been the equivalent of moving to another universe. Everything about the city had seemed foreign to me. And even though I'd told myself I was my own woman, I'd always had my parents or Dwight to lean on. Here I was, all alone for the first time.

I hadn't had a job at the time, and I had no real idea of how I was going to go about getting one—much less have money to eat—while I decided what I was going to do with the rest of my thirties.

But thanks to my ability to save for a rainy day, I'd managed to put aside some of my paychecks from the elementary school I'd taught at each week. I'd be okay for a while. Well, at least I wouldn't starve to death right away.

So, I'd found myself an apartment that I could hopefully afford to keep and had gone to work finding another job that wouldn't remind me of my past mistakes or Dwight.

With a major in elementary education and my minor in English literature, I hadn't been sure how far those would take me in a city that tough. But I'd always been lucky when it came to finding work.

This had brought me to the next important event—taking the job at Martin Publishing, in the accounting department of all things, which was something I couldn't have been less qualified for, unless I'd actually counted with my toes during the interview.

But my new boss, Danielle Kincaid, had seen something of promise—or more likely desperation—in me and hired me on the spot, and since then, she'd also become my best friend in the world.

* * * *

Six years later, I'd apparently been doing just fine. Definitely up to Danielle's predictions, because I'd managed to work my way up to become her second-in-command.

It had been at this stage in my career that another key event had happened—the ending of my year-long relationship with reliable Harry Davison, who'd also worked for Martin in the nonfiction department.

Harry had been a dream come true for a woman who'd been cheated on by her husband. He was the perfect boyfriend—always there for me whenever I needed him to be but never too clingy or demanding. That, for me, had been a must in boyfriends because, frankly, I'd only needed them...well, when I needed them. And having gotten over one bad marriage with Mr. Football Hero back in Texas, not to mention the too-numerous-to-mention boyfriends before Harry, I hadn't wanted to repeat my past mistakes. You know... Get hooked up with the type of guy whose only interest in me was simply for sex or possibly as a mother figure.

So you see, Harry had been perfect—kind, considerate and nice-looking, in that bookish kind of way.

Harry'd had only one flaw that I could find. He'd been boring as hell!

Oh, not to me, of course. For me, someone who'd survived the football hero and all the other superficial guys, Harry had been very interesting.

He'd actually talked to me as if he cared about my opinion and not just how fast he could get me into bed. But for my best friend Danielle, Harry had been as dry as wheat toast and just about as exciting.

But then Danielle's taste for men went in a very different direction from mine. Dani liked men who only wanted to play. Nothing serious for her.

For me, safe Harry had been my new dream guy, in spite of all Danielle's efforts at getting me to live a little—not to mention her pointed attempts at finding out if Harry was as boring in bed as he was out of it.

Okay, so I had to admit, after Dwight and several other mistakes along those same lines, Harry had been... How to put this nicely? Harry had not been the best I'd ever had, but he'd definitely been the most reliable. Harry had been comfortable. He'd never let me down, certainly never cheated on me the way that Dwight had.

I'd actually believed all those things about Harry, right up until I'd found out the truth.

As it turned out, it doesn't really matter how boring they were, most men — given the opportunity — would stray. Harry was the exception to that rule...or so I'd believed.

That event took place two days...yes, two days before my thirty-ninth birthday and just after Harry had returned from a business trip abroad.

That was when my sweet, or at least who I'd believed to be sweet, faithful boyfriend came to my door and announced that he couldn't take me out for my birthday — or any other day, for that matter — because Harry had met the girl of his dreams.

This struck me as kind of funny, seeing that we'd been going out exclusively for over a year now. Harry and I had, on several different occasions, had some serious talks about our future together. I thought I was the girl of his dreams.

"Harry, what are you saying?" I asked, with that all-too-familiar stupid sound of disbelief in my voice. I'd stood in the doorway of my tiny apartment and couldn't believe I'd heard him correctly. This was the guy who'd sworn I was a dream come true for him just a few weeks earlier, right before he'd made this trip.

"Paige, I'm sorry. I know how hard this must be for you, me telling you this. Believe me. I didn't mean for it to happen. I certainly didn't set out on this trip wanting it to. But I've never felt this alive before. I think I love her. She's the most exciting woman I've ever met. It's just that things began, and we clicked in bed, and —"

At that point, Harry picked up my 'hit by a truck' expression, and he realized I was about to get all emotional on him.

"You just met her? On *this* trip? The one you just got back from?" I asked, when I could actually speak again after hearing the worst possible insult any woman could hear. What was I now? Boring in bed as well?

"Does it really matter?" he asked in his best patronizing voice.

"Yes…it matters. You're damn right it matters! You and I have been together for over a year now. How can you go out and sleep with someone you've just met on a trip? How could you do that to me, Harry? How could you?"

I wasn't really sure what I wanted to say at that point, beyond the fact that I really, really wanted to hit him hard — knock that condescending smile right off his face.

But just before I could actually go into action, that voice in the back of my head told me that maybe I was having another narrow escape. I could get away from Mr. Wheat Toast here, before I would become just as boring as he truly was.

"Paige, I'm sorry, but you were stifling me. I mean, could you be possibly *be* more boring?" I think it was then that Harry realized just how close to violence I truly was. He was halfway out of the door when I slammed it hard on him, and I thoroughly enjoyed the sound of Harry's painful yelp.

I wished that was the last I thought about Harry Davison, but unfortunately, after he'd gone, his nasty parting words kept coming back to remind me that maybe all of my past boyfriend mistakes weren't just poor choices on my part. Maybe *I* was the issue. Maybe I was just too boring to hold their interest.

If someone like Harry, someone Danielle had dubbed the king of boredom, was telling me this, then I could have a serious problem — certainly more than just Harry walking out on me. In fact, maybe I should just give up this crazy search for the perfect man before it turned up any more losers.

At that thought, I reached for the pint of Blue Bell Homemade Vanilla ice cream that was hidden in my freezer. That brand was all but impossible to find in New York City. Out of sheer luck, I'd stumbled across this shop close to my apartment that actually carried the stuff. It was owned by a man from Texas.

With spoon in hand, I reached for the phone and dialed.

"Do you think I'm boring?" I all but yelled those words at my best friend before realizing just how late it was, not to mention the fact that this was Tuesday night. Dani always spent Tuesday night in, which meant in bed with her current boyfriend, an investment banker by the name of Mark, at either his apartment or hers. Dani had been seeing Mark for about six months, and I'd never seen her look so happy.

"Hello?" Dani's out-of-breath voice was barely audible.

"Dani, I'm sorry. I completely forgot it was Tuesday. I'll talk to you tomorrow at work."

I didn't wait to hear her answer. I simply hung up the phone and dove, spoon first, into the best ice cream Texas had ever produced.

I was just finishing off the pint when my doorbell rang, and I feared a repeat visit from dear old unreliable Harry.

I was pleasantly surprised to find Dani standing before my peephole, holding up a large bottle of Southern Comfort. I quickly opened the door.

"I'm sorry. I shouldn't have called so late. I didn't realize the hour or the day. What are you doing here anyway? I didn't expect to see you." While I continued to jabber on, Dani pushed me inside and locked the door.

"Don't worry about it. I had to leave Mark's place anyway. I have to be up early for a meeting tomorrow morning, so I was heading home." She walked over to my kitchen cabinet and produced two glasses, one of which she poured half full and the other, all the way to the top. Dani handed me the nearly overflowing one.

"Okay, sister...spill it. What happened?"

Danielle Kincaid was the most perfect woman I'd ever met. Not only was she smart, but she was drop-dead gorgeous to boot. Dani was tall—so tall, in fact, that I'd asked her on more occasions than I could remember why she wasn't strolling down some runway somewhere.

Believe it or not, Dani was one of those urban legends. You know... One of the ones that actually did wear a size zero. And yes, they do make such a thing. I should know. I'd certainly been shopping with her enough.

But Dani was not only beautiful, she was also exotic. Her dark-brown eyes and raven hair, along with her parents' ethnic blending—her father was American Indian, and her mother was Korean—gave her that mysterious, not quite of this world, look. I would have killed for those looks and that body.

Still, Danielle Kincaid wasn't any wilting beauty who was simply happy to go through life trading on her looks alone—not by a long shot. Dani could stand on her own in any corporate environment. In fact, she'd butted heads with the old man himself, Mr. Joshua Martin, more times than most of us around the company could still remember.

Rumor was that because of Dani and all of their previous run-ins with him, the old guy was bringing his son home from the London office to take over the business. Of course, there were also whispers of a recent heart attack, as well, along with various other stress-related health issues that Dani refused to confirm, one way or the other.

She merely told us that the old guy had known what he was getting when he'd hired her.

"Spill it, Paige. Why aren't you out with old what's-his-name? I thought you two had a hot—correction, lukewarm—date tonight?"

Dani didn't know how close to the truth she'd just come with that remark.

"I did... We did. But that's all over now. Harry just broke up with me, Dani," I pretty much wailed, only to see her roll her eyes then push me down onto the sofa before refilling my now-empty glass.

"Good riddance, and congrats on a very narrow escape, I say." When she spotted my unhappiness, she asked, mostly out of politeness, "What happened?"

"He told me he'd found someone else. Can you believe it? Harry found his dream girl. How could he find his dream girl that fast? I thought *I* was his dream girl. Can you believe he actually had the nerve to tell me *I* was too boring for *him*?" I took another slug of whiskey and looked to Dani for reassurance. She didn't even hesitate.

"You mean old Mr. Boring? Oh please! Paige, you were lucky to get rid of him. The guy is all but dead and doesn't know it. And of course, you're not boring. You know that. I've certainly told you often enough. The only boring thing about you was that hundred-and-eighty-pound weight you were dragging around. Harry was holding you back, honey. You changed to fit into his world, Paige. You were such a fun-loving person until you got yourself hooked up with him. Don't let Harry play with your self-esteem like that. Trust me… You have no idea how much better off you're going to be without him. Besides, the only reason you were with him in the first place was that you've met a few bad guys along the way. That will change. You were just green back then…after Dwight. You'll find someone who is right for you, and I don't mean someone tame like Harry. What you need is someone who will set you on fire, melt all that uncertainty away. After all, you have all of New York City to choose from. Don't settle for someone that you work with, Paige. I warned you about that. It doesn't work out usually. Believe me, I've tried it before. And you know what they say? Don't sleep where you work."

"Yeah, well, you don't have to worry about that happening again, because I'm finished with men! They're all a bunch of losers in one way or another, as far as I'm concerned. And don't look at me like that," I added, when Dani rolled her eyes. "You know it's the truth. That's why you never let yourself get serious about any of them."

Now, had I been thinking clearly and not acting on emotion as well as too much whiskey, it would have hit me then that Dani wasn't really agreeing with me. Dani had gone just a little too quiet. But I thought in passing, *Okay she's just letting me get everything out of my system.*

I continued with my ranting, oblivious to the newly emerging, softer side of my friend.

"You don't mean any of that. You're just upset. Paige. You know as well as I do that you didn't love Harry. If you're going to be honest with yourself, you only went out with him because he was safe – aka boring."

"Yeah? Well he must not be too boring, because he's 'in love'! He's met his soulmate. Oh God, I think I'm going to be sick."

By the time we'd killed most of the Southern Comfort, I was close. The room was spinning, and I couldn't really remember what I was talking about any longer. It was then that my good friend hauled my butt off to bed.

More books from
Totally Bound Publishing

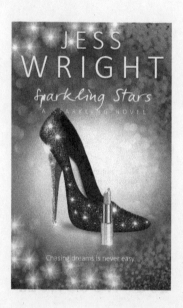

Chasing dreams is never easy.

Samantha Lytton is either going to end up in jail or famous. Maybe both.

About the Author

MJ Eason

MJ Eason grew up in a small Texas town famous for, well not much of anything really. Being the baby of the family and quite a bit younger than her brothers and sister, MJ had plenty of time to entertain herself. Making up stories seem to come natural to her. As a pre-teen, MJ discovered romance novels and knew instinctively that was what she wanted to do with her over-active imagination. She wrote her first novel as a teen—it's tucked away somewhere never to see the light of day—but never really pursued her writing career seriously until a few years later, when she wrote her first romantic comedy and was hooked. Today, MJ still lives in Texas and still writes about romance. In fact, she can't think of anything else she'd rather do.

MJ Eason loves to hear from readers. You can find contact information, website details and an author profile page at https://www.totallybound.com/

Home of Erotic Romance